"And you find yourself helplessly attracted to me?"

Baylor took another step toward her.

"If you come any closer, I might have to defend all of us from me. I might seem a helpless, pregnant thing, but I have to tell you, I'm not." KayLee drew herself up tall and put fists to her hips to take up as much space as possible.

"Never entered my mind that you were." He stopped and leaned against a convenient pine tree, letting her put some distance between them. "Helpless in any way."

"Oh, I shouldn't have opened my mouth. I am so much less censored these days, but I thought if I got it out in the open I could enlist your help in keeping me from doing something we'd regret."

He moved again, stalking unhurriedly toward her like a big cat after prey.

"Darlin'," Baylor said with an exaggerated drawl, "speak for yourself."

D1040963

Dear Reader,

I hope you like reading about the people of St. Adelbert as much as I love writing about them. Thanks to each of you who reads this book.

KayLee Morgan has eight weeks to rebuild her life from the rubble of her past before her child is born. In that short time, she needs to find a place to live and a way to support the two of them. A design project on a ranch outside a small town in Montana offers hope, but winning over Baylor Doyle, the reluctant rancher in charge, is the only way for her to get the job. KayLee soon realizes if she stays close enough to snag the project, she may loose her heart in the process to a man who will be gone before her child is born. It can't be helped. KayLee will risk anything, even her heart, for a chance at a secure future for her child.

I hope you enjoy KayLee and Baylor's story as they each face their own shortcomings and search for a way to say the impossible yes to love everlasting.

Bonus: See how the other people of St. Adelbert are faring, growing, loving, propagating, etc.

I'd love to hear from you. Visit my website at www. marybrady.net or write to me mary@marybrady.net.

Go have a romp with the Harlequin Superromance authors at www.superauthors.com. Enjoy their blog. Comment and you could win great prizes.

Regards,

Mary Brady

Winning Over the Rancher

Mary Brady

TORONTO NEW YORK LONDON
AMSTERDAM PARIS SYDNEY HAMBURG
STOCKHOLM ATHENS TOKYO MILAN MADRID
PRAGUE WARSAW BUDAPEST AUCKLAND

Recycling programs
for this product may
not exist in your area.

ISBN-13: 978-0-373-71730-9

WINNING OVER THE RANCHER

ABOUT THE AUTHOR

Mary Brady lives in the Midwest and considers road trips into the rest continent to be a necessary part of life. When she's not out exploring, she helps run a manufacturing company and has a great time living with her handsome husband, her super son and one cheeky little bird.

Books by Mary Brady

HARLEQUIN SUPERROMANCE

Dedicated to
the intrepid spirit who was Cindy Soerens.

Acknowledgments

To the people of Montana who once again proved
to me they keep in touch with the earth and
appreciate how good life can be.

CHAPTER ONE

THIS WAS EITHER the most brilliant move KayLee Morgan had ever made in her life or it was the biggest blunder. One thing was absolutely certain, they weren't in Southern California anymore. No, two things were certain. She didn't have a warm enough coat for April in Montana. And, for crying out loud, she shouldn't have worn her favorite blue wrap dress in this wind, either.

The early afternoon sun shone brightly, but a chill swept across the expansive porch of the rambling house at the Shadow Range Ranch and had her holding the folds of her coat tightly together for protection. To get herself pumped, she rose up onto her toes and lowered and did it again. Time to be brave.

Do-or-die time.

Do something. Don't just stand there time.

Securing the strap of her shoulder bag in place with one hand, she put her other palm on her belly. "Here we go, kiddo."

"Talkin' to yourself?"

KayLee spun to see a man standing several feet away from the base of the steps—not just a man, a rancher, a real live Montana rancher. He had his cowboy hat pushed back on his forehead and gloriously blond curls spilled from under the brim. His well-worn leather jacket gaped open—didn't he know it was cold in Montana?—and showed off a cream-colored shirt, open at the neck. His jeans clung to his muscular thighs, cowboy boots gave him an inch he didn't need and on his face he wore an expression that could only be described as neutral, though he was only a millimeter away from a frown.

But man, he was—well, by the standards she had left two days ago—beautiful.

"I guess I *was* talkin' to myself." She used his own vernacular and then spread a quick so-pleased-to-meet-you smile across her face. She knew how to look confident. She had, after all, recently come from the land of people versed in becoming the part, any part. "Would you be one of the Doyle family?"

"Baylor Doyle, ma'am." He doffed his hat and the curls jumped loose. And then, oh, my God, he actually ran his hand through his hair.

A new kind of shiver passed through her. Yeah, yeah, she said to her pregnancy-crazy libido. All she wanted from this guy was for his family to hire her for the job. She did not need another pretty face in her life, but she'd deal.

She started to descend the steps with her hand outstretched. "KayLee Morgan of K. L. Morgan and Associates."

Diamond-blue eyes narrowed a bit and a frown came on full bore. Baylor Doyle met her halfway up, engulfed her hand with his big rough one and squeezed with a polite amount of firmness. He studied her without blinking.

"You're K. L. Morgan."

It wasn't a question. It was a disappointment. K.L. was supposed to be some fortyish man with a touch of confidence-building gray at the temples. Most of the people she'd met during this desperate work search kept expecting her to tell them she'd go get the boss and to throw off a curtsy or something. Not her fault she looked a lot younger than twenty-eight or that her "nads" were ovaries.

Oh, shoot. She had forgotten to wear her glasses. She didn't really need them, but they helped her look her age.

"I am K.L." She pulled her spine straighter. She absolutely could not afford to blink even once, as she was positive ranchers were no-nonsense people—and she was working for two, or she would be when somebody gave her a job. "Thank you for agreeing to meet with me in person, I'm excited to show you and your family my ideas for the Shadow Range Eco Ranch project. I think you will all be very pleased."

"I expect everyone else is already in the house." He held his hand out for her to proceed back up the steps.

His soft Western drawl clipped a few of his words as he spoke and she found the sound attractive in an exotic, alien-to-the-Eureka-state kind of way.

Wait a minute, she thought as she crossed the porch. *Everyone else?* She knew there was a son or two involved in the deal. How many more players were there? Were they all going to frown like this one?

He held open the door of the house for her and she stepped into a previous century. Antlers hung from the walls of the foyer and the huge stone fireplace in the adjoining pine-paneled room had discoloration from the heat and smoke of a hundred years of use, maybe more.

He led her into the large room dominated by heavy leather furniture and filled with Western objects from varying cultures and time periods.

"About time you got home, Baylor. She'll be here anytime," a man's voice called from down the hallway.

He grimaced. "Wait here, please. I'll see if they are ready for you."

"Am I early? Do you want me to wait outside?" KayLee regretted the questions as soon as the words were out. They made her seem tentative. Not good in a place where life was serious and flippancy was most likely confined to the children.

He shook his head and strode off down a hallway from where the voice had come. His broad shoulders, it seemed, spread from wall to wall, and could probably hold the weight of the world.

Frown or no frown, if she weren't careful, she'd be in love Hollywood-style with this man—fast, hot and gone as soon as sanity returned.

She took in her surroundings as she waited: pottery on high shelves, stark black-and-white photos of Old West life in groupings on one wall, family type photos hung in a large collection on the far wall. If these were all family photos, there were a lot of Doyles. One photo, if she wasn't mistaken, was Baylor Doyle, with his parents, his two brothers and a sister from at least ten years ago. She walked over to the photo.

She wondered if she'd have to face all of them today.

"They don't bite." Baylor's deep voice came from behind her.

Funny, she thought, coming from a man who looked as if he might, but when she faced him, he wore a deliberate smirk. It made him skew bad boy even more than the frown. Attraction stirred in her and she gathered her full coat around her. A pox on bad boys. That had been why her husband had been so attractive, a rogue producer on the fringes of Hollywood.

"Most of them don't, anyway," he continued, sans drawl, and it was her turn to narrow her eyes in suspicion. "My mother will be here in just a couple of minutes."

"Thank you." Bring 'em on, *all* of them, KayLee decided as she stepped away from the wall of photos and over to a carefully lit painting of a solitary horse, saddled, riderless, standing on a rocky hilltop, proud. If he hadn't been wearing a saddle, she would have thought him a wild stallion.

"This horse must be special to your family," she said as she examined the delicate brush strokes and the colors suffused with light and energy.

"Not the horse so much as the artist."

KayLee glanced at the man again. His playfulness was gone, replaced by something that might be hurt, but also might be "none of your business, so don't ask."

She leaned closer. In the lower left corner in pale blue paint was the name Crystal.

"It's beautiful." She wanted to ask about it, but if she didn't get the job...

He let her wander the room, getting to know the Doyle family a bit more. She tried to affect casually interested and empathetic, not needy or like the fish out of water she was.

If the objects in the room were an indication of the family history, KayLee couldn't help but feel awe at the depth. She moved from the gleaming silver cup sealed in a glass box to a handmade baby gown pinned out on a frame and also protected behind glass. "Some of these artifacts appear to be really old."

"Many of them have been in the family for a long time."

"Those?" She pointed at the pair of rifles hanging above the fireplace.

"They were used on the ranch well over a hundred years ago."

The stocks of the rifles were worn and the barrels dinged but they had been polished with care. She wondered how many lives they had taken and how many they had saved.

"It's all so far-removed from the chrome accessories and plastic fingernails in my life."

He checked her hands and she held them up. "A little clear polish is all."

"Good, I'd have hated to have to throw you out over plastic fingernails." His expression gave nothing away, but he sounded as if he were kidding.

At least she hoped to God he was. Baylor Doyle was a swarming mass of confusing signals. She'd have to steer clear of him as much as she could.

An older woman entered the room from the hallway. She glared pointedly at Baylor, then smiled welcomingly as a tray of chocolate chip cookies just off the cooling rack in grandmother's kitchen.

"Hello, Ms. Morgan. Don't pay any attention to him. He's lookin' to be booted out of the state," she said, giving the man a "be good" look that could only come from a mother.

"You must be Evelyn Doyle." KayLee stepped toward the older version of the woman in the family photo and put her hand out. "This is a lovely home, so full of history."

"The Shadow Range Ranch has been in the family for over five generations. Though it's much larger than the original homestead." Evelyn Doyle's smile broadened and she adjusted the thick gray ponytail that hung down the front of her Western-style plaid shirt.

"And we'd like to keep it that way." Baylor leaned down, placed a kiss on his mother's cheek and then stepped away.

Evelyn took KayLee's hand in one of hers and put her other hand on Kaylee's shoulder, giving her a couple of pats. "I am Evelyn Doyle, but Evvy will do," she said. Then, without taking her hand away, she looked up at Baylor. "Welcome back, Bay, dear. Your buying trip must have gone well."

"They'll be delivering the new stock as soon as it can be arranged."

Evvy let her hand drop and smiled at KayLee again. "I'm afraid there'll be a lot of livestock talk here. We've bred our own line of Angus beef and we'd like to think it's superior to most of what's out there."

"I'm afraid I don't know much about beef that isn't ready to put on my plate," KayLee said and looked from Evvy to Baylor, hoping that wasn't some sort of faux pas.

Baylor made a quiet, derisive sound.

"Baylor." Man and mother held a momentary wordless exchange and then Evvy continued, "I'm glad you made it in time. Bay, take her coat now, please."

Evvy gestured toward KayLee, who shrugged off the heavy shoulder bag and placed it on the floor at her feet. The light touch of Baylor's fingertips on her shoulders as he helped her out of her coat might have felt sensual if she weren't standing between the rancher and his mother. And not at all if pregnancy hormones hadn't tricked her brain into becoming a sex engine. Thankfully, Baylor took her coat and left quickly.

"And your drive?" Evvy asked KayLee as Baylor strode away.

KayLee tugged on the tails of the white sweater she had put over her dress when she realized her coat wasn't going to be warm enough. "I can't get over how gorgeous Montana is. I hope I'm not being insulting if I say you all live in a scenic postcard."

"Not at all. Even those of us who were born here think the same thing from time to time. Well, come, we're all in the den."

"I'm so glad to have the chance to meet everyone." Everyone. Gulp.

When KayLee heard Baylor coming back into the room, she spun around slowly and faced him. His steps faltered and he gave her a long, questioning look with his eyebrows nearly drawn together, but he didn't say anything.

She smiled to herself. This was the moment he realized he was seeing a pregnant woman, that her girth wasn't just from her coat that fell from her shoulders in voluminous folds.

Evvy had not been surprised or, at least, not bothered.

After more smiles and nods, Baylor snatched up KayLee's shoulder bag from the floor, and they all headed down a hallway, Evvy Doyle in the lead.

The ranch house was big—bigger than she expected. Good. They were already used to big spaces inside as well as out. Hopefully, they'd like the wide-open design of her guest cabins the best. If K. L. Morgan and Associates got this job, her design firm might have a future, *she* might have a future and so might her baby, who was the only associate she had.

KayLee buried any sign of desperation under a bright Hollywood smile and kept her place in the parade.

Moments later, they stepped into a den with a knotty pine floor and walls, and a cheery fire in the fireplace. Five more faces assessed KayLee as they stood to greet her—two women and three more men. Seven against one. Fine, she'd faced worse odds when her husband's creditors came after her.

The older man, no doubt the Curtis Doyle from the phone calls and the father in the photo, stepped forward to stand beside his wife. If there were middle-aged, Western-wear wedding-cake couples out there, then this pair had been the model. There weren't two people in the world as well-matched as Evvy and Curtis Doyle, or who looked more honest and upstanding.

Or two people she knew she couldn't disappoint. Well, where did that come from?

"Mr. Doyle, I'm KayLee Morgan. Nice to meet you in person."

He shook her hand firmly and then introduced her to the rest of the family. The younger men and women were dressed in what KayLee thought might be casual-office Western wear, jeans and boots with open-necked button shirts from plain to plaid, and they all inspected her carefully.

Lance and Seth were Baylor's older brothers and the women, Holly and Amy, were their wives. The wives grinned and the men smiled politely. All handshakes were firm, not one limp hand in the bunch. She expected no less and gave as good as she got.

Crystal, the sister from the photo who had painted the stallion, apparently lived in Denver and wasn't able to make the meeting Curtis had said.

When they were all seated, Baylor and his father

flanked the elder Mrs. Doyle like the Fu Dogs outside Grauman's Chinese Theater. She was guarded well. Point taken, KayLee thought. The family was tight.

Good. She'd rather set up an alliance than broker family squabbles any day.

She shifted her gaze from one Doyle to the next. These were not boardroom types. They didn't come here to posture and preen. They came to review the package she had prepared for the development of the ranch project and to make a decision. Excitement frizzling along her nerves let her know she was ready for this.

"Small talk or business first?" she asked.

Lance, the oldest son, barked a sharp laugh. "Well played, ma'am."

Most of the others nodded.

Time was money—their money, not from the bank account of some big corporation—and she knew how they felt.

"I think we pretty much laid out our position in the information we sent to you." This was from Curtis Doyle. "Why don't you show us what you brought?"

KayLee donned her let-me-entertain-you smile.

As she did a quick study of the group, the fire crackled and the sounds of children's laughter filtered in from a distance. "Great then, I'll get started."

She splayed open her leather shoulder bag and took out a half-dozen copies of her proposal, including samples of her past work, her work from her life before Chad. Her old laptop sat on the backseat of her car. Its age wouldn't make her presentation cutting-edge, and she suspected these people were hard-copy types anyway.

She kept one for herself and placed the rest on the

large round wooden coffee table in the center of the room. "I apologize for not having enough."

"We can share," Amy said, handing one to Holly. The husband-and-wife couples snuggled close and KayLee suddenly wanted to cry.

Pregnancy hormones. She blinked, had several soothing swallows from the glass of water on the table in front of her and continued. "In the final plan there are the seven guest cabins you requested and I recommend they be of varying sizes. My proposal is to build one of the medium-sized and one of the smaller ones first. I believe beginning on all of them at once would put too much of a strain on the resources here in the valley. The sheer noise created by doing the project on such a large scale would be unpleasant for the people as well as the wildlife."

She saw a couple of nods and one slight smile. The smile was from Evvy. The rest had remained neutral, except Baylor, who just frowned harder. Tough nut. She wondered what it would take to crack him.

KayLee took another drink of water and then checked to see that her smile was still in place. She'd made harder sales than this one and that was when she was a youngster compared to now.

"I suggest, in keeping ahead of the curve, that all of the building materials be as green, as eco-friendly, as possible." There were a couple more nods with this proposal. "But I also propose that the second medium cabin, when built, be constructed with the materials and ventilation needed to make that particular house a safe environment for anyone who, for health reasons, cannot tolerate what most of us consider normal indoor pollutants."

The faces of the group had all taken on a rather neutral countenance. She searched for a sign. Approval? Bewilderment? Boredom?

Amy leaned forward and refilled the glass of water in front of KayLee. It wasn't much, but she took it as a sign someone wanted her there.

She nodded her thanks, took a drink and then drew herself up and pressed on with the details. She answered their questions as they asked them, giving a solid look of confidence and an honest response. She had built her premarriage business on integrity and expected to do the same now.

As she explained the family area concept where two cabins were located near an all-natural play area, but not near the other cabins, she got nods and smiles from the three women.

She had worked hard studying their wish lists, the absolutes of the landscape, aerial photographs, topographical maps and available supplies in the area. She had a decent idea of what she was facing. She hoped it showed. By the time she had spread out her design of the first medium cabin to be built in a stand of pines, near enough to the stream to hear the burbling water on a quiet night, but not close enough to pollute the water, and the second near the proposed play area, she was sure she had all of them in her corner. Well, all except Baylor.

The more she talked, the more questions she answered, the more confident she felt she had sold herself and her ideas to the others, the more Baylor seemed to scowl. She wondered how much influence he had on the group as a whole.

By the time KayLee was almost finished, it seemed as if the sun should be setting, but only about an hour and a half had passed. She hoped what she had to offer next would make even Baylor sit up and smile.

"I know you all want this project started as soon as possible, and I can arrange my schedule to accommodate an immediate launch if you should choose to go with these designs."

She scanned each Doyle. Evvy and Curtis were the image of warmth and receptivity. The younger husband-and-wife teams held hands and expressions of approval. KayLee gave in to a small shiver of excitement. This was the first real hope she'd had since the accident that had taken her husband.

And then her gaze landed on Baylor.

He sat, arms crossed over his big chest, chin tucked, forehead creased. He had asked many questions, grilled her was more like it, and she'd met every query with knowledge and conviction. She wondered what he doubted now.

The senior Mr. Doyle looked up from the written proposal. "You have been very thorough, Ms. Morgan," he said as he squeezed his wife's hand.

"I like the play area for the children." Amy smiled at her husband with hope and love. They must be parents to one or more of the giggling and chattering young voices she heard coming from another room.

"What would we be talking about as far as a time frame for completion of the first two cabins?" Evvy asked.

"I'll have a better idea of that when we have materials and workers on hand, but with ideal conditions, the middle of summer would not be out of the question."

They all leaned in a bit toward Baylor.

He leaned in as well and folded his hands over the papers on his lap.

"It has been nice meeting you, Ms. Morgan. Thank you for putting so much work into your proposal. We have your card if we have any further questions." Baylor's words were polite, even regretful sounding, but she read body language well enough to clearly read "thanks, but no thanks."

A shock wave of failure overtook her. She hadn't expected a go-ahead, but she hadn't expected outright rejection, either. She knew getting accepted or declined was a combination of personality, design and dollars, but Baylor Doyle didn't even want to give her a chance. He clearly had the power of decision here and she supposed there must be a family reason for that.

She pushed to her feet, rebalancing her weight carefully.

Curtis rose from his seat and so did everyone else.

"You've given us a lot to consider with your proposal. What we're going to have to do now is to talk among ourselves." The patriarch's words seemed to abate the finality of Baylor's pronouncement, but not by much.

Evvy gave her a warm smile. KayLee suspected Evvy was kind to everyone, even a rejected designer. "Your plans are elegant and resourceful, KayLee. You won't be heading for home yet today, will you?"

Home? She almost laughed. She didn't have a home.

"I've got a room at the inn in town. I thought I'd get a good night's sleep and I've always wanted to get to know Montana better." Oh, blab and dither. Stay professional. "Anyway, thank you so much for the opportunity to share my ideas with you. It's been a pleasure. I hope to hear from you soon."

She gathered her bag and the papers she would need, leaving her proposal and credential information for the

Doyles, hoping she had a reason to stay in town and not flee back to…where?

Well, she was competent and strong. She'd find something, if not here, somewhere else. That was her anthem and her prayer, and she was sticking to it.

"Anyone in town will help you with whatever you need." Amy's tone seemed to offer an apology for the group, and her smile their regret.

Her husband, Seth, put a hand on Amy's waist and nodded his agreement. "If you need anything, you can call out here, too."

They truly were good people and from what Mr. Doyle had said, when completed, this project needed to boost the ranch's income, not be a drain on it. Besides cattle and summer cabins, KayLee wondered what income ranches in Montana used to stay afloat.

She really didn't know as much as she thought about the area where she proposed to work.

Her inadequate coat seemed to appear from nowhere and Baylor held it up for her to slip into. When they walked her as a group to the front door, she wanted to grab each one of them and ask what more she could have done. Instead she nodded to each in turn. "Thank you all. You've been very kind."

And then she fled.

When she paused at the bottom of the wooden steps, it seemed as if she were about to leap off with no possibility of knowing if she would ever land, let alone land safely.

She lifted her chin, sucked in a breath of clean Montana air and patted her belly. It's okay, Baby, she thought, Mama's got your back.

She stepped into the oblivion called the rest of her life.

AFTER K. L. MORGAN DROVE away in her tiny blue Ford, Baylor herded the rest of his family back to the den. Though they had come docilely enough, none took their seats.

Standing was a better fighting position.

He shoved the hair away from his face, leaned forward and placed his hands on the back of an upholstered chair. Deliberately, silently, he held the gaze of each one of them. When none of them so much as blinked, he spoke quietly. "Have you all gone nuts? Did you all not notice K. L. Morgan is pregnant? I'm only a good judge of cows and horses, but I'd say very."

"And you'd hold that against her?" Amy challenged as she moved over to stand next to his mother and Holly.

"I think you know me better than that, but we need someone who can get the whole job done and get started yesterday."

"She can do the job, Bay," Holly said as she approached him, Amy and his mother at her side. "And she said she could start right away."

"I don't doubt she believes she can start this job. She might even believe she can get it done, but that doesn't make it so." Baylor took a seat on one of the couches, but none of them followed his lead.

"She graduated from the School of Architecture and Urban Planning at UCLA and she presents herself nicely." His mother gave him a benign mother smile when she spoke. "And her bid was lower than any one else's."

His sisters-in-law glared at him and his father and two brothers were in a tight knot, no doubt trying to figure out how to handle him. Just why he needed handling, he had no idea. They all knew that every single one of their futures rested on this project. He had promised himself and all of them, he'd see to the development of the Shadow Range Eco Ranch, and he was fairly certain K. L. Morgan was not going to be part of that promise.

Now they formed a semicircle around him with arms crossed over their chests, except his mother. She had picked up a stack of papers from the coffee table.

"And what about the baby's father?" Baylor asked.

CHAPTER TWO

"SHE GOT HERE BEFORE you got a chance to read the background report on her." Baylor's father pointed to the stack of papers his mother held. "You should read the information before you make any decisions."

What could possibly be in the report? Something that would make K. L. Morgan less pregnant? The pleading on the faces of the women and the blank I'm-not-moving-an-inch looks on the faces of the men made it pretty mandatory he at least take a careful look.

"I've obviously missed something big," Baylor said as he took the report and straightened it—as if his mother would let anything be messy, "because you people have all but given her the nod for the work."

"We thought you'd be happy when you found out she could start straight away." Lance stated what must have been the family opinion because every one of them nodded. "No one else could offer that. She gets the job underway and you're out of here."

"And if she gets the job started and then falters, or doesn't get the job started at all, that's a lot of wasted time and money we don't have."

"And you'd feel stuck in the valley with the rest of us," Seth said, following up Lance's defense.

Baylor took a patient breath. "We might none of us be 'stuck' in this valley. This ranch has to make enough money to pay the bills."

"I could work more at the attorney's office," Holly volunteered.

"And I could go back to the diner." Amy glanced at her sister-in-law.

"If it comes to that—" Lance started.

Baylor looked up at all of them from the couch and held up a hand. "Wait, just wait. We've been through this more than once. With everyone here working as much as they do on the ranch, we're already falling behind on the work that needs to be done." They needed to get the calving finished and the shed in good repair for the following spring, the branding had just started, the barn needed a new roof, there was a lot of fence to ride before the cattle could be moved and the new stock had to be integrated into the herd when it arrived. There wasn't an end to the list, but they all loved it. "Trey needs you, Amy. And, Holly, the more hours you put in off the ranch, the more we'll have to replace you here."

"What about me?"

Baylor shook his head at his mother. "Mom, even if you hadn't just had your knee replaced, I'm sorry, but there aren't jobs in this valley big enough to bail out the ranch. If we get this project going with the livestock and the lumber, we can pay off debt and provide a decent living for all of you. And then maybe there'll be Doyles on the Shadow Range for another hundred and twenty-five years."

"We hear what you're saying, Baylor, and we're not afraid to look the truth in the face anymore, thanks to you," Lance said as he took Holly's hand. "And we think this woman is what we need to get the project up and running."

"How does she plan on doing that? How long will it be until she can't even make the trip here?"

"We think she plans on living in the valley during the project, instead of commuting," Lance continued. "That gives us her constant attention during the whole thing."

"She plans on living here?"

There were several nods.

"Why would she do that? Isn't there a husband or at least a man who cares about his baby involved in that decision?"

"She moved out of her home two weeks ago and she's been staying in a motel since," Holly said as she tugged a strand of her long red hair.

"And you're all dodging the topic of the baby's father. Why?"

"Six months ago, her husband died unexpectedly," his mother said in a gentle tone.

"And you'll soon find out, it was a week after he had moved out of their home," Holly added.

He tried not to glare at the bunch of them. "She loses her home and her baby's father, so you think we should give her a place in this valley? Why don't we throw in a family, too?"

They had the presence of mind not to snicker at that one. It would please them all if he thought this valley was a place to have a life and a family and not a place to flee from.

"Bay, she needs us and we need her. There's a match meant to be here." His mother took a seat beside him as she spoke and patted his knotted forearm.

"What about the rest of her client list?" Baylor asked.

"We're it right now. The whole kit 'n' caboodle," Seth said as he hooked his thumbs in the belt loops of his jeans and rocked back on the heels of his boots.

"I have to ask you again, are you people nuts?"

Amy stepped forward. "Baylor, Holly and I were talking and we knew you'd be concerned, but we can tell you having a baby isn't any sort of disability. Holly helped birth a calf three days after Matthew was born."

"We also suspect," Holly said as she stepped up beside her sister by marriage, "one of the reasons you want out of this valley so badly is you don't want to bring a wife and a family into this situation, to put more strain on the ranch."

Holly was mistaken about his reasons for leaving, but he wasn't going into that right now.

"You know we're behind you, Baylor," Amy added. "No matter what you decide."

Baylor let his hands relax on his thighs. "I'm not sure there's a third woman in the world like you two—"

"Baylor, you're full of crap," Seth said.

"No language like that in my house, please," Evvy Doyle insisted. They might wade in the muck on a regular basis, but that didn't mean they were uncivilized.

Baylor glared at his brother as he continued. "But someone has to think of what's best for all of us. You all chose me for that."

Lance, always the peacemaker between his two younger brothers, gave a conciliatory wave. "So, do we call her and tell her she has the job or do we wait a day or two so she doesn't think we're too eager?"

"Wait a minute. Wait a minute." Baylor waved both hands in the air. "If she has nothing, then why—"

His father interrupted. "When her husband died six months ago, he owed a lot of money."

"And two weeks ago they threw her out of her home." Amy tapped in what should have been another nail in the coffin of failure for K. L. Morgan and Associates.

But all faces looked, if not hopeful, at least mulish.

"This is even worse." Baylor put his hands behind his head and glared at each one of them in turn, except his mother. He hadn't been able to give her impatience since he was in middle school and he was old enough to know she would never harm a fly. "We're going to bail her out after she made too many bad choices in her life."

"It was more like bad luck." Lance defended her in the name of peace and harmony, of course.

"She seemed to be playing straight with us. Her proposal is more along the lines with what we wanted and she thinks she can bring the project in under the costs of all the others." This was his father again.

"Have any of you checked these references closely?" Baylor asked as he studied each member of his family again.

Evvy extracted a folder from a stack of papers, spread out several glossy prints on the coffee table and handed him a list of names and contact information. "We called them all. They had nothing but praise."

Baylor examined the list and then each photo. They all were impressive. He had thought that the first time he went through them. There were individual homes, and two concept communities, but there was one problem. "You know there is a big gap in her work résumé."

"She apparently let the business slide early on in her marriage," Seth said. "But before that…"

"And she wants to relaunch with us?"

"Baylor, worst case, what if she can't do it?" Holly asked.

"More of us leave the valley than just me, and soon." Baylor's blunt response made the group go quiet.

With no one speaking, the children could be heard playing in the back of the house. His brothers had three children between them. The neighboring ranch had lent their housekeeper to see to the little ones so all the family members could be present for the meeting and not be distracted.

His family was right about one thing. K. L. Morgan was the lowest bidder and that was another reason he wanted to eliminate her. You get what you pay for. Could they afford the lowest bidder? Would it all fall apart before it was completed or collapse in the middle of a stormy night?

Yet she had covered as much and, in some cases, more than the other designers and contractors had covered in their proposals. As far as he could tell, her plans were impeccable.

There was one thing about KayLee Morgan the others did not offer and Baylor was somewhat uncomfortable admitting it even to himself. The woman was hot, hotter than this valley had ever seen—and he suspected she was that way before pregnancy made her curves so seductive.

"She is the most convincing candidate, Bay, and we need her." Lance took his stand. "But, most of all, we need you on our side."

On their side. Ultimately, if Baylor fought hard enough, the decision would be entirely up to him. They had paid dearly in hard-earned cash they could have spent on themselves, but instead they gave him a university education. They sent him out to gather the collective know-how of ranchers and farmers all over the country and bring it back to the Shadow Range. Now their livelihood depended on his being good enough to make the right move.

He helped his mother up from the couch, and she

followed him as he left the room with the paperwork in his hand.

"Did you find out anything about your sister?"

Baylor felt the sharpness of the pain in his mother's voice and shook his head.

He stopped and hugged her. At times like this he wondered how she withstood the pressure of her life. He knew she'd take the blows for each of her children and grandchildren if she could.

KayLee had truly believed she had a shot this time. When tears she couldn't stop filled her eyes, she steered the car off the road and shut off the engine. Crying on mountain roads didn't seem all that smart.

The off-road parking spot had to have been put there for the view, so when the tears passed and since she had no idea what to do next, she viewed.

She stared out at scenery so stunning it almost made her brain hurt. Mountain peaks soared in the distance. The midafternoon sun danced in sparkles off the melting snow around her car. The tops of tall pine trees peeked out from the deep canyon beside the road, and water burbled down from the rock face that shot straight up on the other side of the car.

She shifted her gaze down to the lump where her lap used to be and put both hands on her swollen belly. "I am so sorry, my little peanut. Mommy had great hopes for this gig."

She'd spend the night at the Easy Breezy Inn because she'd already paid for and used the room at the only motel in town. Tomorrow, she could head for her mother's home in Wisconsin. Her mother always said "Anything I can do to help, dear" and always found a reason not to. If KayLee showed up on her doorstep, even her mother might take her in for a week or two until KayLee got a job.

And she'd get a job. She was actually a sane, competent person who was a bit emotional these days. She'd take a firm hold of herself and put things together so they made sense. She always had before and she'd do it again even if that meant leaning on her reluctant mother for a bit.

If her mother wasn't in a hut on Bali or sharing a rustic villa in the south of France with a couple dozen hippie wannabes, several dogs and maybe her ex-husband.

She took out her mobile phone to see if she could find her mother.

"No bars." She patted her belly. "It's us two, baby, baby. As usual."

The warm sunshine bathed her and relaxed her. She had only driven a few hours this morning to get to St. Adelbert from Missoula for the early afternoon appointment with the Doyle family, but she was so tired. She felt as if she had driven the entire route from Southern California in one day, from the old motel in Oceanside to be exact.

The motel where she had taken refuge after losing her home was located right next to the junkyard, complete with rottweilers and across the street from the resale shop where she was lucky enough to find maternity clothes. She hadn't been able to afford a motel in the fancy community of La Jolla, where she had shared a home with her husband.

Chad. Handsome. Crazy in a fun wild way. A genius. And why did he have to die without meeting his child? He might have been able to love their baby someday, even if he hadn't been able to love the baby's mother for a long time.

She leaned over the steering wheel, put her forehead on her clasped hands and closed her eyes against the hurt.

BAYLOR MOUNTED BLUE MOON, his American Paint Horse, and rode past the barn and deeper into the ranch, down the half-rutted, half-muddy road into the pine forest. He had read all the information gathered on K. L. Morgan and carefully reread the proposal she had left behind. He had spoken with family members individually about what they thought and why. He still had no clear idea of what to do, but he'd always found the best place on the ranch to think was on horseback.

He nudged Blue Moon forward and, when he came to the break in the trees, headed out onto the meadow and let his thoughts and the horse wander.

The Paint chose to meander down toward the stream, and Baylor's mind came up with full, rosy pink lips below a straight nose, flanked by flushing high cheekbones and long dark blond hair, begging to be picked up and rubbed between finger and thumb.

Baylor fisted the hand that had started to act as if it were feeling her silky hair, and it would be silky.

There was scant room for debate. K. L. Morgan was sexy. Her round curves pressing against the blue dress had captivated him.

He did like the idea of having the buck-stops-here person in the valley overseeing the job full-time. If everything went well, she could have the project up and running in a couple of weeks and he could be gone from the valley sooner rather than later.

The opportunity he'd been offered overseeing several ranches outside of Denver, and outside of this confining corner of Montana, wasn't going to keep forever.

He could live in Denver and keep his Paint at one of the ranches he was overseeing.

He knew he never wanted to leave the ranch life completely behind. Ranching was what he lived and breathed. He couldn't even imagine himself in a nine-to-five job, but the St. Adelbert Valley offered nothing new, nothing innovative, nothing to catch his interest. He'd wanted out for as long as he could remember.

And he could, without alerting or in some cases alarming his family, try to find Crystal.

J&J Holdings, LLC, had said they'd hold the position for him for sixty days. Nearly half of that time had already passed while they continued the search for someone willing and able to help them build the Shadow Range Eco Ranch at a price they might be able to afford.

The person or persons hired would alter the family homestead forever and ran the risk of destroying the way of life for many generations of Doyles. The decision of whom to hire could not be made on the basis of the looks or the need of the candidate.

With a kernel of an idea, he headed his Paint back toward the barn.

A SHARP RAP ON THE WINDOW beside KayLee's head woke her, and—FCOL—she almost wet her pants. She snapped her head up to see a man in a sheriff's uniform standing outside her car with one hand resting on his holstered gun.

No…no crying out loud or crying at all because now she was going to be thrown out of the county at gunpoint for loitering and maybe even all the way out of the state, if the size of the sheriff determined how far he'd toss her.

Did they throw you out for loitering in Montana?

She tried desperately to clear her brain of the sleep fog and lowered her window.

"Ma'am. Are you okay?" The big man blocked the late afternoon sun so she didn't have to squint at him.

Late afternoon! No wonder she needed to find a restroom so badly.

KayLee unstuck her tongue from the roof of her mouth. "I think I'm okay, Sheriff Potts," she said, reading the name off his name tag.

She took inventory. She must have been asleep for at least a couple of hours.

"Ms. Morgan, there are some people looking for you."

"You know who I am? Of course." She at least still owned the car she drove.

He waited politely for her to wake up some more.

Wait... Some people? "Some people?" Oh, God. Chad's creditors had found her. No. They had already taken everything they could. She was finished with them, at least that's what her attorney had said. "Some people. Who?"

He smiled in at her. A smile was good. A confident smile.

"The Doyle family," he said in a voice she figured could echo through the canyons if he wanted it to.

"Oh, them." Her shoulders sagged, followed by her whole body. At least with the bill collectors it hadn't been personal. With the Doyles it seemed very much so.

"Are you sure you're all right, ma'am?"

"I'm fine. I'm— I was resting." And she'd been rebuffed enough for today.

"Baylor Doyle asked me to keep an eye out for you.

He thought you were headed for the Easy Breezy and when you didn't show up, the Doyles got worried."

The Easy Breezy Inn, small and old, fit her budget and since her home was the pillow in her trunk.... The Doyles most likely wanted to tell her to keep on driving, don't bother to stop in town. She'd get their message when she got bars.

"Well, Sheriff, I thought I'd get to pretend for a while longer that they still wanted to hire me." Why was she talking to this guy as if he were her best bud, her BFF in LaLa Land-speak? He wouldn't care if she got a job in this valley or not. Ha, she might never see him again in her life. BFF.

Tears spilled down her cheeks and she blubbered right there, sitting in her car, in front of Montana law, because she didn't even have a best friend west of the Mississippi River, 'cause she was sure Addis Ababa, where her only friend was currently working on an indie film, was considered east.

Oh, she loved these hormones. They gave her permission to feel anything she wanted to feel and right now she wanted to feel sorry for herself.

The sheriff towered over her, arms folded over his chest, somehow seeming more friendly than threatening. It seemed they all did the arms-over-the-chest thing here in Montana. Well at least he'd let go of his gun.

And he was patient enough to wait while she cried.

"I'll—I'll move on in a few minutes, Sheriff. When the falling water is all on the outside of my car." She pointed lamely at the water dribbling down the rocks.

"Is there anything I can do for you?"

"Got any job openings?" She rubbed her fingers across her wet cheeks.

"You should give Baylor a call."

She pointed at her phone and made a zero with her fingers. "Nada."

"Go back to the ranch."

"I really have had enough rejection for the day." Buddy. Pal. BFF. God save her, she was an idiot.

"You might be done with that."

"What? What are you saying, and if you're saying what I think you're saying, how do you know?"

He laughed at her. She'd laugh at her, too, if she still remembered how.

"Baylor said he needed to talk to you before you got away. The Doyle family has apparently come to a decision."

"He told you that? Why? Is he your nephew or something, I mean why would he tell you?"

"He's a friend. Most people in the valley are."

"Wow. A valley full of friends. Just like California, huh. I'm sorry. That must have sounded sarcastic... mean." But most of her friends in California had been like temporary tattoos. The one friend she had left was out of the country on a movie shoot and the rest had stuck around only as long as conditions were exactly right and then they quickly faded. "Wait! He wants me. I mean, do you think the Doyle family want to hire me to do the job?"

The sheriff laughed again. "At least you're not crying anymore."

She felt her cheeks. Dry. "Oh, thank God about that. I'm a bit pregnant and I— Wait. I'm a lot pregnant." She patted her belly and he nodded. "And I'm a lot influenced by the hormones and nobody tells you the half of it. Sorry—again—to go on. See Baylor Doyle, you say."

"Yep."

"Should I be scared? Is there anything scary about that family? There are so many of them."

He chuckled and shook his head. "You have a good day now, ma'am."

"Thank you, Sheriff Potts. Potts, right?"

He touched his index finger to the brim of his cowboy sheriff's hat.

"Goodbye. I hope you have a great day, Sheriff."

"You, too, ma'am." He nodded this time and turned away.

The sheriff got in his car and sped away. He most likely had cattle rustlers and varmints to catch. Did they still rustle cattle? The world was full of varmints, she could attest to that. Though in Southern California they called them celebrities and star-makers, and even producers if overborrowing, then dying and leaving your wife with the bills and a baby on the way makes you a varmint.

She leaned back against the headrest, but her head popped up immediately. She really did need to find a bathroom.

Which way? Town or the ranch?

Breathe deeply.

Think kind and peaceful thoughts. She was a sane, competent person. She rested her head back and took several long breaths. And all that did was make her have to pee more.

Oh, hell, what did she have to lose?

She started her car and headed back the way she had come a couple hours ago. The ranch had to be closer. Funny, her poor squashed bladder was going to determine her future.

Go. Go. Speed limit. Okay, maybe a bit faster than the speed limit. Besides the sheriff had gone the other way.

She sped down the highway and then up the lane to the Shadow Range ranch house with, she was sure, streaks of mud spraying out from behind her rear tires. Then she leaped out of the car as fluidly as a seven-months-pregnant woman who badly needed a powder-room fix could leap.

"Please, please, please, let me make it," she prayed as she hugged her coat around her, covered the ground from her car quickly and hobbled up the steps.

Rap. Rap. Rap.

The door popped open and Baylor Doyle stood there holding a stack of papers. He gaped at her.

"Let me in." She barged past him. "Which way? Which way?"

Was the man really as dull as his expression?

Holly appeared, glanced at her for a half a second. "That way. First door on your left."

Gales of Holly's laughter followed her down the hallway, and she soon heard Amy join in, too. She knew, given half a chance, she could love those women dearly.

She flipped on the powder-room light and found porcelain bliss.

BAYLOR EYED HIS GIGGLING sisters-in-law. "I don't stand a chance, do I?"

"No," they howled together and then mercifully stumbled off down the hallway, holding each other upright as best they could.

Baylor shook his head and continued to the office, where he had been headed before the person who might be occupying his short-term future pounded on the door and, wild-eyed and sexy, ran on in.

In the office, he found Lance sitting on the edge of the desk waiting for him. His oldest brother shifted to the "visitor" chair as Baylor dropped the stack of papers in the middle of the blotter and sat down in the chair behind the desk.

"Have you decided our fate yet?" Lance asked when Baylor laced his fingers together, rested his hands on the stack of papers and leaned in to study his dark-haired brother.

CHAPTER THREE

BAYLOR GAVE HIS BROTHER a long stare. "We can't hire her because she needs a job," he said. Or because she's good-looking, he thought.

"We can't afford to turn a good option down for the same reason," Lance drawled.

Baylor nodded and wondered if his brother knew the rest of his thoughts on KayLee Morgan.

"Two weeks," Baylor said. "We'll give her two weeks. That should be enough time to make a final decision."

Seth approached, leaned on the doorjamb and gazed between Baylor and Lance. "She was good at facing us all like that and holding her own, answering all our questions."

Lance snorted softly. "She seemed to look forward to the next question, like she'd be easy to work with."

"Eager at least," Seth added.

"Eager's a great quality," Baylor acknowledged to his brothers. "But it's not enough. The first guy we interviewed was eager, and we know how that ended."

"It wasn't hard to figure out he was a crook, but you're not putting KayLee in the crook category."

"No, but I'm the one who's going to be doing most of the work with her."

"And you'll be able to keep a close eye on her." Seth

flicked his eyebrows at Baylor and smirked toward Lance.

Lance grinned, but shook his head to silence Seth. They both knew. This wasn't going to be easy no matter how it went down.

"This is business, guys. No matter what we think of her as an individual, it has to be a business deal. When the project is complete, you all can adopt her if you want." He wouldn't care. He'd be gone.

"We'll have to trust you to give her a fair chance." Seth must have been finished because he walked away.

Lance stared at Baylor for a response.

"It might not even be fair to give her a chance." Baylor restacked the papers on the desk blotter.

"She's good people, Baylor, and you know it."

"And if we give her a two-week trial and she fails, it might spoil her chance of getting a job before her baby is born."

"She'll do a good job and we'll keep her on."

"If I didn't think you had a chance of being right, I wouldn't have called her back."

Lance nodded, got up from the chair and followed in the direction Seth had gone. His boot heels clomped down the hall, through the mudroom and outside. His brothers had gone back to the never-ending string of chores necessary to keep a ranch running and the animals healthy.

Baylor spread the papers and sorted them into piles for filing. Now that he had made the decision, he was going to throw himself at the situation as if it were a worthy stallion needing some tender loving care to be a great stallion. Not that "tender loving" was anything he planned on aiming at K. L. Morgan.

Tempting, though.

Tempting. That was crazy thinking. If he let crazy thinking rule him, unintended consequences happened.

He had finished tucking away the last papers when he looked up to see K. L. Morgan standing in the doorway with her flimsy coat draped over one arm and her hands folded together in front of her as if in apology.

He rose quickly from the chair and made a gruff coughing sound to cover his laughter at his sorry old self.

"Come in," he said when she didn't enter the office.

She stepped inside. "I ruined whatever chance I had at making a great impression, didn't I?"

He hadn't realized how melodious her voice was, but in the small office, it made the air vibrate.

"Is your life ever dull?"

She shrugged and stepped up to the desk. "You'll undoubtedly find out, so I might as well tell you, I met your Sheriff Potts."

Baylor studied the molding around the ceiling, trying his best to bury a smile. Unintended consequences, he thought. "He called."

"I'd hoped he wouldn't snitch on me. Damn."

He snapped his gaze to hers. "Don't let my mother hear you say that word. *Darn* and *heck* are all right if you're highly provoked, but *damn, hell* and *crap* are over the top. Have a seat, please."

Radiating confidence and poise, she draped her coat over the back of the chair and sat down across the desk from him. He couldn't deny his brother's assessment that K. L. Morgan inspired admiration for her courage under fire—but that didn't mean he had to be taken in by it. He scowled and retook his seat.

"Oh, darn." She raised her brow in question.

He gave a slight head nod of approval and she curled

her hands together on her lap. "How much did the sheriff tell you?"

"He said he found you and we should be expecting you soon." He paused for dramatic effect. "And then he laughed."

"How did he know I was coming here? I don't remember telling him." She thought for a moment. "When he left, I didn't even know."

"He knows people. That's why he's so good at his job and that's a reflection on our judgment as well as yours." He paused. He was about to tell this woman she could hold the family's future in her hands, and Sheriff Potts's positive assessment of her had made that decision easier to live with.

"He is so kind to just have laughed at me." She studied her fingers for a moment. "Is it too late to start over?"

"Do you think it would help?"

Alarm spread across her face, and then when she realized he was chiding her, she smiled a smile as bright as a sunny day in the Bitterroot Mountains, and he felt that smile all the way down to the toes of his Sunday boots.

She relaxed her hands on her knees. "I think at this point, it would only muddy the waters."

"My family thinks you're the best choice for this project."

"Okay." She waited for him to explain.

"But they've left the choice up to me."

"I realize I'm not what you expected and that it's a stretch for you to consider me for the job, but if you do give it to me, I will give you more than you asked for."

More than he asked for…

"I'm willing to go along with my family and give you

a chance." She sat up straighter and he continued. "Two weeks. After two weeks, if things aren't working out, you would be paid for your time and, of course, we'd pay you for your designs."

He watched her closely.

"You won't be sorry." Her words indicated her delight while her face showed her focus on the future.

"That's what my family tells me."

She nodded her head once. "Now tell me why your family puts so much stock in your opinion."

Her green eyes, the color of leaves in the light of sunset and rimmed with dark lashes, were highlighted by the merest touch of makeup.

"Because I'm the youngest brother?"

She nodded again.

"Fair enough." The Doyles knew so much more about her than she suspected. It seemed right she should know more about them. "My older brothers wanted no part of college. They were happy working the ranch and their wives were happy with their husbands and their lives. My parents could read the writing on the wall, but my brothers would rather ignore the signs the ranch was faltering."

She listened as though she were gathering facts without passing judgment. He found himself liking KayLee Morgan more and more, at the same time telling himself it wasn't his job to like her.

As he told her about his family sending him to Montana State University in Bozeman and why, she barely blinked.

"Wow," she said when he was finished.

Her lips held the form of the last *W* as she explored the thoughts in her head, and it made him want to kiss those puckered lips—and to smack himself on the back of the head for thinking such a thought.

"So do you still want to work for us?"

"They have put a lot on you." Deep concern dimmed the sparkle in her eyes.

"Someone has to take the reins and I can."

She placed her palms on her knees and leaned forward. "Yes, I'd still like to do the job."

He reached across the desk with one hand and when she put her soft hand in his, she gripped solidly.

"Welcome to the Shadow Range Eco Ranch project," he said, and found himself sincerely meaning it.

Either he was a step closer to his dream and his quest, or he'd chased them out onto the far horizon. Whatever happened, he found himself wanting her to succeed for herself, as well as each and every Doyle.

"Now tell me what *you* think," she said as she let go of his hand and sat back in the chair.

Baylor shifted. Tell her what he thought? That she's hot or that he was already in trouble because he was beginning to see why his family wanted to hire and protect her?

"I like to think I'm an open-minded kind of person. I admit, your—"

"Pregnancy, sex, age?" She grinned.

"Once I realized you couldn't be as young as you look, that was not even a consideration.

"As for your being female, you've met Holly, Amy and my mother and…they don't balk at much." An image of his missing sister pushed into his thoughts. She had one of her defiant looks on her face and her hands were balled into offensive fists. "And they're tame compared to my sister, Crystal."

He could see KayLee wanted to ask about Crystal,

but he wasn't ready to talk to anyone yet because he had nothing of substance to say. So he hurried on. "Your proposal offers the most support and oversight—with the possible exception of a period of time when you will be otherwise occupied. If you are as good as you say you are, I expect this job will go well."

She gave a heavy sigh of relief and a warm smile that a part of him wanted to interpret as sexy.

"I expect the same. If I could, I'd like to look around a bit, see the place I proposed the first cabin be built."

"Now?"

"The sun shines. Isn't that when I'm supposed to make hay?"

K. L. Morgan kept surprising him with her understanding of the situation. She might work out better, though, if he could pretend she was the mid-forties man he had expected.

"Do you have warmer clothes?" he asked.

She glanced down at her blue dress. "I have different clothes. Warmer, probably not."

"Boots?"

She lifted a foot with a shoe meant for a city street. "This is the best I've got. The boots I have are not the sort you're talking about."

"I'll find a warmer coat for you and we'll mostly stay in the truck."

"Do you think Holly and Amy might be willing to advise me on wardrobe shopping?"

"I think Holly and Amy would do anything you asked them to do."

She blinked at him as if she were having a hard time believing what he said.

"KayLee, this is the St. Adelbert Valley. The Doyle women probably already have a place in mind for you to live, a trip to Kalispell for supplies planned and a crib to lend you. Believe it or not, you have already won the esteem of our sheriff. Most of the people here in this valley will need no more than that to welcome you and offer you whatever help they can give you."

She studied her fingers for a long moment and then shifted her scrutiny to him. "I knew I wasn't in California anymore."

"This will sound like some sort of a threat, and it could be. With the exception of a few ornery ones, the people here will believe in you quickly and be loyal."

"Accept me first, and I get to decide whether or not I break their hearts? Warning taken. I'll be careful with them."

He nodded. "I'll get you a coat."

Baylor escaped the office and headed down the hallway toward the mudroom, which was located at the side entrance to the house.

Was that tears he had seen in her eyes? Give him a couple cows having difficult calvings and a runaway mule. Those things he could handle.

He searched the closet for a coat that was big enough to fit around KayLee, but the first two he considered would have swallowed her up.

Now that he had made the decision to hire her, even if it was temporary, he'd do what he could himself to help her. The two of them could finalize the plans, scout out materials and hire laborers. There were locals chomping at the bit to have gainful employment. Calving was nearly at an end, branding and spring clean up would soon be under control, and there would more idle hands around.

The job in Denver was a chance of a lifetime, a stepping-off point to launch him in the world outside the small valley where he'd spent most of his life. If K. L. Morgan could get this job done, she could set him free. He held up a green kid's jacket. He was getting closer.

If she couldn't get the job done, she could end up tying him to this valley until the next chance of a life-time came up. Yep, two once-in-a-lifetime chances. As if that were going to happen.

The lead he had on Crystal hadn't panned out yes-terday, but that didn't mean the next one wouldn't. She was in Denver—that much he knew.

"How about this one?" Holly reached around him and pulled out a work jacket. "I wore it when I was pregnant with Katie about this time two years ago."

"Thanks." He didn't even want to guess how she knew what he was searching for in the closet. Made him crazy when he tried to figure things like that out about Holly and Amy.

"So, is she in or out?" his dad asked from the door-way of the mudroom.

"She gets a chance to try, and she wants a look around."

"Yippee!" Holly clapped her hands together once and sped away, no doubt off to tell the others.

"You don't seem thrilled," his dad said when Holly was out of earshot.

Baylor shrugged. "I'll keep *thrilled* corralled up until we see how things go."

"Fair 'nough."

KayLee slumped in the chair. She should feel excited about this job, ecstatic even. All she felt right now was scared. She'd just promised to make a future for these people. This was more personal than any of the California projects had been. The good feelings must be on their way later.

She'd had things all mapped out in her mind even before she got here. She'd come to the valley, do the job, have a safe and snug place to raise her child for the first year or so, then move on and build her company… probably back in California.

Things had gotten complicated right off the bat, starting with the warm and fuzzy feelings she already had growing inside her regarding the people who lived in and around the town of St. Adelbert. The people at the Easy Breezy Inn had given her a room at ten o'clock in the morning without charging extra, so she could freshen up for her interview with the Doyle family. The gas station attendant at the self-service station had insisted on pumping her gas and washing her bug-spattered windshield and headlamps. That guy—Barry, he called himself—had worked really hard on those dried bugs.

Everyone here was eerily nice.

That gave her pause. Were they too nice? What if they were part of a cult or aliens from outer space?

Whoa! She stopped herself from thinking wild movie-making fantasies.

Worse, however, what if the time came for her to leave, and she still had no place to go, no prospective home? She could do it to her pregnant self, but could she force the itinerant life on a child?

And what if she didn't want to leave the valley at all?

It had been easy letting go of California. When her husband died, her life there had simply evaporated.

She should have made better choices. One of their so-called friends had even accused her of being responsible for Chad's death.

What if it *had been* her fault Chad was unhappy and, who knows, that he'd had a boating accident? She couldn't really fault that friend too much. Some days she blamed herself.

"I'll be everything you need." She stroked her belly and let herself feel the joy and peace her child brought to mind.

Baylor appeared holding a practical, warm-looking jacket. She hoped he hadn't overheard her. He already had enough doubts.

The heavy work jacket he held suspended on the tip of one finger summed everything up. The jacket was nothing she would have ever given a second look at when she lived in California.

Her life was never going to be the same.

When Baylor smiled at her, even though it was a reluctant smile, she found herself wanting to leap up and run into his arms...but she was so *not* flinging herself into anyone's arms. It wasn't going to happen, wasn't even a good idea. She and Chad had flung themselves at each other and look where that got her.

"Hey." She pointed at the jacket and put on a cheery face. "That seems as if it will do the trick."

He held the jacket for her and she slipped inside its warmth. "Hmmm. This feels nice."

"'Bout the time you get used to the cold, the weather will change and you'll be wishing to have it back." He gave her a serious if-you-stick-around-long-enough look.

She'd get used to the weather, or at least, he'd never know about it if she didn't. All he was going to see from now on was the upbeat side of her, the confident side of her she had used in her sales pitch. She hugged the jacket around her and spun in a slow circle, trying to affect comedy. "Ah, if they could see me now."

Another reluctant smile. He was so trying to be nice to her. "You mean the people in California wouldn't appreciate your…ah…style?" he asked.

"Style?"

"Because, for the backside of Montana you look purty trendy."

Yep, she thought, repeating the affirmative she'd already heard more than once in this state. Baylor Doyle was going to give her a chance, a harsh but fair one. Now, if she could live up to his and everyone else's expectations… She shook off doubt and melancholy before they got a foothold. Upbeat. Stay upbeat.

"*Très* chic and ready to work." And she felt better than she'd felt in a long time about anything except her baby, who at that moment seemed to leap to block a soccer goal or something equally emphatic. "Whoa!"

"Are you all right?" Baylor took a step toward her.

She held up one hand up and rubbed her lower ribs with the other. "Nothing to worry about. Sometimes the little one gives me a poke and it takes me by surprise, but I'm great. Better than great. Lead the way."

He handed her a knitted cap, one like her grandmother might have made for her, with a fluffy yarn ball on top, and then he slid on his hat—a Stetson, that's what they wore in one of Chad's movies anyway.

She put on the hat he had given her and tugged it down until it pressed her hair snugly against her ears. Then he led her outside, where she got a spectacular view of the lay of the ranch buildings. To her left and back at the edge of a stand of pine trees sat a pair of log houses. His brothers' houses, she assumed. Straight in front of her, but farther away, sat a barn and several outbuildings. Beyond the barn she could see corrals where horses were eating from a trough. Farther out were open snow-patched areas of what she supposed were grass-lands, and of course, mountain peaks glistened in the distance.

Doyle land spread out beyond fifty-seven hundred acres. After leaving the rich farmland of southwestern Wisconsin that sold by the expensive acre and the pre-cious square footage measured out in inches in Southern California, she wasn't even sure she could conceptual-ize that much land owned by one family.

The seven cabins she would build for the Doyles would dovetail nicely with the two already there. Though the new ones would have more glass and deck-ing, the existing ones had the charm of being more weathered and rustic-looking.

A cabins-in-the-woods kind of thing.

When they filled the cabins for the three to four prime months out of the year, they should do well.

"Less than a quarter mile beyond two small houses is where the cabins will be built," Baylor said after she had spent several minutes gaping. "Ready?"

"Yes, I am."

Baylor held the passenger-side door and she climbed up into the warmth of the truck. Then he jogged around and jumped in the driver's side, and when he did, the truck got even warmer inside. Hormones. Had to be hormones.

"Thanks for having the truck so cozy."

"That would have been one of my brothers, most likely prodded by one wife or the other."

"I knew I was going to like Amy and Holly."

"They're like sisters. It would be a shame for them to have to split up and go separate ways."

"This project means a lot more than income to your family."

"It does."

He took a hard grip on the wheel as he steered away from the big ranch house. "Should I get in my car and run away before I get in to deeply?"

"I wish you wouldn't."

The brim of his hat shadowed his features and she realized she really knew little about Montana and less about the Doyle family. She might have done it again—rushed into something without enough thought.

I'll make it work.

"Hey—" she poked him on the hard muscle of his upper arm "—your Sheriff Potts saw me at my worst and he sent me back here instead of running me out of town. Give me a peek at what's going on, I can take it."

He nudged his hat back on his forehead as if it would help him think better.

"Ranching doesn't support families the way it used to. Income has gone down, but more importantly the cost of living has gone up. We've been able to keep going because the largest part of the income stays in the family. Mostly we're our own ranch hands. We hire on during the heaviest part of calving and when it's time to shift cattle around to different feeding grounds. We let out some logging to a small local company—controlled, environmentally friendly logging that brings in a bit of income."

"And that's not enough." She had asked for the truth and just because it was starting to scare her, she wasn't going to back away.

"It was as long as there weren't any kids' futures to worry about."

"So you decided to try for the tourist population."

"We started a few years ago and it's been popular. We've had a waiting list every season. At the Shadow Range we provide several things not everyone else this far out does. Satellite TV and internet, granted both are intermittent depending on the reception, but it's there enough of the time to satisfy all but some of the teenagers. The houses have electricity, gas and indoor—"

"Plumbing? One of my favorites."

His grin warmed her, a lot more than it should have.

"Then we have features most people's homes don't— fireplaces with an endless supply of wood on the porch, daily wildlife viewing and, although you might hear a train whistle in the distance from time to time, there isn't even a whisper of highway or freeway traffic. And if you want it, you can have maid service and meals included."

"Roughing it the way city people like it. I have to tell you, I'm one of them. Give me a good old pillow-top mattress and a dishwasher any day." But she was finding out in detail she didn't have to have either of those.

"We add horseback riding, fishing, guided trail walks and trips down the river on pontoon boats."

She tried to imagine what it would be like to be a guest at the ranch. What would she want? A picture of Baylor and her floating down a lazy river in a pontoon boat resting in each other's arms popped into her head. Her eyes sprang wide. She sat up and leaned forward as if interested in something outside the window. Talk about *whoa*.

"What are you looking at?"

"I was wondering…" She paused so she could quickly make something up because she sure as heck wasn't going to tell him what she was thinking. "Does the nonranching part get to all of you?"

He was silent while he bounced the truck over the uneven road, out beyond where the two smaller houses sat and onto the edge of a small meadow.

"From time to time, but keeping the ranch for everyone's future is more important than not washing someone's dirty sheets. And we get to help the poor city folk get a glimpse of what a really rich life is like. You know, dirt under your fingernails, getting stiff from being in a saddle too long, sleeping out under the stars with the snakes."

"You make it sound as nice here as I imagined it would. I might have to rent out one of the cabins we're building—but there'd be no snakes for me, please." She wondered what he'd say if he knew how little she was kidding about renting one of the cabins, reptiles or not.

"The wooded area over there…" He'd stopped the truck, and pointed out into the distance.

"Wait. Where do you put the tourists? Aren't those two houses for Holly and Amy and their families?"

"In the spring, while Lance and Seth are busy calving and doing ranch work, Holly and Amy are busy packing up to move out of their homes and into the big house. We all live together in the late spring and summer. There are seven bedrooms and it's, well, we'll call it cozy."

"It's good you all like each other. Maybe we should build more cabins to start with and that might give Holly and Amy a break next spring."

"If we build them all at once, you can invite all your California friends who are looking for a break from the crowd."

Bam. A reality blast thrown in her face. All her friends?

It was bad enough to know most of her so-called

friends had deserted her, but to have to admit it to a stranger—a customer—pointed out a far too dismal future. Blah.

BAYLOR WONDERED WHAT he said that made her face go all long and thoughtful, and then he reminded himself it didn't matter.

He knew himself well enough to know KayLee Morgan could be dangerous territory. Dangerous because he couldn't help himself. Rescuing damsels in distress had been his thing since he kept the bullies in grade school from picking on Abby Fairbanks when he was nine and she was twelve. But damsel rescuing had to take a second seat to this business deal. Rescuing this one could put his family's welfare in jeopardy.

"Over there—" he pointed toward the far side of the meadow "—is where you propose to start the first cabin."

She leaned closer to the windshield and peered at an isolated stand of pine and larch trees. "Perfect. We'll need to set down the roads first so the equipment can be moved easily in and out."

She reached for the door handle.

"Hang on. I'll drive over and you can get a closer look. It gets muddy out there when the snow melts."

She nodded. Her expression held a mixture of concentration and excitement. He wondered if he would have gotten that reaction from the other bidders.

Baylor realized she had a hand on her belly. She seemed to be speaking to her baby and that simple gesture made her seem totally invested in the project. At that moment, she seemed more like a partner than a vendor. He wasn't sure whether that was bad or good.

Bad if it made him lose his objectivity, and good if it made her care more about his family's future.

Suddenly, she seemed very attractive and not just because she was sexy. He stopped the truck. The heat must have been making him stupid. He needed fresh air and badly.

BAYLOR STOPPED THE TRUCK at the edge of the stream and leaped out, but KayLee climbed down before he could get around to help her. She didn't need help, she couldn't allow herself to need help, but she wanted to stand where one of the cabins would be built, feel the site, make sure it was as perfect as she had hoped it would be.

While Baylor rummaged around for something in the toolbox in the bed of the truck, she made her way across the uneven, somewhat icy terrain to the middle of the grouping of ponderosa pine trees. Their sweet scent filled the air and she inhaled deeply and let herself imagine.

She could see a cabin nestled between the largest trees where there was a natural space. There was enough access from the side of the lot away from the stream that only one small sapling might have to be removed to make way for the heavy equipment.

It was the perfect spot for a cabin, a home, her mountain home. She shook her head at the futility of that dream and swiped a rascal tear from the corner of her eye.

"What do you think?" Baylor spoke softly from behind her as if he knew he was intruding on the mood.

Upbeat, that's all she'd show him, not tears. In fact when she wasn't pregnant anymore, she vowed to never cry again for any reason.

"It's perfect," she said when she was sure her voice wouldn't squeak or waver. "I'd put the cabin right here, offset from the middle."

"That's where me and my brothers would pitch a tent when we wanted a wilderness adventure and our mother thought we were too young to be too far away."

The sound of his voice drew closer until she could feel the heat of his breath against the back of her neck. KayLee fought a sudden intense craving to have him touch her, put a hand on her waist—well, where she used to have a waist—or put his lips to her neck. Oh, heck and darn. She took a step away.

"This is a special place, and I think a cabin here would be great. We could call it the Whispering Winds Cabin because the wind swishes like a whisper through the pine needles."

"Maybe not," he said and chuckled.

"No?" Why not? Why was he laughing? Was he going to squash all her ideas?

He nudged her shoulder with his fingertip to get her attention. "It's a fine name, but Whispering Winds is the name of the neighbor's ranch. Thinking of names as you build them is a good idea, though. Cabin one, two, three, et cetera is kind of boring."

She shifted to look directly into sky-blue eyes that studied her face. She dropped her gaze to keep him from reading her soul.

The sparkle of golden hair in the V of his cream-colored shirt beckoned her with a "come on and touch me." She wanted to put her fingers in the V and loosen the rest of the buttons so she could press her palms into the middle of that soft hair, feel the ridge of muscle where his pecs bulged. She fought to keep her eyes from moving even lower and then with a hormone-balancing force of will brought her gaze back up to his face.

She smiled and shifted from one foot to the other. "You know…"

"What do I know?" He was amused and not embarrassed by her assessment.

"Besides the obvious handsomeness of your face, speaking from a Hollywood perspective, you have uncommonly nice individual features."

"A Hollywood perspective?"

"I saw enough of the people my husband cast in films to know a great jaw and a sexy camera-friendly mouth when I see them."

"Sexy, too?"

She parted her lips to speak again, but stopped when she realized she wanted to ask him to kiss her.

She stepped backward.

Ask him to kiss her? Yeah. That should send him fleeing back to the ranch house, where he could call the sheriff to toss her out of Montana for good.

But he didn't look upset. He might even look… interested?

Not good.

They were both being silly, not just her.

Worse.

They had known each other only a few hours. She had an excuse—pregnancy.

She tried to put distance between them but he stuck to her side. When in the center of the clearing, she slipped on an icy patch and found the electric touch of his hand on her arm long enough to stabilize her—long enough to make her burn inside and out.

That's it. A drastic intervention was called for.

"Thank you." She stuck her hands in the pockets of

the jacket. "Okay. All right. I want to be upfront about something so I can keep it from growing out of proportion."

He gave her a skeptical look. "Go on."

"I'm attracted to you and I want you to know the pregnancy hormones racing around inside of my body are doing that to me. I'm sure you're a perfectly nice guy who is perfectly attractive to most women."

"But you aren't most women?" He stepped closer, she was sure he did that to make her step farther away… and she did. She wanted to skitter away, but she didn't do skittering very well these days.

"Unfortunately, I am most women, and right now, I could eat you up without even sitting down."

He grinned. "This is turning out to be a very interesting day."

"I'm afraid it's not really me talking."

"It's the hormones?"

"Afraid so. I usually have more control than…"

"Than what?"

"I know you're yanking *my* chain now, but I've been around pretty faces for years and I've always been able to keep a lid on feeling anything about any of them, because a pretty face is just that."

"I'm a pretty face?"

She stepped closer to the stream. "Oh, you are such a pretty face."

"And you find yourself helplessly attracted to me?" He took another step toward her.

"If you come any closer, I might have to defend all of us from me. I might seem to be a helpless, pregnant thing, but I have to tell you, I'm not." She drew herself up tall and put fists to her hips to take up as much space as possible.

"Never entered my mind that you were." He stopped and leaned against a convenient pine tree, letting her put some distance between them. "Helpless in any way."

"I shouldn't have opened my mouth. I am so much less censored these days, but I thought if I got it out in the open I could enlist your help in keeping me from doing something we'd regret."

He moved again, stalking unhurriedly toward her like a big cat after prey.

"Darlin'," he said with an exaggerated drawl, "speak for yourself."

CHAPTER FOUR

KayLee felt her muscles tense. She couldn't budge, even to flee. Baylor approached where she stood by the burbling stream.

Stuff had come tumbling out of her mouth today, stuff that horrified her to hear out loud even if it was the truth.

The big rancher took another deliberate step, concentration suffusing his features.

He was coming—she knew he was—to grab her by the borrowed jacket collar and throw her off the ranch himself. And she'd be lucky if that's all he did.

He took another step, and then he stopped and threw his head back and laughed.

She did a slow fish-mouthed gape. *What the hell—heck—are you laughing at?* hung frozen, unspoken, on her tongue.

"KayLee."

"I'm sorry. I'm so sorry." She hated to be in a position to apologize, but there was nothing for this situation except to beg forgiveness and hope Baylor Doyle had a big…um…heart.

"You have nothing to be sorry for." His sincere expression told her he wasn't joking or being dismissive.

Relief sapped nearly all the energy from her legs. She leaned forward and put her hands on her wobbly knees and then straightened. "I know it's—I'm so idiotic to…"

"KayLee." He stopped her with a raised hand. "You will so fit in around here."

"What?"

"It's good to know you won't be horrified by the goings-on at the ranch. There are fewer inhibitions way out here than people think—at least it's true on this ranch."

"Uh, it's not the cow and horse sex is it?"

He made a face as if her words shocked him and laughed again.

She grabbed the sides of her borrowed knit hat and tugged it down until it hid her eyes. "I can't believe I just said that. If you threw me out right now, I wouldn't blame you."

"It'd be easier to keep you than to try to explain to my family. Did you make everyone in Southern California blush?" He sounded too kind, and...well, maybe tolerant when he spoke.

She lifted the edge of the hat and blinked at him. "I didn't. Really. I used to be sane and nice, even intelligent."

Shade from the windblown pine branches flickered across his features. "You're still nice. It's all the things going on in your life that're making you a little—"

"Extreme? Crazy? One brick short of a load?" She narrowed her eyes. "And what do you mean? All *what* that's going on in my life? How much do you know about me?"

"More than you know about us, I'd wager."

What had she said? She had practiced her presentation so often, she was sure she hadn't dragged her personal life out for them all to examine. What had they done? She turned slowly away and stared into the partially ice-covered brook. The water flashed and coursed in plain view and then sometimes hid beneath a layer of snow-covered ice.

The sheriff trusted these people or he wouldn't have sent her back…unless he was one of those bad cops from the movies and these people were all psycho. Too extreme? Yes, it was. She took a deep breath of the cold air to ground herself.

If she had stepped into a horror movie, she wasn't going to wait until some dark night to find out. She'd demand of Baylor what was up and judge his reaction. She could only hope he didn't pull out a chainsaw from his back pocket.

Cold seeped trough the toes of her shoes and the seams of the well-worn brown jacket. She started to shiver, but she faced Baylor. "How much do you know about me and how?"

He reached into his jacket pocket.

Oh, God.

He studied her for a long second and then produced a battered old red camera.

"You're cold—" he handed her the camera "—but I thought you might like to take a couple photos before we get in the truck."

"It's not a chainsaw," she said as she breathed out a sigh.

"No. I keep all my gas-powered tools in my work-coat pocket," he said very seriously.

She did so deserve to be mocked, but it was better than being thrown out.

She scanned his face and the sincere expression warmed her and then she shivered harder. She didn't know how much was cold and how much was mortification, but she took the camera. "Thank you."

Grateful to have a diversion, she started clicking

photos of the stand of trees, of the clearing where the other cabins would be built, of the stream and forest, of the mountains against the blue sky. The more she shot, the more excited she became, and the colder, until her hands shook too much to get a decent picture.

"Ready?" He held a hand out in the direction of the truck.

When they were settled in the toasty cab he shifted to face her. "We checked into all the viable bidders' backgrounds."

"Ah."

"Checking out candidates seemed prudent."

"And you're still willing to give me a chance." Awe and wonder filled her, and then her mind spun with the possibilities of what the investigator might have found. "I think I'm going to accept that for now, but I might never want to know what you discovered."

"To my family, you seemed the most...human I guess."

"I...um...try."

"They trust you and I've decided to listen to them."

"I had the feeling trusting me was difficult for you." She drew her lips inward. "I won't disappoint you, Baylor Doyle, because you're a good man."

He lifted an eyebrow but didn't say anything.

"Thank you for everything." KayLee closed her eyes briefly and imagined the happy feelings filtering down toward her baby. Everything that was good in her life, she tried to share with her unborn child.

She noted his expression and tried to figure out what he might be thinking. "You could have given me such a hard time for opening my mouth about being attracted to you."

"Still might."

"Or take advantage of me."

"Still might."

It was her turn to laugh and she did and then faced the window when new tears formed in her eyes.

"Do you cry all the time?" he asked.

"Pretty much." She sniffed.

"Isn't that normal?"

"Normal? Nothing about me is normal, if normal is the way I was before I was pregnant." Her breath steamed the window as she spoke.

"Here." He reached around and handed her a large soft hankie with a red-and-white paisley pattern, the kind she used to wear as a scarf, but this one was softer and the color had faded so much, it must have been washed a million times.

She blew her nose and dabbed her eyes.

"Thanks." She tucked the hankie in the pocket of the jacket. She'd have to remember to take it out and wash it.

"Amy cried for seven months straight before she gave birth to little Trey two years ago," he said, his voice kind and soft and she so appreciated the gesture of comfort. "Good news, though, KayLee."

She sniffed again. "What's that?"

"Now she only cries when she's sad."

"That's good."

"Or when she's happy."

She laughed again. Baylor Doyle made her laugh. Not much did these days and she loved him for it—well, liked him for it. When she pivoted in her seat, he was still facing her, arms folded, hat pushed back so golden curls framed his face.

She had never seen anything that looked as good as

he did at that moment. Trouble. Sexy and roguish at the same time. A bad boy. Deep trouble.

"I can do this job and you will like what I've done." She smiled and placed a hand on her belly. "Now, I need to get back to town and get some rest."

"The family will want to say goodbye before you leave."

When they got back to the ranch house, the Doyles, including three children, had gathered in the kitchen to see her off.

Holly and Lance introduced their two-year-old daughter, Katie, and a five-year-old son, Matt.

"Hi, Katie. Hi, Matt," KayLee said. Katie grinned and hid behind her father's leg. Matt stuck out his hand and she shook it.

From the other side of the butcher block island Seth and Amy introduced her to their shy two-year-old son, Trey. Amy held the frail-looking boy in her arms, and he kept his head on her shoulder.

Evvy hugged her, and Curtis shook her hand. "Thank you for working so hard on this project for us," he said. This must have been where Baylor got his blue eyes.

"Don't be fooled by all this, KayLee." With the sweep of his hand, Baylor included every Doyle in the room. "We all have our company manners on."

"Speak for yourself," Holly shot back. "I'm always nice."

"You are, Mommy," the red-haired boy beside her said. "Can I have pie now?"

Curtis laughed. "You keep it up, boy," he said to the child. "You never know what you'll get by asking."

"Thanks, a lot, Dad."

"So, can I?" Matthew patted his mother on the arm.

Holly made a fierce face at her father-in-law and was met with grandfatherly innocence.

"After dinner, sweetie. If you're hungry now I'll get you an apple."

"Me, too," Katie cried and jumped out into the open.

While the other children romped, blond, curly-haired Trey sat quietly in his mother's arms and seemed to get more attention than he needed. KayLee knew she'd be like that. The first-child syndrome.

"I'm glad you're going to work for us," Evvy said from the table where she had taken a seat.

"Me, too," said Amy.

"We all are," Holly added, as she washed an apple at the sink.

The brothers and sisters-in-law all looked to Baylor.

He shook his head. "Yes, we all are."

"Is she your girlfriend, Uncle Baylor?" Matt asked, accepting an apple slice from his mother.

"She's going to build more houses here on the ranch," Holly said to distract the boy.

"Wow. Real houses."

"Cabins. Seven of them." KayLee loved the boy's enthusiasm.

Lance leaned down and nudged his son with an elbow, and Matt giggled. "Maybe we'll have to get you a hammer to help."

The boy's eyes lit up.

The simple exchange between father and son exacerbated a yearning inside KayLee, a tearing at her heart that almost took her breath away.

Her nuclear family consisted of her mother, herself and sometimes her father, and they never filled the kitchen or any room with gales of laughter and teasing.

She wanted for her child what the Doyles' children had.

"You okay?" Baylor asked beside her.

KayLee smiled. "You all seem to have so much fun as a family. I was thinking about being a family to my child."

Holly patted KayLee's hand. "You'll do fine."

"Thank you, Holly." She knew this was small talk, but she hoped anyway that Holly was right.

Trey suddenly coughed and both his parents gave him their complete attention. Seth put one hand on Trey's back and Amy put one on the boy's chest and whispered something into the boy's ear. Trey shook his head and smiled, a tiny smile that held—distress.

A hard, deep twinge squeezed KayLee's chest, and dread flipped on like a switch. There was something going on with the youngest Doyle. Something seriously wrong.

Baylor took her elbow. "You must be tired. I'll see you to your car."

When Baylor finally got K. L. Morgan on her way back to town, he paced the porch. The taillights of her small Ford retreated and he wondered if he was going to lose his mind in the next few weeks.

When the tiny red specks blinked out, he stepped off the porch and headed toward the barn to saddle Blue Moon. There were chores to be done that had been delayed by the meeting and he'd volunteered to do this late-afternoon round by himself because he didn't feel like discussing a certain woman at the moment.

It was bad enough he'd gone mad and let his guard down long enough for her to slip inside. He remembered how sexy she had looked with the sunshine in her hair and the ranch on her mind. *Darlin',* even in jest. He wasn't just mad, he was a stark raving lunatic.

The barn door gave its usual comforting low groan as he slid it aside and Blue Moon nickered as Baylor approached in the dim light. Blue was a cow horse and a good one and no horse on the ranch, or in the county for that matter, could cut pairs or help bring a restless unwilling cow in labor into the calving shed like Blue could.

When he finished saddling his horse, Baylor paused to lean his forearms on the old, ride-worn leather.

The sound of KayLee's laughter had blended with the rest of the family's as if it had always been there. Once when she had looked up at him, her long curling hair had tumbled over her left eye and he had wanted to tuck it behind her ear.

He straightened.

"Come on, boy." He led the horse out of the barn and climbed into the saddle. Without more than a touch of the reins on his neck, the horse knew they were headed to where the cows that would soon calve were kept in a small field adjacent to the calving barn. "We got work to do and I got a woman to not think about."

KAYLEE ARRIVED AT THE Easy Breezy Inn with only enough energy to flop on the bed. With the exception of the day she waited to hear if Chad was alive or dead, this had been one of the longest days she could remember.

She would have thought growing up as a latchkey kid would have prepared her for life's knocks. It wasn't that her parents didn't love her, but as soon as they thought she was old enough to see to her own needs, they weren't there much of the time. With her mom's rotating shifts as an aide at the hospital and her dad's many different jobs, their hours were unpredictable.

One of them usually showed up sometime in the evening. Her father always brought burgers or fried chicken and her mother brought tofu and sprouts. She was very young when she began to wonder why they ever got married in the first place.

She wondered what kind of mother she would make. Would she grow tired or bored with her child?

Her baby chose that moment to kick her and she laughed. "Oh, baby. Mommy will love you always. In fact, you might not be able to get rid of me. I'll be a class mother. I'll be a prom chaperone. I'll move to wherever you go to college."

She thought of another baby, little Trey. She hoped the boy was all right. She couldn't imagine having something happen to her child. "You'll be happy and well, won't you, little one?" It was a wish for her own child as well as for Amy and Seth's son.

The voice-mail signal from her mobile phone jangled.

It could be Baylor calling to make sure she made it safely or to say good-night.

She clicked on the single lamp, and checked her phone. Sharring and Hack the caller ID said, her attorney's office.

"Ms. Morgan, this is Randolph Sharring. I need to speak with you. I'm out of the office for the rest of the day. Please call me tomorrow morning."

She folded her phone and dropped her chin to her chest. She had engaged Randolph Sharring to help her through the maze Chad had left with his death. Three days ago she told Randolph she was leaving town for St. Adelbert. It seemed wise for someone in the world outside this remote valley to know where she was. She'd left a message on her mother's voice mail but had no idea when that would be picked up. If she went missing, at least Randolph might eventually notice and call the police.

What Randolph wanted, she had no idea. The last time he personally called her, it had been to tell her she was broke, totally and irrevocably. Maybe the creditors were after her again. She had little money or possessions to give up. Maybe they wanted blood.

Well, if that's what they wanted, Randolph would have to send them to St. Adelbert to get it.

She took off the work jacket Baylor had insisted she keep until she got a good one of her own and hung it in the closet. She stuffed the hankie in the bag of laundry she had attached, by the plastic straps, onto a hanger.

Shower and bed were all she had energy for and hopefully enough for that.

The tub was old and had patches where the black of the metal beneath peeked through, but the water came out hot and fierce. She dawdled in the heat of the shower for as long as she could stand, which wasn't long. Then she dried off with a rather thin towel and crawled gratefully into bed, where she tugged the brightly flowered quilt over her. Blessed sleep would take her to a new day.

For the first time in months, maybe even a couple of years, she was going to drop off to sleep knowing things were looking up.

She closed her eyes and Baylor's face floated into view. What a great bedtime story. Then Chad's face floated in. Soon, the two men began to carry on a dialogue about something she couldn't quite hear.

"But she's damned cute." Baylor's words were the first to register.

"Everybody in our circle was cute. Doesn't count for much," Chad replied as he took a sip of his favorite single malt scotch, which KayLee now noticed he was holding. "She used to be smart...."

Randolph Sharring's image appeared between Baylor and Chad and added, "Too bad." He shook his head, a morose expression on his long, jowly face. "So sad."

An ex-friend of Chad's, a groupie actually, named Farly Longwood appeared beside Randolph and pointed a finger at her. "Our Chad wouldn't be dead if it weren't for you. It's all your fault," he screamed.

KayLee's eyes flew open and the images fled.

She sat up in the dark. That it had been a twilight musing between wakefulness and sleep did not make what they said any less plausible.

She used to be smart.... Could she attribute those words to Chad? Had she heard him say such a thing or was it from her head alone? *Too bad. So sad...* That she used to have a brain? Is that how she interpreted the tone of Randolph's phone message?

Had she had everything and let it all go?

Was it all her fault?

CHAPTER FIVE

A STUNNINGLY BRIGHT Tuesday morning sun against a stark blue sky greeted KayLee as she stepped out of the Easy Breezy and started down the broad, curbed street to take her morning walk.

She strolled past a log-cabin gas station with a convenience store where she had bought gas yesterday. The man—Barry—waved at her. She passed the post office, a town square with park benches and an empty lot with a very old and dilapidated sign that touted the soon-to-be-built community center.

Half an hour later she let herself into her room, placed a bowl of steaming oatmeal and a banana from the motel's breakfast bar on the table and hung her warm borrowed coat on the back of the chair by the window.

She ate her food and then called the ranch. When Evvy answered, she told the matriarch she had some business to conduct and would be later than she thought. Then she bucked up and called her attorney.

"Randolph, please," she said when the receptionist answered the phone. "It's KayLee Morgan."

"I'll see if he's in."

KayLee waited. She was used to "I'll see if he's in." It really meant "I'll see if he wants to talk to you." Most people in her previous life used the ploy.

"KayLee—" Randolph sounded like his usual

somber self. "You need to come back to California. Right away."

That was extremely enigmatic, even for Randolph.

"I've started work with a client and I can't leave now, Randolph."

"Apparently there is a letter for you."

"You're speaking in riddles." This wasn't like the dot-and-cross Randolph she was used to.

"Your husband's attorney has a letter he says has to be delivered personally to you."

A letter from his creditors? Something regarding Chad's death? Someone else blaming her?

The accusing expression on Farly Longwood's face popped into her head.

Acid scalded the back of her throat. Chad's death had been declared an accident largely because no suicide note had been found. What if this was…?

"Who is it from?"

"It's allegedly from your husband personally."

"No," she blurted out. Her husband had been driving his speedboat too fast and when he crashed, witnesses said it had burst immediately into flames.

"KayLee, are you there?"

Randolph's stern tone brought her to her senses.

"Do you know what it's about or can you overnight it to me?" She had to know if Farly Longwood had been right. Was she somehow horribly complicit in Chad's death?

"He couldn't say what it was about, but it seems as if it might contain your husband's last wishes."

KayLee sat up and sucked in an involuntary breath as Randolph almost confirmed her terrifying suspicions. "Randolph, you don't think… I have to know if Chad did this to himself on purpose. If he…"

"Let's not go there, KayLee. His attorney says he's had the letter since a few weeks before Chad's accident."

That had to be right after Chad found out he was going to be a father, she thought. "But what if it's…"

"It could be any number of things—information about his estate for instance, or a summary of his financials. But anything is purely speculative right now."

"You're sure his attorney doesn't know?" She sat back in the chair and propped her puffy feet on the edge of the bed. How could this secret letter be anything but bad news? What if it was some horrible genetic secret that might affect their child?

"His official stance is he doesn't know what's in the letter."

"Why did he wait so long to let you know he had it?"

"Apparently, there was a stipulation attached to the letter to give it to you six months after Chad's death as long as you are not—"

Now Randolph's end of the phone line went silent.

"Randolph? As long as I'm not what?"

"Attached. As long as you are not attached to a new man."

She felt Chad reaching out from his watery grave, clutching at her. "And if I was attached?"

"His attorney was to deal with the contents of the letter in a responsible manner. I assured him there was no way there was a man in your life."

Thanks a lot, Randolph.

"Randolph." She tugged on her hair and then brushed it back behind her ear. "Can he send it to me?"

"He's supposed to deliver it to you personally. When you come and collect it."

"I can't do that. Not in the near future. I have six weeks, seven at the most, to get this project well-established and then I'll be even busier for a while. It'll have to wait."

"Well, the attorney said he could stretch things since Chad is…er…passed. He will have it delivered to me, if you sign a release form for me to represent you in this matter."

"Thanks, Randolph. Let's do that."

"Do you have a fax or a printer available?" She thought of the office at the Doyle ranch, but decided it was way too personal. She couldn't open up even more to people she didn't know very well, especially since she would be working closely with them for the foreseeable future.

"Drop the form in the mail." But to where? General delivery to the post office in St. Adelbert? She hesitated and then gave him the address of the Easy Breezy Inn. She'd have to stay here until she found some place in town to live.

Randolph said he would send the forms right away and then they rang off.

She dropped her phone on the table and rested her head in her hands.

She could take it if Chad blamed her. She really could. She could take a lot these days as long as it didn't harm her baby.

As for Farly Longwood's accusations, she could drive herself crazy with such things. If she let herself.

BAYLOR COAXED THE REST of the mud from the crevice in Blue's left front hoof and pried at the stone jammed along the edge of the horse's shoe. When the small pebble popped out, it clanked against the metal rail of the corral and dropped to the ground. For the second day in a row the brilliant blue of the sky was a boon to the livestock and the ranchers who tended them. He and Blue could be outside in the glorious sunshine because the eight to ten inches of snow that had been predicted for today had been delayed for a day or two.

"That feel better, boy?" he asked as he patted the horse's flank. Then he rotated to the next hoof to clean out the debris collected during the morning ride to check a problem spot in the fence where the cattle would soon be turned loose. Chances were, he'd not get back on the horse again today until much later. This was to be the first big planning day with KayLee.

And she was supposed to be here bright and early.

Since she had called to say she would be late, he'd gotten the day's chores started with his brothers and was glad for the distraction while he waited.

Every time he let his mind wander this morning, he found himself thinking about the woman from California. Thoughts of her had kept him from sleeping last night when he wasn't on calving duty. This morning when she didn't show up, he found himself unreasonably disappointed and not just because his planned departure from this valley might be put off. If she had changed her mind and had gone back to California, she was putting his family's dreams on hold. And he found he anticipated seeing her.

Not good.

He went back to scraping the bottom of Blue's hoof like he was supposed to be doing and not letting his mind gallivant off to think about a woman.

"Come on, boy. You want some hay?" Baylor lowered the last hoof to the ground, happy they were all in good shape. A sore foot would put a horse out of commission and neither horse nor man needed that kind of trouble.

"You about done babying that animal?" Seth stood several yards away, boots in a wide stance, arms folded over his chest.

Baylor led Blue up to where his brother waited near the barn.

"You come all the way out here to give me and Blue a hard time?"

"That and there's a car coming up the ranch road. A little blue one that looks like it could blow away in a mild breeze."

KayLee's teensy Ford. And it was a small car. He had thought that last night as she was leaving in the dark. He was used to either being on a surefooted horse or having a substantial amount of metal wrapped around him. Either was safer than the car KayLee had driven all the way from California into the outback of Montana.

Hands on his hips now, his brother made an exaggerated assessment of the sun's high position in the sky. "She must still be on California time."

"She called. Said she had some unexpected business to deal with this morning."

Seth laughed. "You wanted life outside the valley. This one'll give you a taste of that."

"Yeah, she might." Dark-lashed green eyes had haunted his night and thoughts now of long dark blond hair tossed around by the wind made him feel things he didn't need to feel right now.

Seth laughed again and lightly punched Baylor on the arm. "She's pretty easy on the eyes, Bay, and all the wives like her."

"She's a good choice for the job."

Blue nudged him on the shoulder, impatient for the

promised hay, no doubt, and Baylor rubbed the scuffed toe of one boot on the leg of his jeans.

"Hey, she's gotten to you, hasn't she?" Seth asked.

Baylor planted both boots firmly on the ground and before answering, reached around and rubbed Blue's nose. Then he gave his brother an exasperated snort. "You're having a good time with this, aren't you?"

"It's a funny thing to see my calm-and-collected little brother lose his cool."

Baylor shook his head and purposefully examined his mud-caked hands. "Suppose I should wash up a bit, and I did promise Blue some hay."

"I'll see to Blue. You go greet Ms. Morgan."

Baylor nodded and gave Blue a last pat. "How's that heifer coming? She was getting awfully restless."

"Got her all safely tucked in the calving shed. We'll soon know if she needs our help."

"Yeah, it might come to that."

"We're ready if it does. Holly's with her. Said she didn't want her skills to get rusty."

"Lance isn't back from town yet?"

Seth shook his head and took Blue's reins.

"That isn't the kind of…"

"It's risky? I got it, Bay. I'll go back when I'm finished here." Seth patted Blue and held up a carrot. The horse abandoned Baylor for his brother.

Seth smirked.

Baylor left his brother and the horse behind and headed into the barn, where there was a sink to wash his hands. If it was obvious to his brother that K. L. Morgan affected him, he might want to soak his head, too. See if he could get some clarity.

After he'd washed his hands without sticking his head under the faucet, he cleaned his boots from top and bottom. Then from the barn, he watched KayLee get out of her car and walk slowly up to the house.

Today she wore well-fitting jeans with the brown jacket he had lent her and a bright green scarf around her neck. She looked like every dream that had awakened him last night.

If a woman's physical attributes were all that mattered to him—he'd met plenty of great-looking ones inside and outside the valley, and enjoyed their company—he hadn't found one who made him restless. KayLee made him restless.

He was going to have to get over that. She was here to do a job and she was going to have a baby. The first would help him and he didn't hold the second against her. A woman and a baby didn't fit into his life right now. He had too much to do, too much uncertainty. Let her stay in this safe valley after he was gone. His family would love to take care of her.

Someone answered the door and an arm came out and pointed directly at him. KayLee swung toward him and waved.

He waved back and headed toward the house. Might as well get started. His parents would be there to sign papers and then he and KayLee would be left alone to put their heads together and get to work on the details.

As she waited on the porch for him, the wind lifted her hair and laid it back down so it flowed over one shoulder. The same feeling of heat shot through him as it had last night in the dark.

If you'd have asked him yesterday morning, he'd have said there was nothing about a pregnant woman he'd find sexy. That had been before he met K. L. Morgan.

When he realized he was staring directly into her

eyes, he dipped his chin and removed his cap. Hats came in handy sometimes.

"I'll leave you two to get to it." From the doorway Amy watched him closely, a small, knowing smile on her face. God, he hated that smile.

"Thanks, Amy," he said. She nodded once and retreated. He then said to KayLee. "Good morning. I trust you had a good night's sleep."

"It did the job well enough." She waited a beat and then continued. "So tell me, are you glad I came back?"

There was the real question, and it had only one answer.

"Well, I can tell you, you made a whole houseful of people happy by coming back." He held the door open so she could enter the foyer. The smell of her, suggesting a gentle herbal shampoo, floated up at him and had his nose wanting more.

He slowed and let her get farther ahead of him. For a house that was supposed to be full of people, this one seemed deserted.

"And you? Did it make you happy?" KayLee asked as she walked into the living room.

She stopped short when a small head, face half-covered by a blue kerchief, popped out from behind one of the large wood-trimmed leather sofas.

"Hey! We've got a bandit of some kind holed up here," Baylor said as he stopped beside KayLee.

She smiled at the boy and the little head ducked out of sight.

"Matthew, are you in the living room?" Amy called from the direction of the kitchen.

The head popped out again, handkerchief sagging down under his chin and with a finger to his lips.

"Don't tell, Uncle Baylor. Aunt Amy wants me to help make the beds," the child whispered.

"I bet she thinks you're great when you help her."

The features in the boy's face drooped comically and he lowered his chin to his chest. "Yeah. She does."

Baylor knew how he felt. Do it because it was the right thing to do. "And she means it. And I think so, too."

The boy smiled from ear to ear, then he got up and ran from the room. "Here I am, Aunt Amy."

Baylor chuckled. "Gotta hand it to him. He does a good job of figuring things out."

"Like his uncle?" She studied him with a deeply probing gaze, her lips parted slightly, and Baylor found himself wanting to dip his head and take a taste of her mouth. Her soft pink lips would be…

He forced the image from his head and gave her what he hoped was a benign smile. "Everything is in the office. My parents should be there by now."

"I'm here bright and early after all."

The grin hit him as a hard smack and sent every sense he had rushing downward.

Damn.

He cleared his throat. "Yeah, that's what I was thinking. How early you got here. It's barely noon."

"Sure you were."

The office was empty when they arrived. No parents. If he let his natural instinct rule, he'd take her in and lock the door.

CHAPTER SIX

K<small>AY</small>L<small>EE</small> <small>FOLLOWED</small> the invitation of Baylor's outstretched hand and stepped inside the brightly lit office. The anticipation of starting the job warmed her, as did the sight of the sunlight streaming in by way of the generous casement windows.

"I'll go find my parents," Baylor said and then he disappeared down the hallway. She stepped into the warm rays of sunshine as the sound of his boot heels faded.

More of the brown grass and rocky ground showed through the snow today and the vision of what she could build for the Doyle family became clearer. She envisioned the cabins off in the distance sprouting from the ground, settling mostly in the open spaces surrounded by trees. The first and last to be built sprang up fully dimensional in her mind amid the trees where quiet night would offer the whispers of the larch, the lodge pole and ponderosa pines, the smell of wood smoke and earth, and the soft laughter of lovers.

Her breath caught in her chest. Lovers. She wondered if she and Chad had ever really been lovers, if they had ever been more than humans suffering the urges of survival of the species and tricking themselves into thinking they were in love.

Chad, what did we do?

The click of the outside door interrupted her thoughts and Holly stopped in the office dressed in work clothes.

"Hey, KayLee. Glad we didn't scare you off," she said with a big smile.

Holly's welcome gave KayLee a boost of courage and she laughed. "I'm looking forward to getting things started."

"Bay will be a lot of help. He's pushy sometimes, but it's just his way, so don't let it get to you."

"I'll keep that in mind."

"Holly?" Evvy called from a distance.

"Sorry, gotta go." Holly waved and disappeared down the hallway in the direction Baylor had gone.

KayLee walked away from the window and sat down in one of the three chairs arranged in front of the desk. She forced away thoughts and feelings of precious lost chances. For better or worse…she and Chad had at least stayed together.

She dug in her briefcase and extracted her glasses and her copy of the contract. Regardless of her promises to fulfill the Doyles' dreams, she found she wanted more than ever to work for them, to be a part of something solid with roots and history.

She put the documents on her lap and twirled her glasses by one stem.

And then there was Baylor.

He smelled good this morning, like fresh air and horses.

Wildly handsome, smirky and good with kids? Too good to be true. There must be something about him that made him off-limits. Maybe it was the pushiness Holly had mentioned. She didn't need pushy. She needed to be the balanced foundation her baby's life could be built on.

She slipped her glasses on with a bit more force than necessary and opened her copy of the contract.

She knew it by heart, knew the estimated time frame. She also knew, no matter what it said, she'd get people started as soon as the ground could be worked and in the meantime, she'd make arrangements for the materials to be brought into the valley and ready to be delivered to the site when needed.

The cabins would be a dream for city dwellers who wanted to "rough it." To recline in front of the fireplace, covered with a wooly blanket, letting the ambiance soothe her as she sketched her next project, the smell of the pines, the singing of the birds, the crackling of the fire in the stone fireplace...

Her head bobbed.

She snapped her eyes open, sat up straight and cleared her head with a couple of deep breaths.

The clock on the wall said she'd been alone for over twenty minutes. She couldn't think of a reason that could be good.

Footsteps thudded down the stairs and hurried toward the office. A moment later, Holly flew past and a blink later, the door leading outside slammed shut. There were undoubtedly many ranch emergencies that required hurrying. KayLee assumed she'd see much hustle here, a totally different kind of hustle than she was used to in Southern California.

She picked up the contract again and checked to see that it was in order. She had left behind copies yesterday so the Doyles could review them, run them by their attorneys again if they wanted to.

Everything appeared to be in order and ready to sign.

The outside door slammed again and this time Seth passed the office alone, striding purposefully, toward the family living area and then she heard boots thumping up the stairs. She wondered if Holly carried out a message to him, an urgent one.

She smoothed her hair with her hands. No matter what, she intended to present a normal face to the Doyles today, engender confidence, promote feelings of reliability.

Faint voices speaking soothingly carried in from the living area and then stopped abruptly with the closing of a door. Someone had left the house. The crisis, whatever it was, might have passed. At least she hoped it had.

She'd been planning, designing and wishing for so long, putting most of her eggs in this particular basket— mostly because it was the only basket she could find— that it seemed as if moving to the next stage would never come. Thinking about the Doyles signing the contracts and the job getting started had still been a bit surreal.

Footsteps again.

Evvy and Curtis Doyle entered the office, followed by Baylor.

KayLee rose, letting a smile slip across her face, but Curtis wore a grim expression and the corners of Evvy's mouth were turned down. KayLee dropped the cheerfulness and swallowed the quickly rising fear that her dreams were about to be dashed.

"It's good to see you." Curtis took her offered hand and shook twice, firmly, but his words sounded more like an auto response than a greeting.

Okay. Whatever this was, she could deal with it. She had an answer, she had to have one.

"Welcome, KayLee." Evvy held KayLee's hand longer than might have been necessary and a small tear leaked from the corner of her eye.

If she had to walk away today, she'd go. A flash of a baby in her arms crossed her mind. And she'd do whatever she had to do to make things work for her child. Evvy was so sweet to feel sad for her.

She sat because she knew Curtis and Baylor wouldn't sit until she and Evvy did.

Maybe it wasn't her at all. Maybe there was trouble in the Doyle clan. She realized she cared about these people already, and for more than just the work. It was as if deep feelings had lain hidden within her and were waiting for a reason to spring forth. She cared for her own sake, and she cared for theirs.

Evvy settled solemnly in her seat and Curtis followed her lead. Neither spoke. She looked to Baylor, but he offered no relief as he sat down in the chair behind the desk.

"Let's get the papers signed and get things under way," Curtis said firmly.

It wasn't me, KayLee thought. Or at least she hadn't done enough damage for them to put off the job.

Curtis picked up a pen and began to scribble his signature. When he finished a line, he positioned the papers in front of Evvy.

KayLee couldn't find any satisfaction in the problem not being of her doing because anything that involved her "new family" would be of concern to her.

Her new family. She was so gone. These people were her job, her livelihood, her child's future, not her family. Her mind was lost to her via pregnancy hormones, and she fervently prayed she'd get it back in time to be a good mother.

When Evvy finished signing, she pushed the papers silently down the line for KayLee to sign. KayLee passed each set to Baylor to finish off the round.

The dramatic signing of the contract, the event that would change her life and begin her future, ended quickly and the Doyle parents hurried away, Evvy leaning on Curtis's arm, even before KayLee could rise from her chair to thank them.

"Are they all right?" she asked Baylor when the footsteps faded away to silence.

He stacked papers and put them in folders as if he were deliberating on what to tell her. When they were neatly tucked inside, he put one folder in the drawer of the desk and handed the other to her.

"There's a family concern," he finally said.

"I'm sorry to hear that. I hope things turn out all right," she said when he didn't embellish.

His answer was to hand over the check for the down payment. She would divide this up between the expenses she would incur to get things started and the amount she would need to live on.

While she stowed the check in her bag, Baylor spread out an enlarged set of plans containing the general scope of the project. "The building contractor you picked to get started with the site excavation and road work is a good choice. The owner, Allen Martin, hales from one of the ranches in the valley."

With her silence, she knew she was making a tacit agreement that they would ignore the elephant in the room, at least for now. Whatever was the matter in the Doyle family was none of her business. She tried to tamp down her concern for the Doyles and nodded in agreement with what he said about the area contractor.

When she stood and leaned over the plans Baylor spun them so she could see them right side up and stepped around the desk to join her.

"I have a few suggestions for materials suppliers," he said after a few seconds of contemplation, "but we are going to have to go into Kalispell to take a look at what's available to get started and how much will have to be special-ordered. It's different here than in California. Not quite as many resources at hand."

"I welcome any suggestion you have. I'll contact Martin Homes right away. I spoke with Mr. Martin last week to get an update on his schedule and he said he would make his arrangements based on, he said, 'Whatever the Doyles need.'"

It was Baylor's turn to nod.

"And after having been in the area less than two days," she continued, "I realize it was not lip service. I'd like to get Martin Homes started as soon as possible."

"That would be good."

"I could use a little more enthusiasm," she said quietly as if she might not want him to hear.

He smiled broadly this time. "Great. I mean it would be great."

"Whew. I didn't want to be the only one excited about getting started."

"I'm going to have to leave you to begin making your arrangements." His smile disappeared and pensiveness took its place. "Use the phone here as much as you need. Stay as long as you like. I'll be out in the calving barn and I'll be back in when I can."

With that, he strode out and left her alone at the desk. KayLee wasn't sure what she had expected—chatting, camaraderie, people who might spend time with her adding to their list of wants and needs.

She tugged her list of contacts from her briefcase and studiously avoided feeling deserted. She'd do her job and make it look easy so the Doyles would be sure they had done their best in choosing her. Much of her life might be a mess, but in this one area, she knew what to do.

She dragged the desk phone toward her and dialed Martin Homes. As she waited for Allen to come on the line, she suddenly found herself fighting the feeling that signatures on the contracts or not, if something dire happened in the Doyle family they might have no choice but to cancel the project.

"HOLLY, I'M HERE," Baylor called as he stepped inside the comparatively dim light of the calving shed and hung his jacket on a nail.

"Are they on their way?" Holly called from inside one of the calving pens.

"Yep," he said and stepped around the wooden dividing wall. Holly's back was to him. She was applying lubricant to help the heifer with a calf that might be too big for her to deliver on her own.

He retrieved his work jacket from the nail and draped it over Holly's shoulders. In her haste to fetch Seth, she apparently hadn't bothered with a coat.

"Thanks," she said. "I lose my mind when it comes to Trey's illness."

"Dr. Daley is meeting them at the clinic and the chopper will be here as soon as possible, weather permitting." Baylor bent down and started scrubbing his hands and arms with the soapy water in the bucket on the floor outside the birthing pen.

"God, I hope so." She expelled a breath.

Every Doyle worried about the youngest, and every one of them felt as helpless as the babe.

"You look like you have things under control here."

Holly snorted softly in dissension. "She doesn't think much of my assistance."

"The calf still okay?"

"The calf is better than I am. Seems comfortable right where she is. Knows it's cold and hard out here."

Baylor dried his hands and arms with a clean towel and hunkered down beside Holly. "Are we going to need the calving chains?"

"Seth said the calf's in good position but big and he left a message with the vet that we might need him today, but I hope not." Holly stood, her teeth chattering.

"Go, clean up. I got this."

A few minutes later, Holly was clean and dry, and she slipped her arms into the jacket. "I didn't realize how cold I was."

Baylor made sure the calf was still all right. It was.

"I always knew my brother was strong," he said. "I had no idea he'd ever have to be this strong."

"Things happen so fast with Trey." Holly spoke with gentle outrage in her voice. "Amy said it seemed that one minute he was playing and the next he was fighting for breath. I might be selfish, but I hope for all our sakes the doctors are able to do something definitive this time."

"He's a strong-willed kid. I can't see him doing anything except making it through all this and coming out the other side ready to rope a steer."

"Yeah. Roping a steer is the first thing Amy will want him to do." She gave a short, appreciative laugh at his attempt to lighten the mood. "I'd settle for him being able to run and play the way he wants to."

They kept a silent vigil, eyes on the cow, thoughts with the sick child and his parents.

The cow shifted and huffed and Baylor gave his attention to her.

"Come on, girl. You can do it," Holly crooned to the cow.

Contractions came and went and there was no progress in spite of using more and more lubrication. He told Holly she didn't have to stay but she couldn't seem to abandon cow, calf and man. The cow was tiring and Baylor knew they were running out of time.

"Chains?" Holly asked.

"Got one more trick to try. I didn't get this big for nothing."

"Your magic-towel trick." Holly smiled. She left and came back with a stack of clean, dry towels.

With the next contraction Baylor used a towel to grab one slippery calf leg and pulled, maintaining tension and pulling until he felt a shoulder "pop" through the pelvis, and then he relaxed when the cow did.

He smiled as his spirit lifted. "This is going to work."

"I am so not strong enough to do that," Holly said as she leaned in to check the calf. "This pair is lucky to have you here."

"I got more brawn's all."

"You get the papers signed?"

"You mean do I have brains, too?"

She nudged him on the back with her knee.

"Yep, and she's in the house making some arrangements right now."

"I like her."

"If that's an invitation to talk about her, I'm going to ignore it."

When the next contraction started, Baylor tugged the second shoulder through. Then he rotated the calf to help the hips clear.

Holly laughed. "You make that rotating-the-calf thing look so easy."

After the hips cleared, the calf slipped completely out. The soft mewling sounds indicated it was breathing.

Holly untied the cow and the tired mother struggled to her feet to give instinctual attention to her offspring. The calf bleated his dislike of his new world.

After a few more minutes, the calf began his struggle of trying to stand. He failed on his first try.

"Nice job, little brother." Holly patted Baylor's shoulder.

"My brothers married well," he said as he stepped away from cow and calf. Then, when he was sure the pair wouldn't need any more help, he washed his hands and forearms.

"It's supposed to happen like this, Bay," Holly said, indicating the new mother patiently licking her calf dry while it struggled up onto wobbling legs. "It did for Lance and I."

Baylor didn't say anything. He could see the toll Trey's illness had taken on his brothers and their wives, on his parents. Even Holly and Lance's children knew there was something seriously wrong with their cousin.

"I wish there was more I could do for the three of them," he said as he dried off.

"Me, too."

He put a hand on Holly's shoulder and she stepped in and gave him a tight hug.

"Hey, you two. If that's all you got to do, I can take over." Lance stepped into the pen and hugged his wife when she went to him.

"'Bout time you got back." Baylor reached into the bucket and pulled the unused birthing chains out to dry them.

"I stopped at the Whispering Winds and dropped

off a couple things I'd picked up in town for Bessie. So what's up?" Lance pointed at the happy cow-and-calf pair.

It was that moment Baylor saw KayLee. From the look of horror on her face, she had spied the chains.

"Hello."

CHAPTER SEVEN

KAYLEE SHIFTED IN the doorway of the steel-sided shed and then drew nearer to where the three Doyles seemed to stand guard over a mother cow and her newborn calf. A baby born with the use of the chains Baylor held in his hand? The thought made her shudder.

No doubt about it, Montana was a different way of life than she had ever imagined.

Baylor dropped the chains into a bucket with a splash of water. Holly and Baylor looked at her and she wondered again if she had done something wrong. But the Doyles wouldn't have signed the contract if that were true.

Would they?

There was nothing to do but remove the doubt, by force if necessary. She ramped up her courage. "It's none of my business, but since I'm…um…probably going to find out anyway…"

"What?" Lance furrowed his brows.

Holly's shoulders slumped. "It's Trey."

A chill gave KayLee goose bumps in spite of the warmth of the borrowed coat. She hugged her arms tightly around her. The boy whose parents doted, the one whose smile held the ghost of anguish, was in trouble.

"What's up?" Lance asked with a seriousness that belied the casual question.

Holly glanced at KayLee before she spoke, apology in her expression. "He started having trouble breathing after breakfast."

"They left for town a couple of hours ago," Baylor added as he dried his hands on a towel.

Holly looked at the brothers and then again at Kay-Lee. "We didn't want to worry you."

"He's so young. Bad things shouldn't happen to one so young." KayLee knew she had said the words, but they sounded tinny and distant to her, as if from inside a deep cave.

She begged her knees to stop wobbling as she put a hand on a nearby metal railing.

"The plan is to send him to Helena," Baylor said, not taking his eyes away from KayLee, as if he were afraid she'd fall over or break apart if he looked away.

And she might. She made ice fill her veins so terror could not and steel fill her legs so she would not give away how frightened she felt for the little boy and his family.

"Helena is so far from here." Five hours or so away. KayLee knew because she had verified her resources before she left California. They wouldn't take a child all that way for a cold or the flu or any childhood illness. She remembered the looks on the boy's grandparents' faces and her heart squeezed until she was deathly cold.

Holly stepped away from Lance. "It's okay, KayLee. Come and sit down for a minute."

"I'm all right." KayLee froze to the spot of hard-packed earthen floor. She had already shown these people she could be pitiful. She would not do that anymore.

"Are you sure?" This was a demand of assurance from Baylor.

"I'm sure. I'm so sorry." The words sounded inadequate under the circumstances.

If there were ever expressions of buried feelings, Baylor and Lance were poster boys. Their faces, even their demeanor, gave nothing away. She knew they were reluctant to supply details that would help her form a picture in her head of what could befall any child if bad luck had a hand.

"He was born with a heart defect," Holly said softly. "They're fixing the problems in stages as he grows."

KayLee crossed her arms over her chest above the bump of her stomach. "Will he be all right?"

"He's an intrepid little fighter and he couldn't have better parents."

Holly retreated back into her husband's embrace and Baylor stood near them as if in solidarity. When the other woman smiled, KayLee wanted to believe what she said.

"It must be hard for all of you." Her own deep terror kept her at a distance from the others.

"Bay and I were talking." Holly leaned into Lance as she spoke. "We're sure he'll come out the other side of this."

"I, um, have to go into town. Is there anything I can do?" The empty offer was all she truly had.

"They'll have called for the medical evac helicopter to pick him up, and they'll all be gone shortly." Baylor crossed the gravel-and-dirt floor toward her.

She retreated a step. She wasn't sure that human touch would not shatter her in this instant. She had worked so hard to learn to comfort herself in recent months and there was no way she was willing to give that up. "Of course, they'd send him where he could get the help he needs."

"He'll do fine. He's hardy pioneer stock from both sides of the family."

At the sound of a long, low moo, Baylor faced the cow and calf pair. The others followed suit. The calf was standing, having a first drink of what KayLee knew would be colostrum—first milk—from its mother.

"You two did a good job here." Lance closed in with his arm around Holly for a better look.

Lance's optimistic tone and Mother Nature's show of how well she could get the job done offered KayLee well-needed encouragement.

"Yep, Holly's a good midwife."

"Thanks." Holly smiled and pointed at Baylor. "But he did the hard stuff."

"I just finished up."

"Speaking of finishing things, we'll leave you two to clean up." Baylor smiled at Holly and Lance. "And do whatever it is you two do when you catch a moment alone."

Holly and Lance grinned at each other. Holly grabbed the damp towels and Lance grabbed the bucket.

"We work," Lance said very seriously as he rubbed a hand on the thigh of his jeans.

"Yep. I gotta get me some of that work."

Holly and Lance both glanced at KayLee and she felt her face glow more than usual.

Baylor made a noise that sounded like a cross between a growl and a cough.

"Ignore them." He took KayLee by the arm and turned her toward the exit.

She waved over her shoulder to Holly and Lance and promised she'd be back soon.

Outside in the cold, the wind whipped her hair around and bathed her face with coolness. She took a deep breath of the air scented by the ranch. "No smog. No rich perfume. I like how it smells out here."

A gust of inopportune wind blew in at that very moment.

"You like the smell of cow manure?"

"Very funny. Not that part, but I've smelled worse in the city, much worse. At least you know what that stink is from." She laughed at the disgusted face Baylor made and continued. "I like the smell of the trees, the fresh air—when we're upwind from the barn, the wind that smells as if it's come right down from the mountains and across the clean snow."

As they headed toward a rutted area, she leaned heavily into Baylor's hand for support. She was never quite sure where her feet were these days and as they traversed the uneven ground, she was glad to have the help.

Should she be making anything of that? she wondered. She hadn't known him for long and she was already glad to lean on him. She mentally shrugged. She was pregnant, and heck, she'd take good help when she needed it and be glad of it.

Although she worked hard to ignore it, with each step her awareness of him surged—his size, his strength, his male allure. What would it be like to have sex with someone like Baylor Doyle? She suspected there would be less soft groaning passion and more...what? A wild stallion came to mind and she put it swiftly away.

"Trey is such a little man about things. I sometimes think it's harder for his parents than for him," Baylor said as they neared her car.

Of course, he was thinking about the boy and she was thinking about sex with a near stranger. She was so demented.

She forced herself to consider the boy and not the man. "I have a better idea these days of what you're talking about. I can't imagine anything going wrong with my baby."

"Trey sort of accepts things as they come."

"They say kids are resilient. I hope that's not just something 'they' say." She rested her free hand on her belly and her baby shifted inside her as if the child knew she needed reassurance. "I hope Trey comes back soon, happy and lively like the other children."

"We all hope that."

When they stopped beside her Ford, Baylor reached for the handle and then let his hand fall back to his side.

"Are you sure you're all right to drive back to town?" he asked as he reached up and brushed back the hair that had blown into her eyes.

"I'm fine." The touch of his rough fingertips on her skin sent a jolt of sensation through her. She found herself yearning for him to reach up again and put his hand on her cheek, to have him bend down and kiss her mouth.

He studied her as if he was considering the same thing. "Then we should get you on your way."

"We should." She slid into her car. "I have an appointment to meet with Allen Martin in a couple of hours. We'll go over some of the supply and labor details, and he says he'll set up a meeting at the diner in the morning and bring some of the people in the area that I need to know."

"Good." Baylor rested both hands on the top of her car and smiled in at her. "Al can get you in contact with all the right folks. He has a good idea of who's available and when."

"Thanks for giving me a chance at this project." Kay-Lee felt her energy begin to flag.

Baylor shifted, reached into his pocket and produced a folded piece of paper and a flash drive. "These are preferences, thoughts, ideas and things to bug the designer with. One set is mine and the other is from my parents. Meant to give them to you earlier. You do have access to a computer?"

"A laptop. I'll study them carefully."

"Good enough." He patted the top of her car. "Drive safely."

"Always."

The sun had traveled halfway down toward the mountaintops in the west by the time she departed the ranch. Trey would be in Helena by the time she got to St. Adelbert. She wondered if they let the boy's mother and father ride in the helicopter.

She couldn't imagine sending her child so far away with strangers.

KayLee puffed out a breath and concentrated on driving as she continued down the muddy road toward the highway. She traversed the small valley where the Doyle ranch and several others sat nestled between mountain ranges. The scenery was as inspiring as ever, but soaring peaks and the deep green of pines against the snow couldn't blot out her memories of the distressed looks the Doyle grandparents had worn earlier, nor the pained innocence on Trey's face yesterday.

As she crested the last hill near St. Adelbert, a vivid image of Baylor Doyle as a noble knight on a large steed flashed into her head so clearly, she almost felt as if she were floating. She let off the gas and the car slowed.

"Wow."

What was it about Baylor Doyle that had her feeling so light—and so what? Hungry? Needy? School-girl crushy? Not that she didn't appreciate knowing she could still feel such things after not having felt them for so long.

By the time she got out of her car at the Easy Breezy, she *so* needed that nap. She stumbled into the room, dropped her briefcase onto the chair, went to the bathroom, of course, and then propped two pillows against the headboard. Without taking her coat off, she lay down on top of the spread clutching her mobile phone.

But couldn't sleep and got up.

Standing at the table, she held the check from the Doyles up to the light. Uncertainty tugged at her until her knees weakened and she sagged down onto the chair. She held the future of so many people in her hands.

It had all seemed so doable. She had been so sure of herself, but until she held the down payment in her hands, it had all seemed like it could be a movie, somebody else's script.

It was up to her to reach into her drawings and pluck out the dream other people's lives would be made of.

She should nap first to take the edge off the sleepiness.

She had just set her alarm, when the phone rang in her hand. Too tired even to startle, she gripped it tightly and lay back against the pillows. When the phone rang again she glanced at the caller's name on the screen.

Cindy Sorenson. Her friend was back in the States. She had to be. Cindy's mobile didn't work in the desolate area outside Addis Ababa, where her friend's shoot was taking place.

She flipped open her phone. "Cindy! Hello. How are you? Where are you?"

Her friend laughed. "Hi to you, too. I'm fine. I'm in California, but they tell me you're not."

"They're right." KayLee leaned back on the pillows and wiggled over on her side so she could pin the phone between her head and the pillow. "I'm in Montana."

"The state?"

"Yes, silly. I have a job here."

"What kind of job? But…wait—aren't you pregnant? I mean, you are still, aren't you? Pregnant? Because knowing you, you wanted so much to be that baby's mother."

"I am seven and a half months and counting. You should see me. I'm rather houselike." KayLee wasn't sure she wanted the conversation to stay on her, so she changed the subject. "How was your shoot?"

"Long. It's way cooler in Addis Ababa than I ever imagined, it being so close to the equator and all. Elevation, you know. But, I'd rather hear about you."

"Your life is more exciting and mine is…" KayLee stopped.

"Hey, as the reigning queen of low-budget indie films, I get to pass on talking about the process if I want to. We'll save it for a day of deep red wine and artichoke-anything under a palm tree. Hell, a forest of palm trees, gently lapping waves…men rubbing our feet."

"Okay, okay. Uh, so far the baby's doing well and so is the mother, most days."

"Yeah, it's hard to believe Chad is gone. I wish I could have come to his memorial service."

"Your flowers were beautiful. So was your offer for me to come and share your apartment in Addis Ababa. It seemed kind of far away under the circumstances."

"I still think Chad would have come around once he saw his baby's face."

"He might have, but that's all over now." Everything was over and gone: the matching Mercedes, the living room with an ocean view, the parties... But Cindy had seen the rise and fall so many times in the California crowd, there was no need for details.

"I didn't expect you to be back so soon," KayLee said to swing the conversation back to Cindy. If she talked very much about the ranch, Cindy would ask about Baylor Doyle and KayLee was sure she didn't want to go there now. "Your kids must be ecstatic."

"FYI, I know you're dodging. Yeah, speaking of my little love buckets. I missed my kids. Mom brought them to England and we had a nice visit, but it's not the same as being home with them. The weather there is not too unlike Southern California, but it's way easier to find peace and quiet there for a shoot, even without a sound-stage."

"It's a bit colder here in Montana. I was so pitifully dressed when I got here, they lent me a coat."

"And they still hired you."

"Imagine that."

"Any men?

KayLee's thoughts immediately flew to the image of her standing in front of her car staring into Baylor's eyes, wondering if she saw the need there that she had been feeling. "Um—there's…"

"What's his name?"

KayLee let out a purposeful sigh. "His name's Baylor Doyle and every time I see him things begin to happen, things I can't afford to act on right now."

"You can't afford to find a man you can fall in love with?"

"It's complicated."

"Simplify it for me."

"What I'm doing here isn't a casual thing. An entire extended family is depending on this project to make money for them so they can all live happily on the ranch forever."

"That cooperative community or whatever it was called—"

"Concept community."

"Yeah, that. Those people all pooled their life savings to get that place built. And you made that happen."

"If it had failed, they would have had to go back to their former lives."

"But they didn't."

"There's a sick child involved here."

"That's harsh."

"Sometimes I wonder if I'm being fair to me and my baby to be into something that could turn into a tragedy on many levels."

"Dark alert. Dark alert."

KayLee laughed again. A dark alert meant the speaker had two minutes after the alert was sounded to feel sorry for herself and to be as dark and depressed as she wanted to be and then she had to stop. "All right, I'll be quick."

"Hey, we've never gotten the chance to talk about you and Chad, and if we're gonna go dark…"

"Our marriage was torn apart by not being able to change lust into love. I don't recommend it."

"Ha, you dated him for almost a week before the nups."

"Yep." Tightness in her throat swelled to nearly choke off her breath and she coughed to free the air and then forced the words out. "'I give up. It's over. We need to get a divorce.' That's what Chad said."

"And?"

"The pregnancy test had come back positive that day, and when I told him, he said he'd stay for the baby—if he could."

"Girlfriend, you should have gotten a hold of me. I know I said I'd be out of touch for months, but here I am and the film people could have gotten a message to me."

"I thought about it, but it's hard to say any of this stuff in an email, let alone across an ocean on the phone."

Something thumped loudly on Cindy's end of the phone. "It's also nuts to think Montana will be harder than what you left behind."

The thumping sounded again, louder this time.

"Okay," Cindy continued, "my little ones are circling and we don't have much time, so I'm canceling dark alert. Tell me about the man you've met there."

"He's one of the clients."

Thump. "We can't hold that against him, can we?"

"It's just pregnancy hormones anyway."

Baylor Doyle. She smiled at the thought of the big rancher alighting from his steed. She saw herself stepping up to him and putting her hands flat on his chest. Might as well remove his shirt. Putting her hands on his bare chest, his muscles flexed, the crisp hair tickling her fingertips. She'd let the feelings have free reign in her body, let everything that wanted to, clench and swell. Then she'd inhale deeply, raise up on her tiptoes...

"KayLee?"

"Er...I missed that. What did you say?"

"Were you thinking about him just now?"

"I was. He's hot by any standards, Cindy."

"So what I said before, blaming it all on your hormones is a load of crap. Remember, I've been there three times and the hormones only amplify what's there."

"Exponentially?"

"That bad, huh? Or should I say good."

"Moooom-meeee!"

KayLee laughed. "How are the kids anyway?"

"They're great. I promised we'd go to the place where they have the big pipe organ and nearly edible pizza."

"Sounds yummy."

"Laugh today, lady. After your baby is born and for the next twenty years, you will eat things you never believed would ever cross your lips."

"And yet I am looking forward to it."

"You are going to love it. Listen, I'm glad you found work even if it is on the other side of the mountain."

"I'm so glad somebody wanted to hire me or I'd be living in Marshside with my mother."

If the Doyles hadn't hired her, she'd be making the bleak trip to her mother's tiny home in Wisconsin right now.

"You could move in with my mother and the kids."

"Mommy, mommy, mommy…"

KayLee knew the offer from Cindy was a joke as her mother lived in an apartment with the grandchildren while Cindy was off earning a living. "I'm so glad you are back stateside. It will be so nice to have someone to talk to."

"Oh, honey, I'm not really home."

"What do you mean?" KayLee shifted on the pillow.

"The director let me off for only a few days. We're shooting the sequel right away. Presumptuous, but since the big movies are all doing it, he says it'll be more cohesive—read *cheaper*—in the long run. I leave early tomorrow morning."

What could she say? Hadn't she just thought about what a good job she'd done in learning to prop herself up.

"You can do this. You were married to Chad, after all."

"And what does that mean?"

"It means nothing. I'm just talking, that's all."

Her usually forthright friend was backpedaling fast and KayLee wondered what that was all about.

"But, Cindy—"

"Mommy."

"I am so sorry, I really have to go. I love you, sweetie. Email me and let me know how you're doing."

"Thanks, Cindy, you're the best."

They said their goodbyes and KayLee put the phone on the bedside table. *You were married to Chad, after all.* What the heck? Was she blind to some huge fault Chad had? Or she had?

She stifled a yawn and willed her eyes to stay open. She had to meet with Allen Martin in fifteen minutes. Enough time to fix her makeup, brush her teeth and head out.

You were married to Chad, after all. She couldn't hide from the echo of the words inside her head, nor from the possible implications.

WEDNESDAY MORNING, KayLee drew her natural bristled hairbrush through her almost dry hair. If she brushed it when it was dry, the lack of humidity would make half of it fly out as if it were trying to get away while the rest stuck to her head. Not very appealing and this problem hadn't happened to her when she lived near the ocean.

By the time she had headed back toward her room last night, she had been so tired a deli sandwich from the gas station convenience store had to do for dinner and she barely finished it before falling asleep. During the meeting, Al Martin, the building contractor, had promised to arrange breakfast with a couple local suppliers for this morning.

She put the brush away and leaned closer to the mirror to apply a few light brushes of mineral makeup to help tone down the more-than-healthy glow pregnancy had given to her cheeks, and then she smudged on concealer to hide the faint dark circles under her eyes.

With the exception of Cindy, people wouldn't recognize her today. She used less makeup in a month now than she used to use in a day, but Cindy had seen her with makeup and without.

It hurt to think of her friend so far away. She'd be on a plane, over an ocean somewhere by now. Cindy had been the first person she had met in California. Already the mother of two, she sort of adopted the stray from Wisconsin. She and Cindy didn't run with the same crowd—Cindy mostly ran with her kids—but their friendship seemed to survive anything.

KayLee stroked a bit of color on her lids and mascara on her lashes, but used no dark liner, no six shades of shadow and sculpting blush, no liquid, sponge-applied foundation.

Her flashy blond hair was now its natural dark blond and because she kept the straightening products and flat iron away, it fell in soft curls.

She almost didn't recognize herself sometimes, but

she liked what she saw. She saw a mommy, not a peripheral member of the glitterati.

The alarm on her mobile phone beeped. Al Martin et al would meet her at Alice's Diner in ten minutes. She tugged on a pair of low-rise jeans that she buttoned below her belly and slipped on the only warm sweater she had. Then she nabbed her long, flowing coat from the closet and stopped without putting it on. It wasn't right for going out today. She'd wear the borrowed coat to the diner. Wearing it might lend her some Montana respectability.

She could use all the help…

She left her car at the motel and headed down Main Street. Heavy cloud cover kept the morning dark and gloomy and the wind made her glad she had chosen the work coat no matter how she looked.

It was cold today. No melting going on and it would snow soon, but the idea of driving out to the Doyle ranch in the snow didn't bother her. When she got rid of the two sporty Mercedes to pay creditors, she bought a car she could drive in Wisconsin if she had to.

A gust of wind blew a shiver right through her. Funny how fast a pregnant woman can trot when she's propelled by cold. Another block and she was at the lovely white building with blue trim that had flower boxes below the front windows waiting for the spring to warm up enough.

KayLee found herself wondering when exactly that would happen.

When she entered the cheerily painted diner, many heads turned in her direction.

CHAPTER EIGHT

KayLee CLOSED THE DOOR of the small diner against the cold wind and smiled at the people who stared at her from tables, booths and the red vinyl-covered stools at the counter.

Al Martin rose and motioned to her, and as she made her away from the entrance to a round table in the corner, more faces examined her. She nodded to each and hoped this assembly of her new friends and neighbors gave her passing marks, as she had no doubt this was an inspection.

"Hello, KayLee." The greeting had come from a stranger, a thin fortyish woman with long, deeply auburn hair, who could only be described as vivacious-looking and was sitting with a picture-of-decorum man in a three-piece suit.

Several others called her by name and with big smiles as she passed. Okay, so did they all know her name?

These people meant no harm, right? Al had seemed very normal during their meeting yesterday.

She continued to smile and nod, wondering which faces would be employee, friend or vendor. A big man with a salt-and-pepper beard smiled as if she were an old friend. He had *Fred* on the front of his shirt, and as it turned out when she passed him, *Fred's Fix-It* on the back. He was undoubtedly the owner of the very big, very "chromey" tow truck parked out front of the diner with the license plate that said BIG FRED. She might not be able to put too much stock in the size of his grin as it seemed he did everything big.

Fred sat at a table with several other smilers and greeters, whom she suspected might be the regular crowd, including one very elderly gentleman with a bright purple cast on one arm. Another breakfaster grinned, a middle-aged woman who could have been in a black-and-white western, inclusive of a checked apron, large girth and a pleasant, friendly face. The other three at the table were of varying age.

"Good morning, Al." She sat down across the table from the contractor, feeling as though she had run the gauntlet, unsure how she felt about people she didn't know calling her by name. Smiling was okay, but acting as if they knew her... A little creepy perhaps.

"Good to see you again this morning, KayLee."

Or she was being impracticable. It was a small town, after all, and the grapevine in St. Adelbert must be a thriving one.

As soon as she sat down, a waitress with a name tag that read *Vala* swept up and handed her a menu. "Orange juice or milk, honey?"

KayLee smiled in spite of the waitress's obvious familiarity with her condition. "Both, please."

Vala nodded and flitted away.

The table was set for five and before she and Al were able to start a conversation, a man and a woman came around the table to the two empty seats near KayLee, smiling, of course.

"Hi, KayLee. I'm Rachel Taylor and this is my husband, Jim," the dark-haired, middle-aged woman said and sat in the chair next to KayLee.

"I'm pleased to meet the two of you." KayLee shook

the woman's hand and then the man's. Rachel's husband looked to be an amenable person. He was mildly paunchy and had barely any hair to speak of.

"We own Taylor's drugstore, down the street. We're all excited about the project at the Doyle ranch. Oh, and there's John Miller."

Rachel pointed at a tall, thin man—probably well into his seventh decade—approaching the table at a purposeful clip.

"Good morning, Mr. Miller," KayLee said as the man with the near perfect eyebrows approached. A good barber or was he born with it?

He grinned at her and took a seat. "You catch on fast, but please call me John. I figure we'll be meeting a lot in the next several months. Hardware emergencies seem to crop up all the time when there are buildings going up."

"Or not going up," Rachel said and everyone laughed as if there was history to the comment.

Al leaned toward KayLee. "A reference to the new community center we've been planning for how many years?"

"Four," John said as he perused the menu.

When John was finished speaking with the oh-so-efficient Vala, the conversation ranged from the design dispute over the community center to the local sights, including a lovely and secluded waterfall, to people's families. Somehow, thankfully, the table talk always managed to come back to the construction project at the ranch.

"Those Doyles are all such nice people. Why, Baylor used to be one of our volunteer firemen." Rachel seemed like a healthy branch of the grape vine.

Jim leaned in toward Rachel and did a stage whisper. "Firefighter, Rache."

"Anyway, we can hook you up with any safety equipment and supplies you might need." Rachel added more sugar and stirred her coffee. "One of Jim's hobbies, so to speak, is to find vendors who give the best bang for the dollar."

Jim leaned toward his wife. "Buck."

"What?"

"Bang for the buck, Rache."

Rachel laughed with a touch of bawdiness. KayLee liked it.

Breakfast dishes had been cleared away, and KayLee was about to excuse herself to get started on some of the wants and needs on the Doyles' list when a couple entered the diner. Soon elbows and whispers were engaged until everyone paid attention to the couple who walked in arm in arm.

Apparently, lots of interesting activity for the diner today.

"The Dawsons," someone said with a touch of awe.

KayLee found her own jaw dropping. The woman was the epitome of statuesque with more than her fair share of glistening blond hair and a figure most women would like to have even for just one day. She was gorgeous, and the man, dressed all in black, was equally good looking, but seemed like a no-nonsense local rancher.

Her previous life was peppered with such women, but how did one end up here?

"That's Cole Dawson and his fancy New York model wife," Rachel Taylor said in a whisper louder than KayLee was comfortable with.

"I thought she left town," Jim Taylor said in low tones.

"She's come back to try to talk him into coming to live in New York. I heard he said New York was no place to raise their daughter, but I think she only asked so she wouldn't feel guilty about leaving her kid behind."

"Rache!"

"Oh, hush. It could be true," Rachel said to her husband.

KayLee watched the couple as they made their way to the table and wondered if she and Chad had looked that mismatched.

Or if she would ever find anyone who matched her and if she did how long it would last. She and Chad had thought they'd last forever. The couple by the window, almost glaring at one another, probably thought they would last, too.

KayLee leaned toward the others at her table. "I do need to go. I have a lot of work to do."

She told them all how pleased she was to meet them, and she was, and how very much she anticipated working with them, and she did. Then she rose from the chair and made her way to the cash register.

KayLee held cash and the breakfast check in her hand while Vala finished filling the large takeout cup for her.

"They aren't who you think they are." The voice came from one of the counter stools. "None of them are."

KayLee realized the man was speaking to her.

"Excuse me?" The Dawsons? The townspeople?

"Yeah, I'm talking to you."

KayLee recognized the smell of last night's alcohol.

He must have drunk so much he could not yet be considered sober.

The man who sported untamed curly red hair and a well-worn suit coat continued. "You should leave while you still can. The rest of us are stuck here."

"Hush, McCormack," Vala said to the man, turned then to KayLee. "Pay him no mind."

"Those Doyles think they're better than the rest of us," the man continued in spite of Vala's admonishment.

When KayLee tried to ignore him, he tugged on her arm. "Especially that Baylor Doyle, he went and got himself educated and he can't wait to leave."

"Please, have some manners," KayLee said as she removed his hand from her arm.

"All Baylor wants to do is get his family off his back and he's leaving this place behind. We should all leave this piece of—"

"Michael McCormack, leave her alone." A woman's quiet authoritative tone from behind KayLee commanded the red-haired man into silence. He snapped to attention and then hunched over his breakfast without uttering another word.

KayLee faced the woman. She was tall, with shoulder-length brown hair, and a white lab coat sticking out the bottom of her heavy winter coat.

"We're friendlier than that, really," the woman said and thrust her hand out. "Hi. I'm Maude DeVane."

"Good morning, Dr. DeVane." Vala held a cup in each hand. "How's that little one of yours?"

"She just started walking and she looks more and more like her cousin Lexie every day. All those red curls."

Vala smiled at both of them and handed a cup to

KayLee. "One decaf and one regular," she said as she handed the other to the doctor.

KayLee held up her decaf in a salute. "I believe you *are* friendlier than that."

Dr. DeVane smiled.

"Thought I'd get that up front," KayLee continued. "Because I hope you'll be my doctor while I'm here in the valley."

"I'd like that, especially since you're all my patients want to talk about today."

"Oh, my gosh."

"Not to worry. It'll wear off soon. Don't hesitate too long behind the green-bean display at the grocery store, though. You'll hear more than you ever wanted to hear about yourself."

"Green-bean display?"

"Kind of a local gossip hub. Call the clinic and set up an appointment. I'll be looking forward to seeing you." She handed Vala cash, smiled at KayLee, bade them goodbye and headed confidently out of the diner without giving Michael McCormack another look.

Rachel Taylor approached and explained. "That's Dr. DeVane."

"Yes, we introduced ourselves."

"This one—" Rachel stopped and pointed at Mr. McCormack, who was still busy with his over-easy egg dripping yolk all over his fingers "—will do what she tells him. She stood up to him alone in her clinic late one night. Brave lady."

"It was good to meet you, Rachel, and thanks for the info about the safety supplies." KayLee smiled again.

She wasn't all that comfortable with gossip. Yes, where she had come from people thrived on talking about people and especially loved being talked about.

No matter how much they protested, their careers were made because they could generate buzz about themselves, but she always preferred to stay with Chad behind the cameras.

It definitely didn't comfort her, though, to have her vague suspicions about the people around here revved up by a drunken man.

She hurried out into the street. Were these people what they seemed?

All Baylor wants to do is get his family off his back and he's leaving this place behind.

Was anything the red-haired man said true, or even have a grain of truth to it?

KayLee started back down Main Street toward the Easy Breezy Inn. If the plans needed to be revised based on the new requests Baylor had given to her yesterday, she needed to get them completed before she ordered supplies.

She hadn't gone another ten feet when a pair of women rounded the corner at the end of the block across the street. One of them pointed in her direction and then they crossed at the town's one stoplight and made a beeline directly toward her.

Run away was her first thought.

Okay, KayLee realized she was being paranoid, as she had been in the diner when most of the people knew her name and a drunk tried to chase her out of town. Put like that it sounded as if she might have reason to be cautious.

The two women closing in on her could be on their way to breakfast, and instead of pointing at *her,* maybe the woman had pointed at something *behind* her.

Of course, that was it. She had to stop thinking she was the center of the world, and get over herself.

These were only people.

Nonetheless, as the women approached, she had to stop herself from fleeing in the other direction.

The two women weren't smiling, but they weren't exactly frowning, either. They seemed very determined and they were close enough now for her to see they had gray hair, but older didn't mean harmless.

She squared her shoulders. Not to be more cynical than your average Californian—only they called it worldly—she might soon find out what this town's *über*-friendliness was all about.

Maybe they were after her money.

Surprise! She didn't have any.

When the determined looks on the women's faces tipped decidedly to the friendly side, KayLee found herself expelling a breath of nervous anticipation. She wouldn't exactly consider herself timid or easily frightened, at least not before she had become a mother-to-be, lost her husband and faced the prospect of a new job in a new state or starvation or living with her mother.

Okay, she could do this.

Bring it on, ladies, she thought and squared her shoulders as Dr. DeVane might do under the circumstances. If they were space aliens, she'd deal.

The determined pair stopped a few feet in front of her and grinned.

Sure they would. Didn't all axe murderers smile at their victims.

"Hello." KayLee smiled.

The two women in their late sixties appeared to be sisters.

"Good morning, Ms. Morgan," said the one in the rose-colored hat.

Sure they knew who she was.

"Good morning, ladies."

"Holly Doyle called us and told us we should find you and meet you because you're going to be our new tenant," the other woman, the one in the turquoise-colored hat, said.

"Holly did? Hmmm." *The Doyle women probably already have a place in mind for you to live,* Baylor had mentioned. This might have been really scary if she were still in California. Still, it was a teensy bit. "Well then, we'd better get acquainted."

The two women's grins seemed to spread completely across their faces, lighting them up from the inside out. "We'll walk you back to the Breezy and talk on the way if that's all right with you."

"I'm Cora," said the one on her right, a five-foot-four-ish woman with gray hair, gray eyes and a knit cap that matched her turquoise-colored coat.

"And I'm Ethel," said the one on her left, a five-foot four-ish woman with gray hair, gray eyes and a knit cap that matched her rose-colored coat.

"You're sisters?" A rhetorical question about the two peas in a pod.

The women looked at each other and then back at KayLee. "We're friends," Cora said.

Not sisters? Okay, KayLee thought. There's a story there, but it might be too early to talk about such things.

"The Breezy is nice enough for a few nights, but there's only that tiny table for you to do your work at," Ethel said as she started the group moving toward the inn.

"Holly said we shouldn't pressure you, but we wanted you to know you'd be comfortable living in the apartment on the second floor of our house," Cora continued. "It's the whole second floor with a separate entrance, so you'd have some privacy and it's furnished, including linens and everything you'd need in the kitchen. Washer and drier in the basement, too."

"And a clothesline out back if you like that kind of thing. Lots of nice neighbors, too, and we love babies." Ethel bobbed her head as she spoke, as if to lend credence to her words. "Just ask Sally Sanderson—we've seen to each of hers from time to time."

"All five." Cora again from her right.

"Wow. That's a lot of children." KayLee thought people in California moved fast. These ladies had already gone from housing to childcare and they'd walked less than a block. For someone who liked to think she could figure things out for herself, this was a tiny bit disconcerting.

"She's the best mother around," Ethel said, interrupting her thoughts. "Sally Sanderson is. Almost lost one of her little ones a couple years ago. Never gave up hope, though, not for a minute. Best kind of mother a child could have."

"I hope I can say the same about me someday." What was it about these people? They scared her, but she could tell them anything. That kind of thinking did not help abate the uneasiness, the feeling that she was falling down the rabbit hole and there was no way to stop, only hints that she should not even try.

"Time will tell, dear." Cora patted KayLee's shoulder as she spoke. "Now, we know you will be very busy. If you take the apartment at our home, you'll have an office and a nursery."

"And we can provide some of your meals if you'd like."

"That would be fantastic," KayLee said. If Cora and Ethel cooked half as well as she'd imagined...she'd end up a blimp, that's what. A happy blimp stuck at the bottom of a rabbit hole.

"Certainly, you'll want to see the place first and there's no pressure." Ethel grinned. "Except what you put on yourself when you realize it's the best place in town. Obviously, you won't have to do any yard work or snow-shoveling or anything like what you'd have to do if you rented a house."

When a nervous laugh caught in KayLee's throat, she coughed to cover her unease. Even though they walked haltingly down the street, these ladies took her breath away. Caution. Caution. This town could still have some big hairy secret that she should be running from.

"Oh, we're rushing you, aren't we, dear?"

"Well, to be honest, yes." KayLee knew she was probably nuts and these women were as nice as they seemed.

"Take as long as you want." Ethel touched her arm briefly. "The place is available anytime. We don't usually rent it out except to people we know."

"But you don't know me."

Cora laughed. "We know you well enough. The Doyles hired you, after all."

"We make it our business to get to know people." Ethel grinned.

Was that a maniacal grin? "Okay." Now it was time to run. Tabloid reporters had hounded her after Chad's accident and she didn't like it at all.

"But we won't bother you if you don't want and if you ask us not to tell something," Cora said hastily, "we won't speak a peep."

KayLee halted in front of the motel and thought about her lonely room. Do or die. Dive-in or run-away time. "When might I see the apartment?"

She could always flee later before they trapped her and locked her away in the basement. Great, now she was making up B-movie plots in her head.

The friends stopped. Each turned to face her.

"Now if you'd like," Cora said.

"Or later today or even tomorrow, if that's better," her friend-but-not-sister offered.

"I do need to get out to the Doyle ranch. I told them I'd be there early this afternoon." And it would give her time to think about the offer of a place to live.

The women nodded.

"Well, we'll let you go. Here's all the information you'll need to contact us." Cora handed her a sheet of paper with their names and contact info.

KayLee suppressed a smile when she realized the sheet was addressed to her personally and contained a list of references, including Sheriff Potts and the Doyles. The references usually went the other way around where she came from. Busy women, indeed.

"Come to dinner tonight," Ethel said as she put a gentle hand on KayLee's arm again.

"I couldn't. I couldn't put you to so much trouble."

"Shucks, call it a sales tactic. We're offering you a service, after all, and a sample might clinch the sale." Cora's grin, KayLee noted, was much wider than Ethel's, and Cora in the turquoise cap and coat used it now as persuasion.

"In that case, I suppose I could come to dinner." And they could lock her in their basement never to be heard from again.

"Come about six-thirty."

No pushing? KayLee thought.

"If that doesn't work for you, let us know."

"Could we make it tomorrow night? Since I'm going to the ranch, I don't know how late I'll be back in town."

"Tomorrow night, six-thirty," Ethel said and Cora nodded.

"Tomorrow."

The women started off down the street and KayLee toward her room, feeling as if she were walking away from hurricane force winds.

She let herself in and sat down in the chair at the table near the window and sighed. The room smelled like musty old motel. The sooner she got out of the inn, the better for her baby's health and well-being.

Cora and Ethel had come with Holly's recommendation, after all. Maybe they were a couple of dears offering to be her godsend in the way of a safe haven, and she had to live somewhere.

She tugged on the drapery cord to let in the muted daylight.

The sheet from the sisters had a price that KayLee at first took to mean weekly, but the price was another indication she wasn't in Southern California anymore.

"We're going to make it, baby," she whispered as she rubbed where her child kicked against her ribs. "We are. I promise."

She sat for the next hour and a half going over the lists Curtis and Baylor Doyle had assembled. She wondered if they had conferred at all. The lists looked as if they somehow purposefully came up with opposing goals.

She took a deep breath and squeezed her eyelids shut. She might have to wear her glasses more if she was going to have to try this hard. She gathered the papers and popped the flash drive from her laptop. The best thing to do at this point was take the lists and her computer and head out to the ranch. Baylor was expecting her this afternoon. Getting there by noon should get her back on track with the Doyles as an on-time person, someone they could put their faith in, someone who would more than get the job done.

She packed up and put on her borrowed coat.

When she stepped outside, big beautiful fluffy snow-flakes were falling from the sky, as if from a snow maker on a movie set.

How beautiful. She hadn't seen a snowfall since the last time she went to Wisconsin in the winter and that had been almost ten years ago. It was so beautiful out in the street, it had to be a good omen.

She found the long-handled brush she'd bought at a gas station in Missoula and brushed at the snow that had already accumulated on her car's windows.

BAYLOR WASHED UP in the bucket of cooling soapy water, for what seemed like the five hundredth time this calving season. He'd leave Lance to deal with this after-noon's birthing calves. His brother knew well enough to call if he needed help.

There were always mishaps and flukes of nature during birthing season, but so far they'd been lucky, only one stillborn calf. The last of this year's batch should be born this week and put an end to the year's birthing incidents.

He stopped, dripping soapy hands suspended over the bucket. There would be one more birth this year. Kay-Lee Morgan had brought that to the ranch. The births of the three children living here had been highly anticipated events and when Trey had nearly died on his first day, it had sent a shock wave through the family.

Seth and Amy were still in Helena with the boy. He'd

have surgery as soon as he was stabilized, Seth had told him—possibly tomorrow, hopefully the next day if not.

KayLee should be here in an hour or so to do what she called a "walk-off" of the site for the first two cabins. With luck the snow would hold off.

He dried off his hands, secured the cap on his head and stepped outside.

Snow was falling with flakes so large they made audible plops when they hit the ground. He looked up at the sky and wondered if they were finally about to be dumped on. Heavy gray clouds hung like the bellies of pregnant cows.

Yep.

He'd better call KayLee and tell her to stay in town. She had no idea what a spring snowstorm in Montana could mean.

CHAPTER NINE

BAYLOR STRODE ACROSS the frozen ground toward the house. If it was snowing in town, KayLee might stay put. With any luck someone would have warned her about driving in the mountains during a snowstorm.

No sooner had the thought crossed his mind, when the blue Ford appeared out of the snow, windshield wipers flapping furiously, and rolled to a stop near the house.

She'd better be prepared to stay the night.

As he headed in the direction of the car, she leaped out and waved. Hair the color of burnished bronze in the snow-filtered light fell in ribbons over her shoulders, the ends dancing in the wind. The big brown coat wrapped around her never looked so sexy and as she neared him, he could see the flush in her cheeks.

"It's so surreal," she said in a hushed voice as she approached, her footsteps crunching with every step.

She stopped in front of him with wonder on her face. He could smell the sweet scent of her, see her green eyes sparkle with excitement. Then she closed her eyes and lifted her face to the falling snow.

Yeah, Baylor thought of the dream in front of him, surreal.

Flakes fell into her hair and onto her eyebrows and her nose. They melted on her pink lips, forming small fascinating droplets of water, and he found himself wanting to taste them.

Then he found himself wanting to smack his sorry self on the back of the head in frustration at such thoughts.

With her eyes still closed, she stuck her tongue out to capture flakes.

A shot of hot need flashed through him.

Oh, darlin', please don't do that.

She opened her eyes and dropped her chin as if she knew what she was doing to him.

"I thought you might stay in town today." He cleared his throat of the unwanted huskiness he found there and hoped his head—and everything else—might clear soon, too.

"I haven't been in a snowfall since I lived in Wisconsin." She stretched out her arms and spun slowly. "I didn't realize seeing it again would make me feel so giddy."

It didn't make her look giddy. It made her look sexy, sensual. He wanted to take her somewhere—anywhere but the family ranch—and make love to her in front of a blazing fire, all day, until the snow melted into summer.

He really could not afford to be thinking that way. Thinking that way would not get the job completed and get him on his way out of this valley and off to Denver. "The snow might make it harder to do what you came all the way out here to do today. You could wait and do it tomorrow. Evvy and Holly would love your company."

"Oh, I don't want to bother anybody and the snow is so pretty. I love being out in it," she said as she dropped her arms to her sides and smiled up at him.

Yeah, the snow's pretty until you try to drive your

itsy-bitsy car in a storm that has more blow and drift than anything you've ever seen in your life. The thought of her driving that car in a mountain snowstorm stirred the foolishness deep within him, brought up his need to protect—and sometimes in order to protect, one had to conquer.

"Have any problems driving out here?" He hoped to God so. It would make talking her into staying for the duration easier and if he didn't already think it was a good idea, Evvy would insist he do so.

"My car has all-wheel drive and it's not like I've never driven in the snow, and to me this is one of nature's gifts."

"It'll be a big gift wrapped in sparkly paper and tied with a giant red bow if we can get the last of the calves born safely and not have them out in the middle of a blizzard."

She tilted her head to try to look up at him without the flakes falling into her eyes and then blinked when they did. "A blizzard. Will it get that bad?"

"It might. You need a hat." He tugged the bill of his Miller's Hardware cap that kept much of the weather out of his eyes and resisted the urge to put it on her head. The last time he had done that, his sister, Crystal, had smacked him hard and told him to mind his own business, she could take care of herself.

He hoped it was still true, that his sister was out there somewhere taking care of herself.

"Walking the sites will give me a good feel of what I need to change, if anything, and I can't wait to see the plans start to become real." She set her fists on her hips in determination. "So I'm going to go out and do the walk-off quickly so I can still get back to town this afternoon."

Back to town this afternoon? So it would be a fight. "You need some overshoes."

"These shoes'll be okay." She held up the toe of a totally inadequate-for-the-weather light blue running shoe. "Your mother wears this kind of shoe."

"My mother wears athletic shoes inside the house because she had a knee replaced. If you have another pair to wear when you need to throw that pair out, then you're good to go. The ground is not all frozen and pretty white snow."

"Sarcasm. I deserve that for being unprepared."

She offered no excuses, though he could think of a couple she might use, like she didn't know she was getting the job, especially not right away and, according to the report, she had lived in Southern California for almost a decade.

She examined her athletic shoes and then looked up at him, blinking as the snowflakes pummeled her face. "Do you have a pair of overshoes I could borrow?"

"Four buckles enough for you." He almost laughed at the thought of the city woman clomping around in four-buckle overshoes. But the longer she stayed out in the snow, the sooner she would admit she shouldn't drive back to town today.

"I guess. If I knew what that was. Buckle overshoes are somewhere in my memory, like my grandfather had them or something."

"Let's go in the mudroom and I'll get you a pair."

"Thanks. As soon as I can get to a bigger town, I'll get myself some proper gear."

He nodded and escorted her into the mudroom, where the closets of the tile-and-wood-paneled room held enough communal hats, boots, coats, etc. to supply an army.

As he sorted through the footwear, she asked about Trey and he told her what he knew. It was hard to tell a woman expecting a baby about a child who was desperately sick.

He held up a pair of boots.

She grinned and nodded. "Four-buckle overshoes. Montana is chock-full of new experiences for me."

He knew the quickest way to get these boots on her was to do it himself, so he knelt on the rug in front of her and held the boot for her to stick her foot inside. She put a hand on his shoulder for support as she lifted her foot from the floor. Her small hand barely applied pressure as she kept her balance, but he had to work really hard to keep from thinking what it would feel like to have her press her palms to his naked shoulder, massage his bare back with her small fingers.

After he'd clipped all four buckles on each boot closed and was still kneeling in front of KayLee, he glanced up to see his mother in the doorway, smiling all angelic-like.

"Hi, Mrs. Doyle," KayLee said.

"Give her a hat, too, Bay, dear."

On her own insistence, KayLee headed out alone to where the cabins would be built. It wasn't very far from the main house, but the snow was beginning to fall harder. She had heard the Wild West stories about people tying a rope between the house and the barn so they didn't get disoriented in the blowing snow and wander off never to be found again.

As she ventured forward, snow obscured the trees and turned their spread branches into dark hulking figures, nearly hidden in the white. There were two or so inches of snow under her feet, and she was glad Baylor had found boots for her.

She stopped in the all-encompassing white.

What if she couldn't find her way back? What if she was one of those people who wandered off?

She did an about-face to check to see if she could still see the outlines of the ranch buildings.

She could. She could also see the form of a man heading toward her. She had assured Baylor she could do this by herself, that she actually preferred to do it by herself, but she stopped and waited for him.

Hands in his jacket pockets, he had a cowboy hat on now, a bigger version of the one he had found for her to wear. *It'd keep the snow from going down her neck* he had said as he plopped the hat on her head. *Keep the snow out of your eyes, too.* Then he tucked her hair behind her ear and she hadn't been able to stop herself from leaning into the gentle touch of his fingers.

She watched as he approached in long strides, eating up ground quickly and looking powerful, like a big cat, a big sexy male, alpha cat. Not a cat, a wolf.

He drew closer.

No, a man.

The kind a woman would be drawn to if she were trying to propagate the species. Or wanted protection for a child already in progress. She doubted many females ignored Baylor Doyle—only the blind ones, and only as long as they couldn't touch him.

She smiled at the thought of how the hormones of the female body created a different kind of thinking. To her pre-pregnant self, this thinking would have been over-the-top, even bordering on irrational. Knowing she had a real reason for being irrational—no matter what

Cindy said—she grinned wider. She liked it. It was fun, even exhilarating.

KayLee squeezed her hands into fists and tried to calm her breathing. She wanted Baylor Doyle, but she was not going to have him. She had other priorities, and he was a client. Having him could mess things up on many levels. Not the least of which, for her baby's protection, she had to maintain some kind of boundaries for herself.

Having him wouldn't be fair to him, either. She doubted he was the love-'em-and-leave-'em type.

He strode right up to her and leaned down to kiss her.

No, that was her imagination. He actually stopped a few feet away.

"Had enough of being out here alone?"

She smiled at him. "How'd you know?"

"When she was little, my sister, Crystal, would freak out when she got too far away and the snow obscured the buildings." He pointed toward the stand of trees by the stream. "One day when she wandered too far and the snow started coming down hard, she stood in that bunch of trees and screamed until one of the dogs started howling."

"How long was she out there alone?"

"A long time. At least ten minutes."

Even with his teasing tone, KayLee could tell he had great affection for his sister. She might ask him about her someday.

"I was starting to feel uncomfortable, but thank you for letting me come out by myself. Being...well...frightened of being alone out here is one of those things I wouldn't have believed if I hadn't experienced it. It's creepy, but somehow exciting on a primal, woman-against-the-elements kind of way."

He chuckled.

His laughter had been tinged with a yeah-right kind of tone, most likely about the woman-against-the-elements remark.

"I'll hang around, keep an eye on you, won't let you wander off into the woods and get lost."

As much as the necessity of having a caretaker rankled her free-spirit sensibilities, sometimes—protection of the innocent child being one of those times—it was wiser to let it happen. What better guardian for an unborn child than Baylor Doyle?

She left him standing under a pine tree and wandered the area, counting measured steps, jotting notes on paper with a pencil. There were some things one of her instructors at the school of architecture and urban planning had told her she would always have use for—a blank paper and a pencil with a decent point. The woman had been correct. Soggy but functional where nothing else would have worked as well today.

She looked up and around every now and then to see Baylor keeping vigil some distance away. Male guarding female.

He waved and she waved back and continued walking off the perimeter of the second cabin site near the stream. Being up close and personal with her projects gave her an organic, almost biologic, connection that drawings, notes, aerial photos and even drive-by site visits could not offer.

This cabin was going to be the most beautiful of all, with its breathtaking views and relative isolation. Many a romance would prosper here.

Crackling fire in the stone fireplace, comfy long-stranded flokati rug under a naked couple, sweat glistening on their bodies as they professed their love in words and actions…

"Are you warm enough?"

The sound of Baylor's voice so close drew her out of the fantasy. She recognized she had been standing in one spot for a while. Snow had collected on her coat while she'd been thinking of things she'd be better off not thinking of at all.

"I am, thanks to my borrowed coat." She brushed at the snow on her shoulder and shuffled her feet.

He was such a caring man, thoughtful even. It seemed part of his nature to be in charge, to look after things. He was the kind of person she needed in her life right now.

She took two steps closer to him and reached a hand up to his shoulder.

She had meant to tell him how thoughtful she thought he was.

Instead, she tipped her head back so the brims of their hats wouldn't crash together and kissed him on the mouth. His lips chilled by the cold air quickly warmed and she pressed harder. The surge of need closed out the other thoughts in her brain except for this man, of kissing him, of wanting him until she wanted to drop in the snow and make love to him.

She jerked away. "I, um, I didn't mean to do that."

She studied him to see if she could tell how much damage she had caused.

"It felt like you meant it."

His diamond-blue eyes made dark by the muted light somehow burned scorchingly hot. She took a step back from the fire.

"I, ah, have to go."

She headed for the safety of her car. She had to get out of here and regroup. No way was she thinking with a rational brain.

She needed distance and she needed to get it fast.

His boots thudded rhythmically behind her, sometimes muted by the not yet frozen ground of the small meadow. Wisely he left some space between them so she couldn't turn suddenly and throw herself at him until they tumbled down to the cold ground and made hot…

Stop it.

She covered the distance to her car in what might have been record time for a pregnant woman and yanked the door open as if salvation itself could be found within. Once inside, she tossed the mittens and the hat on the other seat and dug in her pocket for her keys.

She found the big red hankie he had given to her that first day. She had hand washed it, even ironed it with the iron in her motel room. She should give it back to him. She touched its softness to her lips and then shoved it back in her pocket.

She had just poked the key into the ignition when the door beside her snapped open.

"What the hell are you doing?" A scowling, angry Baylor Doyle frowned in at her.

"Your mama wouldn't like you talking like that."

"You can't leave."

She ignored that order and tugged on the door. It didn't budge.

She looked up at him. "I've been here less than an hour and the roads were perfectly fine when I drove here."

"Perfectly fine can change fast in a spring storm. You should stay here for the night."

"There are already ten of you staying in that house, and I need to get back to town."

"I'll drive you if you think you need to go now."

"I'll drive myself."

"It's a spring snow. It'll be gone in two days."

He was trying rationality on her. Didn't he know she was far beyond that? Besides, if she got through the one high pass between here and town, she should have no trouble at all.

"I'll drive slowly and very carefully."

He reached in and put a hand on her arm. "I'll drive you in the truck." Instead of angry and impatient, his tone was warm and sincere. She wanted to leap out and tell him she'd stay as long as he wanted her to. She'd live in a tent with him until she could get a cabin built for them.

Her mental imperative to flee intensified.

She shook his hand from her arm and when he moved away, she took the opportunity to close him out. She resisted engaging the locks to keep him out. This wasn't a battle and she could still behave in a rational and civilized manner.

If she left Baylor behind, she'd have a fair chance to get her brain organized again.

If she stayed she might lose everything she thought she had achieved for her baby's future. It wasn't, after all, her child's fault she couldn't seem to control herself when it came to Baylor Doyle.

When he backed away, she started the car. She was grateful he let her leave without any more of a fight.

The road leading out to the highway was still quite passable, especially with the AWD her car had. When a hulking SUV that could have eaten her car as a snack positioned itself behind her, she knew why he had given up so easily. She kept driving. She could not afford to stop and discuss his misgivings about her leaving.

She had a few regrets of her own but not as many as she had about staying at the Doyle ranch with him so close.

When after five minutes, he hadn't tried to close the gap between their two vehicles, she figured out he intended to follow her until he thought she was safe. All the way, she was sure, to the Easy Breezy Inn if he believed he had to.

Snow bombarded her car, but the daylight gave her courage. If she had never driven the road before and it had been nighttime, she would have had to acquiesce and stay at the ranch.

As it was, she was doing fine. She relaxed and let her car do the work it had been built for. Once in a while there was a slip, but the car kept her in her lane and headed back to town.

Her rearview mirror told her Baylor was still behind her. A couple of times she wondered if she should stop, thank him and tell him he could go home because she'd be fine, but she could imagine how that would go over and kept driving.

She thumbed the volume switch on the CD player and let soft music give her shredded nerves something to concentrate on besides the snow falling outside her car.

Eventually she grew used to her guardian. As the snow fell harder, she even started to appreciate his being there, especially when the wind turned bold and began to buffet her car.

Sometimes she had to fight to keep the forward

motion of the car controlled and acknowledged he had been right to follow her. Okay, so she might have been rash to leave the ranch. She certainly had been when she kissed him. Now he offered her and her baby reassurance if she lost her nerve on the mountain road.

As she rounded a bend in the road, a particularly strong gust of wind blew the snow sideways and tried to do the same with her car. She held on to her will and her car held to the road.

It didn't take long to begin the climb into the pass she had thought might have more snow. At one point she had to drive halfway into the oncoming lane to avoid a deep drift, but since she hadn't seen a vehicle besides hers and Baylor's, it didn't cause her too much concern.

As she progressed painstakingly upward in the pass, she gripped the wheel tightly and leaned closer to the windshield, as if that would let her see the road more clearly. As the elevation rose, the snowdrifts grew in height and breadth. The already muted daylight was made dimmer by the shadow of the mountain and impaired her ability to judge the depth of the drifts, but she plowed on.

Baylor stayed on her tail. His big truck probably had little trouble with the drifts or the wind.

A marker told her she had reached the tip of the pass and she smiled. The worst was over. If she continued winding her way down toward town, she'd be at the Easy Breezy Inn in no time.

With her goal achievable, she grew more confident. Driving in the snow was apparently a skill you didn't completely lose, like riding a bike.

"Your mama rocks, baby." No patting. This time she kept both hands on the wheel.

A dark shape moving up ahead caught her attention. As she drew closer a deer—legs at odd angles of indecision, eyes wild in the headlights—loomed in the roadway directly in front of her.

She let off the gas and tapped the brakes. Just as the collision seemed almost inevitable, she steered the wheel gently away from the deep drop into oblivion and away from the deer.

When she was sure she wouldn't swerve and go over the edge, she braked harder. The chugging of the anti-lock brakes said she was getting all the braking power she had.

The car halted inches from the rock face on the opposite side of the road.

She didn't feel the fear she should have been feeling. All she could do was rejoice that she and her baby were safe. She tapped the wheel a couple of times in gratitude and in celebration and breathed a sigh of relief.

She started to shift into Reverse, but stopped when the door on the driver's side whipped open and cold and snow blasted in, followed by Baylor's angry face. Hadn't he ever heard of climbing in the car to chat?

He had left his hat in the truck and snow filled his hair and she was sure was going down the back of his neck.

"You again," she said and grinned, still feeling the giddiness of being unharmed, until he stuck his head inside the shelter of the car, his nose inches from hers.

"Are you all right?" His eyes were so close to hers she could see the darkest of blue striations. She wanted bedsheets made of that color so she could...

"Am I crazy, you mean?" Yes, yes, indeed, she was.

He didn't speak. His warm breath bathed her face and kept the cold away. His blond hair darkened by the melting snow dripped water on the back of her hand. ✴

He studied her for a long moment and then leaned down slowly, capturing her breath.

An invitation. She knew she would be better off if she resisted. Better off, but not satisfied.

She shifted toward him.

He withdrew suddenly, banging his head on the frame.

He said something Evvy really wouldn't like and then leaned back down with his hands on his thighs. He glared in at her from a safe, nonkissing distance. "I don't suppose you have chains for your tires?"

"It wasn't anything I ever thought I'd need."

"Get in the truck—please."

"Isn't this the worst of it? Won't the rest of the way be safer than this?"

"No."

Well, that wasn't the answer she wanted, but it didn't change anything, except to make her more determined. "If I can get my car backed out of here, I'll be fine."

He didn't seem to like it, but he nodded. He most likely figured he could pluck her out of a snowdrift in ten minutes as well as now.

"I'll be fine. You can go back home while you still can."

"Yep, that'll happen."

He strode away, tugging the collar of his jacket up against the snow getting inside.

She backed easily out onto the road and headed down the mountain with headlights shining in her mirror.

She drove slowly enough to maintain control and fast enough to avoid getting stuck in drifts that piled snow on the road. The unrelenting, windblown white combined with the dull light sometimes made her have to guess where the road was.

When she hit a particularly large drift and her car took the second half sideways, Baylor flashed his lights at her.

She stopped in the roadway and he pulled around her, motioning for her to follow him. When she got too far behind him, he'd slow. His big truck took the drifts much better, spewing out rooster tails of snow, but leaving a path for her to follow.

The rest of the fifteen-minute drive took almost an hour of breath-holding, wheel-clenching, teeth-grinding driving.

She parked her car outside her room and Baylor parked beside her. She sat for a moment and let some of the adrenaline rushing around inside her ebb.

There were at least eight inches of snow in the parking lot and it came down harder than ever now.

She pulled on the borrowed knit hat and gloves while Baylor sat inside the cab of the truck talking on his phone.

If she were lucky—if they were both lucky—he'd leave now. When she opened the door of her car, however, he jumped out of the truck and came around to take hold of her arm.

"I'm really okay now."

His fingers held her arm gently.

He didn't say a word, and he didn't let go until she was under the overhang of the building and had her room key in her hand.

When he didn't walk away she slid the key into the lock and opened the door. The musty air and the stained carpet seemed like home and she was glad to be back.

He followed her into the room and when she spun slowly around to face him, he looked dangerously angry and the look made laughter bubble up inside her. She would have doubled over if she didn't think she'd topple.

"Is that steam coming from your ears?"

CHAPTER TEN

KAYLEE DROPPED THE HAT and gloves on the table and shed her coat.

"You make me crazy," Baylor said. The words came out as if he had to force them. His voice was husky and it made KayLee's breath catch.

Her jacket was damp from the melted snow, so she hung it on the back of the chair by the heater under the window. He had purposely left the door slightly ajar, KayLee thought, to protect her reputation.

He was angry as hell and frustrated and yet he thought of her.

Who'd see into the room from outside? By the time the two of them had pulled into the parking lot of the motel, snow was blowing by so furiously that they were surrounded by a solid sheet of white.

A gust of wind puffed in and showered them with snowflakes and then sucked the door shut with a bang.

The door issue settled by default, KayLee put her fists on her hips and faced Baylor. "You made me crazy first."

He stepped toward her so that they were toe-to-toe— almost as close as he could get—and put his hands on her shoulders. Water dripped from his blond curls and dusky blue stared at her, searched her face. She wondered what he saw.

Did he feel any of the desire she was feeling? Was he thinking he was too polite to yell at a pregnant woman?

He drew her toward him for what seemed like an eternity. When he lowered his mouth his soft lips took hers, an ache started—a deeply profound ache low in her belly, a good ache, an ache of hunger and need like she'd never felt before.

She leaned into his kiss and gave back one of her own. He moved his mouth over hers and reached up to cup her head with his big hand, a gesture that made her feel treasured.

Oh, she was so gone.

As his mouth possessed hers and his hands made a slow tantalizing raid down her back, she ceased to care about even the vaguest idea of snow or the rest of the world. She wanted him to touch her, to caress her already sensitive breasts, but when he lowered his hands and squeezed her butt, that was good, too. Angling her body, she pressed herself against his long muscular thigh.

Still he kissed her softly, caressed her gently. If he felt half of what she was feeling, his reserve was the result of hard and resolute control. She wanted him. She wanted to be all over him. She wanted to celebrate being alive and knew there was no better way than with Baylor Doyle.

When she pressed closer, more intimately, her reward was to feel him hard against her.

He lifted his mouth from hers. "KayLee, are you sure?"

"I'm only sure that I want you now."

He held her at arm's length and then let her go.

Oh, well, that wasn't the answer she was looking for.

"I'll be right back." He kissed her hard on the mouth and since he hadn't bothered to take off his coat…

He was gone.

Was "I'll be right back" a joke? Was that like "I'll call you sometime"? Was he coming back at all?

She peeked out the window to see him disappear in the snow, but he was heading in the general direction of the motel office and not climbing into his truck and racing away.

She'd have to wait and see.

In the meantime, she'd do what every pregnant woman needed to do, often. She used the bathroom. When she came out she was still alone, and then she heard a vehicle door slam. Considering she and Baylor were the only two vehicles parked outside her room, she assumed it was Baylor's truck.

Good sense ruled at last. Goodbye, Baylor. Thanks for seeing me home.

The door swept open with a cold blast and Baylor stepped inside, grinning at her. He held up a room key of his own and a strip of condoms.

She laughed. "You have condoms with you?"

He closed the door and slipped off his coat, again covered with snow—melting snow—and hung it on the doorknob.

"Since there is a baby in residence, I thought it prudent to give you the option so you wouldn't have a reason…"

"To turn you down?" He nodded and she continued. "No worries."

She found a devil grin and gave it to him.

He reached out and ran his hand from her shoulder, down the side of her aching breast and below her stomach, where he pressed into the warmth with his fingertips.

KayLee let the heat rush through her.

"The ranch vehicles all have a condom supply. My brothers and their wives insist," he said as he strode forward. "They say there are many secluded places on the ranch where having sex is inevitable."

"*They* say?" He knew what he was doing to her and when he drew her to him, she went eagerly and buried her hands in his hair.

"I've never had the need to dip into their supply."

She brought his mouth down to hers and he brought his arms around her. When she explored his lower lip with her tongue, he kissed her harder and answered with exploration of his own.

She reached between them and lifted the tail of his shirt from his belted jeans. There was nirvana under there and she intended to have it. When she pressed her palms into the hot hard muscles of his chest she felt an odd sense of coming home, of deep relief, and the feelings were soon eclipsed by the desire to have all of this man as soon as possible.

She unbuttoned his shirt and pushed it back off his shoulders and as she did, he kissed every inch of her neck and nibbled her earlobe. She shivered and then pressed her cheek into the bed of curling blond hair on his chest.

"You are everything I imagined you would be," she said as she buried her nose in the warm scent of him.

"You have been imagining me?"

"Since the moment I saw you."

"You California women are forward."

"If that's what it takes to get what I want."

He didn't ask what she wanted. He did lift her sweater

over her head and unhooked her bra. Her heavy breasts, unfettered, swayed and she ached to press into the heat of his bare chest—and she did.

"Oh, Baylor, you feel so good."

"Yes, ma'am, I do."

She leaned back and curled a big grin up at him and when she did, he brought his hands up under her breasts and held each one as if it were a precious gift.

"Perfect fit," she said of his big rancher's hands and her enlarged breasts.

"Plain perfect," he said as he marched soft kisses down the swell of one breast to her nipple. When his mouth closed around her she sighed, and when he suckled gently she gasped.

He drew harder and she groaned.

"Baylor, that feels so very good." She laughed. "I didn't know I was a groaner."

He smiled, his mouth still on her nipple, and reached under her belly to unzip her jeans. Not wanting to be left behind, she unzipped his and tugged them down, followed by his underwear. When he sprang free, she grasped him in one hand and brought his head against her chest with the other, then buried her face in his damp curls.

He whisked her jeans down and swept her off her feet in almost one motion. Then he tugged down the sheet with her in his arms as if she weighed nothing.

KayLee enjoyed the struggle for control and she didn't particularly care who was alpha at any given moment. It was all good.

As he placed her gently on the bed, the cools sheets were a shock, but she scooted over quickly so he could crawl in beside her and take her past warm—way past.

But he didn't crawl. He left.

He went into the bathroom and came out a few minutes later drying his hands.

He grinned at her. "Habit."

She smiled as he edged in and pressed the length of his body to hers.

Sigh, and sigh again. She had never felt anything so right.

He leaned his taut body over hers and kissed her deeply, took her with his tongue. When she was completely breathless, he spoke. "KayLee, you are so beautiful."

She looked down at herself. "You're right. I have loved every change my body has gone through."

He grinned and lowered his mouth to her breasts and then to her belly.

"There is one very lucky person in there."

"Or a very brave one."

He chuckled. "The babe's mother is brave to the point of foolhardy at times."

"I can't disagree with that."

"She is happy in the body she has."

"Or that."

"She doesn't make excuses for things."

She thought for a moment. "I guess. It's not something I've really considered much."

"Trust me."

"I do trust you, Baylor."

He kissed her mouth and this time he drew up the sheet and blanket and then reached his hand under and gently caressed her breasts, massaging one nipple between his fingertips and thumb, and then the other. By the time he lowered his hand to explore between her legs, she was aching for his intimate touch.

She pressed her body rhythmically into his hand, until his fingers went deeper and deeper with every thrust.

"Now, Baylor, please. I want you inside me now."

She had heard of wild abandon. It was a movie thing…a myth…up until now.

Her brain was already there and her body was a willing companion. She wanted him with all the yearning and need she could ever imagine.

"Turn on your side," he said and when she did, she heard the rustle of a plastic wrapper.

She waited for what seemed like an eternity until every inch of her throbbed with anticipation.

When she thought she'd explode, he moved in behind her and pressed gently between her legs, where he was welcomed. He dipped inside her and pulled out, and she wanted to yell, "Unfair! Unfair!" She wanted all of him now, but she found she had no voice, only need.

She reached behind to press him deeply inside her. His every forward stroke brought her higher, drawing a soft groan from her lips.

The world could have ended at that moment and she wouldn't have known.

Ecstasy exploded inside her—body and mind—and she frantically searched for every nuance, extracting every sensation.

Wave after wave crashed over her and she savored each wash of golden pleasure until she was left with completion.

She lay quiet, gripping Baylor's hand against her chest as he held her close.

When she got her breath back and found her voice, she whispered, "Your turn."

A deep chuckle and slow rhythmic movement an-

swered her. Then he reached down and pressed his
fingers between her legs, framing her, exciting her
again.

They moved together, rocking and riding the rising
surge.

She never expected to become completely aroused
again, but it happened so quickly she cried out, and as
she did, he stiffened and ground out a low primal sound.

Soon the sound of nothing except their breathing
surrounded them, bathed them in the opulence of great
sex.

She smiled, gratified to know he felt as strongly as
she did. "How much longer do you think we could have
ignored this?"

"I can't say I've ever been so grateful for a snowstorm." He stroked inside her and she could feel him
hard again, pressing her for what she wanted so much
to give.

Soon they were moving again…and then again.
When they eventually drifted into fatigued sleepiness
the room was dark, and when she closed her eyes, Kay-
Lee was sure she had found some little part of heaven.

The next thing she knew, daylight was streaming into
the room from the crack between the curtains. Before
she opened her eyes, she knew she was alone. When
her exploring fingers found only cold bed, she smiled
and sighed. She had expected Baylor to leave before
the town woke up. She wondered if he was successful
in slipping out unnoticed.

On the bed beside her she found a note on bound
tablet of Easy Breezy Inn paper.

> Good morning. You haven't been deserted. Call
> me at the ranch. Baylor.

She smiled at the sentiment. He wanted her to have options. She already knew this town well enough to know it would be a short leap between seeing the Shadow Range vehicle parked next to hers, to Baylor and her having sex.

He probably didn't just get up and leave. He most likely went down to his room and mussed up the bed, even took a shower there before he headed out. She didn't have to look out the window to know the big SUV would be gone.

She sat back against the headboard and smiled. If they hadn't shoveled and salted the sidewalks, his boot tracks would give them away anyway.

She called the ranch and left a message with Evvy to have Baylor call to talk about a trip to Kalispell to check out the availability of building supplies.

She stretched and yawned. Regrets? She had a billion but not about spending the storm with Baylor Doyle.

She had loved Chad, but she never had feelings of total consumption even in the very beginning when they couldn't seem to get enough of each other. What she had with Baylor was wild, and pregnancy aside, she couldn't imagine anyone stirring such feelings in her.

She hugged the pillow to her naked body and wondered how long she could stay in bed without feeling guilty. If she stayed here she could smell Baylor, close her eyes and imagine he was still sleeping beside her.

Was he really planning on leaving town as the man at the diner had said?

Didn't matter. She had no strings on him, nor he on her. Last night might have been the only time they would get that close. She wanted more and hoped he did, too, but things could get very complicated, very fast. He lived on the ranch with his extended family, and she would be living with the women who professed to be the eternal spring that gave life to the grapevine of gossip in this town. She and Baylor would have few secrets.

Besides, she needed to settle down and provide a safe, stable environment for her child. If Baylor planned on leaving the valley, well…she'd make no judgments based on the ranting of someone who might well be the town drunk.

Showered and dressed, KayLee let herself out of the room and into the crisp air. The sun shined brightly and the reflection off the snow had her quickly putting on her sunglasses.

"It's very bright out here, baby."

At least a foot of snow had fallen and it was already piled everywhere. Main Street was passable, but the sidewalks were a patchwork of cleared and snow-covered. That settled whether she'd walk down to the diner or stay and get food from the breakfast room at the motel.

She dined on oatmeal from the microwave, a hard-boiled egg and an apple, but the sun streaming in the window onto the table in her room let her believe she was on the veranda of her oceanfront home feasting on ambrosia.

Of course, last night may have influenced her outlook a bit.

When she finished breakfast, she found the information sheet from Cora and Ethel and dialed their number.

"This is Cora, is this KayLee?"

Either the woman was psychic or she had caller ID and picked up on the California area code.

"Yes, it's KayLee. I wondered if I could still come over before dinnertime tonight to see the apartment."

"You sure could." Cora muffled the phone as she called to Ethel. *KayLee's still coming today.* "We thought you might have gotten stuck out at the ranch."

KayLee smiled. The grapevine must have trouble working in the snow, or the pair hadn't been to the diner today, and not the grocery store, either, if they hadn't seen her car in the motel's lot.

"It was an adventure getting back, but I bought a car I thought could do a decent job in the snow."

Good. They wouldn't know Baylor had been there, either. Good. Good. Good.

"I told Ethel we should have warned you about the snow coming."

"Thank you, I already knew about it. Baylor mentioned it the day before."

"That Baylor, he's quite a catch."

Ethel's voice came from the background. "Cora, now don't you go pestering her."

"He's a very nice man. All the Doyles are." Bringing up Baylor was a mistake and she needed to extricate herself quickly. "I have work to get to, so I'll see you about six o'clock for dinner."

"That would be lovely, dear. Are there any things you can't eat?"

A twinge of discomfort squeezed low in the front of KayLee's belly and grew as the seconds ticked by.

"KayLee?"

"I'm...um...pretty much an omnivore," she said, trying not to feel alarm or to cause Cora to think something was wrong. "I eat almost anything."

"We thought a nice roast chicken." This was Ethel. She must have picked up an extension.

KayLee decided to pace the room while she talked and the squeezing seemed to ease.

"That would—" Suddenly the squeezing grew intense and her footsteps faltered. She stopped and put her hand on her abdomen. Her belly felt more like a basketball than usual "Oh, my."

"What is it, dear?" Cora asked.

"It's the baby. What else could it be?" Ethel answered.

"Oh, how would the two of us know?" Cora asked and then said to KayLee, "Do you need us to call an ambulance for you?"

KayLee lowered herself into the straight-backed chair near the table and tried to relax, but the squeezing continued. "I think I'm okay." It wasn't really painful, not really, but she found she couldn't sit still and heaved up from the chair.

"Tell us what's happening, dear. What can we do?"

"Wow, that was interesting." KayLee expelled a breath of relief. "It's gone now. I feel fine."

"Are you sure? We could send the EMTs."

"It's gone, Cora, Ethel. I'll rest and if I have any more problems, I'll call someone."

"If you're sure, dear."

"I'm sure."

"Call us if you need anything."

"Thank you, I will."

One question kept going through her head as she closed her phone and slipped it into her leather bag. What if having sex with Baylor had caused some harm to her baby? Sex over and over? The books had said it wouldn't cause a problem.

She sat on the edge of the bed. She hadn't done much yet today and she was already tired.

She thought of Baylor's smirk and his bright blue eyes.

An ache squeezed in the middle of her lower abdomen and intensified until a dull pain spread down the front of her belly.

BAYLOR WHISTLED AS HE and Blue nudged the cow in labor toward the chute leading to the calving shed. Sometimes for the rancher's peace of mind, a cow was better off if she birthed her calf indoors. A foot of snow made muddy by too many hooves was one of those times. But that didn't make the cow grateful for the interference.

As the cantankerous cow waddled into the chute a grinning Lance appeared in the shed doorway. And the cow, well, she had confirmed her second thoughts about going inside and tried to bolt for the open field.

"Thanks a lot, bro," Baylor called to Lance, who ducked out of sight.

Blue was too smart for the cow, and with hardly any guidance from Baylor, quickly cut off her retreat. This time man and horse followed her up the chute and into the building.

"You look pleased," he said to Lance as he dismounted.

"Seth called. They did Trey's surgery early this morning and he's in recovery. The doctor says he's going to do well."

"Were they able to fix the problem this time?"

"Seth said they got it all done. Closed the hole in his heart completely. He might have to have a new valve some day, but right now everything looks good."

"Hallelujah."

Between him and Lance and Blue, they got three more dams into the birthing shed.

Baylor had left Lance behind and was cleaning up in the barn when Holly came rushing in.

"They took KayLee in to see Dr. DeVane about a half hour ago. Cora called. Said she thought we ought to know."

Baylor leaned over and braced both palms on the edge of the sink. He might as well have been kicked in the gut by a mad bull.

"I'm sure she'll be fine," Holly hurried to say. "Things happen a lot toward the end of pregnancy and most of the time it's nothing. I'm sure she'll be able to do the job."

Baylor shook his head and faced his sister-in-law. "I'm not worried about the job, Holly."

"So she got to you, too, huh?" Holly sighed and her shoulders slumped. "It's like this is happening to one of us."

"I'm sure you're right. She'll be fine." He gave Holly a reassuring smile he didn't really feel. "You have more experience with such things than I do."

"Cora said they called the EMTs and they took her to the clinic in the ambulance. I feel—" she paused and raised one shoulder "—helpless. She has no one in town, no one for a thousand miles."

Baylor dried his hands while he studied his sister-in-law. Her features were drawn with worry. It didn't seem fair that the good news about Trey was followed so soon with another baby in jeopardy and a woman this family already thought of as a friend.

Baylor hung the towel on the hook. "I'll go tell Mom we're leaving, and you go tell your husband I'm taking you to town." If he took Holly with him they couldn't wag their tongues as fast. After last night, if he didn't know that KayLee and her baby were fine, he'd be a rampaging bull. "Lance can see to the ones in the birthing shed and Dad can help if he needs it."

The roads had been barely passable this morning and weren't much better now.

He and Holly rode mostly in silence, while music about heartbreak and hope played softly as the truck's big tires hummed out of tune.

Forty-five minutes later, Baylor stopped the SUV in the parking lot of the clinic and Holly leaped out before he had shifted into Park. He let her go first, selfishly, it would make him seem less eager even though he doubted he was.

The waiting room was a flurry of activity. Many of the doctor's appointments would have been rescheduled, but the snow seemed to have raised the number of injuries. Dr. Daley was in the waiting room speaking to the parents of a teenager with a bandage on his head.

He didn't see Dr. DeVane.

He did see a pair of feet of some unknown patient reclined on a cart in one of the treatment rooms, and Arlene, the clinic's secretary, was already speaking with someone who apparently had a hand injury and she had two others waiting to sign in.

A curtain popped open and Abby Fairbanks, one of the nurses, strode out of the treatment room and crossed over to see them.

"Hi, Holly. Hi, Baylor." She smiled broadly at them and gave them each a friendly hug, her dark curly hair its usual unruly self. "Not you guys, too! Seems no one remembers how to use snow removal equipment today."

"We're fine," Holly assured her. "We heard KayLee Morgan was brought in."

"She's here." Abby's smile was encouraging but

Baylor knew they'd get scant information about a clinic patient. "She's being seen right now."

"Would you tell her we're here," Holly said and Baylor could tell she wanted to demand information. He wanted to do the same thing.

"I'm sure she'd like to know someone is here for her," Abby replied very noncommittally. Abby was good people. No friend was happier for another than Baylor was the day Abby married the out-of-towner Reed Maxwell. Abby would give them information if she could, and she would certainly deliver their message.

"Thanks, Abby."

Baylor paced at Holly's side as they waited. Dr. DeVane was tops and her backup—her husband, Dr. Daley—was equally qualified. The town of St. Adelbert had lucked out when they got that pair.

"Whatever is happening with KayLee, she's in good hands," Holly said as they waited.

Baylor thought of how breathtaking KayLee looked last night, of how eager she was to have him. How much he'd learned to respect her courage in the last forty-eight hours. "Doesn't help much."

Holly gave him one of those don't-I-know-it smiles.

Dr. DeVane came out of the room at the end of the hallway and ducked into another room to see her next patient.

Holly sighed. They couldn't expect the busy doctor to give them time when there were injured people.

A couple of minutes later, Abby came out of a room at the end of the hallway, smiling, and when she spotted them huddled near the office, she strode right up to them.

"You can go in and see her now."

Baylor would have worried about knocking somebody down if Holly hadn't already blazed a trail for the two of them.

As they entered the room he took in a pale and resting KayLee on the exam table.

"How are you, sweetie?" Holly asked as she took KayLee's hand.

"Feeling silly." Her face held an apology and relief. That was good at least. The gown she wore and the blankets that covered her made her chaste looking. But he knew better—much better—and wondered if their lovemaking had caused this problem.

"Braxton Hicks?" Holly asked.

KayLee nodded.

"Well, that's okay then."

"Anybody want to tell me what you're both so happy about?" Baylor asked.

KayLee gave him a lingering look before she said, "False labor."

"False labor? Not much help." If it was not real labor, then why was she here? Was there something she wanted to tell him but couldn't with Holly in the room?

He must have appeared as concerned as he felt because Holly gripped his arm and grinned. "She's okay, Baylor. The uterus contracts during pregnancy and toward the end those contractions can get rambunctious. They are normal and usually cause no harm."

He rubbed the back of his neck. "Cows are easier."

KayLee and her baby were okay. He wanted to take her in his arms and hold her. Not sure he could trust himself at all, he took a step away.

"What's the plan?" Holly asked.

"I'm to stay until Dr. DeVane checks me again." She gave him a quick glance.

"Is there anything I can get you?" Holly asked her.

KayLee let her gaze pass over him again and then smiled at Holly. "I'd like some decaf coffee if there's any around."

Holly pursed her lips and gave Baylor a long, appraising look. Then she turned her appraisal on KayLee. Then back to him. He could see her collating data and then try very hard not to laugh out loud. When she was dismally unsuccessful, she raced from the room.

"Coffee, it is," she called over her shoulder as she ran.

"Subtlety, that's the quality I like best about my sister-in-law."

"Technically, I'm not supposed to eat or drink anything until Dr. DeVane says I'm okay to go."

He folded his arms over his chest so he wouldn't grab her up off the cart and hold her in his arms. "And Holly knows that."

KayLee nodded and reached a hand out to him. "I'm sure she does."

He wondered if he should be running for, if not his life, his freedom.

CHAPTER ELEVEN

WHEN BAYLOR CAME CLOSER to her again, KayLee took hold of his hand and studied him. He wore an old jacket, a work shirt, faded jeans and his old scuffed boots. He's been torn away from his work at the ranch. For her.

He had every reason to run the other way as fast as he could and here he was.

"I'm so sorry I made such a lame request of Holly. I wanted to tell you Dr. DeVane says what we did yesterday didn't cause the baby any harm."

He leaned a thigh on the edge of the exam table, where she sat propped up and wrapped in multiple blankets. His concern had changed to a look of bemusement. "What did we do yesterday?"

"Well, what you did." She tugged the sheet up under her chin. "I was an innocent bystander."

He gave the sheet several gentle tugs. "They must have a different definition of innocent bystander in California than we have here in Montana. By our standards you might be some sort of outlaw."

"Maybe—" She tucked her fingers inside the edge of his belt and tugged.

When he leaned down and kissed her she welcomed his lips with an open mouth. When she wanted more, she tugged his belt through the buckle.

He broke the kiss and straightened.

"Hey!" He engulfed her hand in his to keep her from

exploring. "Do you want me to have to take my shirt off and tie it around my waist?"

"You could do that. I wouldn't mind."

He reached for the top button.

"No! Stop!" It was her turn to grab his hand. "Holly is a sweetheart. She doesn't deserve to come back in here and find her brother-in-law half-naked."

"She is a sweetheart." He lowered his hand and tucked his thumbs into the pockets of his faded jeans. "She called you one of us."

KayLee swallowed at the sudden tightness in her throat.

"So what do you think?" he asked.

"About?" She knew he was trying to lighten her mood.

He picked up her restless free hand and kissed her fingertips as he talked. "Are we some kind of—" He sucked her thumb into his mouth and swirled his tongue around it and then he grinned up at her. She jerked her hand away and stuck it under the sheet. "Space monsters in costume," he continued, "and you already have your bags packed 'cause your gettin' outta town as soon as you're released?"

She didn't answer, but held a pose of contemplation. "I admit. You all scared me at first."

"If you want to leave I can call you a taxi," he offered.

"Can't afford a taxi," she said in her best gangsta voice, "until the check from the Shadow Range clears the bank and then I'll take a limo."

Someone knocked and she sat up straight. Baylor took a step away from the bed as the door opened.

"No luck." Holly quite purposefully avoided looking at the two of them as she pretended the sheet around

KayLee's feet needed rearranging. "The coffeepot was dry."

"Thanks for worrying about me, Holly, Baylor."

Holly shrugged. "It's what we do for each other."

"We—baby and I—" KayLee patted her stomach through the blankets "—don't have many in our corner these days."

Holly smiled encouragingly at her. "You have more people rooting for you than you think. Cora and Ethel are in the waiting room. They said to tell you if there is anything they can do for you, just to ask."

"They're so kind."

"They are and their place is a steal, even by St. Adelbert standards. And Rachel Taylor stopped by and said to tell you Taylor's Pharmacy will deliver anything you need, just call."

"It's like a village in a storybook."

There was another knock and Dr. DeVane and nurse Abby entered.

"If you'd wait in the waiting room." She spoke to Holly and Baylor, but she smiled at KayLee.

The Doyles departed quickly.

Dr. DeVane's smile made it all the way up to her light brown eyes. "How are you feeling?"

"Still pregnant and relieved."

"Good." She placed reassuring hands on KayLee's belly and applied light pressure. "Any more discomfort?"

"No."

"I'd like you to come into the clinic tomorrow and then every week from now on."

"So everything's okay? I can go now?"

"You can get dressed and Abby will have some instructions and some phone numbers for you. Is there anything else I can do for you?"

A tear slipped from the corner of KayLee's eye. "Thank you for seeing me and being so nice."

"See you tomorrow." Dr. DeVane smiled again and left the room.

"Do you need any help?" Abby asked when the two of them were alone.

"Yes, I do have a problem, but I'm afraid there's nothing for it."

Abby grinned. "If you move in at Cora and Ethel's, you'll be my neighbor and we can discuss your problem. He's a friend of mine."

MONDAY MORNING, a week after she had arrived in St. Adelbert, KayLee stood at the front window of the charming apartment on the second floor of Cora and Ethel's house. The roomy apartment took up the whole second floor of the house and that made it so un-California like, but very like the village in Wisconsin where she had grown up.

A separate entrance leading to a stairway to the second floor meant she could see the sisters if she chose when she returned home, or not, if she wanted to be alone. It truly was a great arrangement.

It had taken her very little time to be convinced living with the sisters was the right thing to do. She had needed a safe place to learn to trust her body again and this ruffle-curtained place with the 1950s furniture and flowered carpet was as safe as she'd found in a long time.

Her new landladies were the fountain of information they claimed to be. Amy and Seth Doyle's son, Trey, was doing very well, and KayLee had to admit knowing this gave her great peace. She also found out that Mr. McCormack, the rude man from the diner, had left town for rehab in Missoula, and the drugstore was going to have a huge sale next week so she should wait for those kinds of purchases if she could.

She pulled the ruffled living-room curtain aside and looked out onto the porch roof and street below. Holly would be there in a few minutes to take her shopping "at the best places" in Kalispell, she had said. KayLee would take the opportunity, and she hoped they would have time to introduce herself in person to some of the suppliers she had already contacted.

When her mobile phone twittered, she answered based on the caller ID. "Hi, Mom. Good to hear from you."

"You're in Montana, your message said. Is that a good idea?" her mother asked. There usually was never a hello.

"I am and I see you're back in Wisconsin. And if by 'good idea' you mean for the baby, we're both doing quite well. How long have you been home?"

"I get tired of the crowds sometimes. So what's in Montana?"

"A design and construction job."

Her mother laughed. "I just pictured you on a ladder with a hammer."

"Very funny. I hire that kind of stuff out these days." And she always had. And her mother knew it. "So are you alone or is Dad with you?"

"That's another reason I left. Your father showed up with the love of his life."

"Sorry, Mom. I know you never quite gave up."

"I like to punish myself. You must be due in a few weeks."

"Five and change if the doctor's calculations are correct."

"You got people there to back you up?"

"Are you volunteering, Mom?"

"I would, but I've got a thing I just started and I need the money."

It was KayLee's turn to laugh. "I know that one. And, yes, I have people here." She thought of the sisters downstairs, Holly who had stopped after work to check up on her twice since the visit to Dr. DeVane's clinic, and Baylor. He'd do whatever was right—for anybody.

She had final drawings worked out for him to sign off on. She was going to have to see him soon whether that was good for either of them or not.

"Well, speaking of that thing. I have to get going."

"Wait, Mom."

"I'm here."

"I just wanted to say I love you."

"Love ya, too. If you need anything…"

"Yeah, Mom. I know." *I know you'd like to want to help.* Her mother wasn't a bad soul.

The phone line went dead. Her mother did love her, the best she knew how, anyway. She closed her phone, tucked it back in her purse and looked out the window again.

No Holly yet.

She checked over her lists, one of what she wanted to acquire while in Kalispell, and the other named the people she wanted to meet with regarding building supplies.

When she glanced up this time and saw the ranch SUV round the corner and head up the street toward the house, she couldn't help but remember the reassuring headlights in her review mirror. Today, it would be Holly at the wheel.

The truck stopped, then backed into the driveway, and Baylor got out. The shock of seeing him had her heart beating faster and her mind racing. Kalispell with Baylor.

He went around to the back of the SUV and opened the tailgate. She couldn't see what he was doing, but when he came back into sight he was carrying a baby crib and a changing table. He put them on the porch and went back for a high chair, a stroller and a baby swing. By the time he went back for the third load, Cora and Ethel were on the porch collecting things and bringing them upstairs.

KayLee hurried to let them in. "I can help."

The women blocked her way. "Let us do this for you. It'll make us happy," Cora said, and Ethel bobbed her head in agreement.

By the time they were finished carrying things in, she also had a portable crib, a box of baby toys, a diaper pail, a large stack of small diapers and three boxes of tiny clothing and linens.

"Wow," she said as she surveyed the stuff. "I can throw one of my lists away."

She thanked each of the women, who insisted there was someplace they needed to go and split.

"Are you ready?" Baylor asked when he came upstairs with one more thing—a multicolored mobile that had been assembled and was ready to hang.

"I am. Holly's not coming?" A rush of anticipation told her all her weekend rationalization was about to be trashed.

"Said she wanted to spend time with her children

now that the calving is nearly finished and we don't have to worry about Trey anymore."

"How are things in Helena?" She needed to know the answer to this question, but she had others she wanted to ask, like, "Are you still hot for me?" and "Will you do me now?" And then she told herself fiercely to behave.

"Trey's been recovering from his surgery quickly. Doctors are happy, so Seth says they will all be coming home sometime this week."

"That is good news." She grabbed the ranch jacket and her leather bag and hurried outside to let the fresh air help clear her mind about what this trip could mean for her and Baylor. It was a buying trip, that's what it was.

At the first store in Kalispell Baylor took the coat she was trying on for fit and hung it back on the rack. "Don't bother."

"Why? Am I going back to California?" Sitting beside him all the way here and not touching him had nearly killed her. If she was leaving, she wasn't going without a fight.

"Only if you sneak away in the middle of the night. There are coats, hat and gloves enough for an army at the ranch. If you want something besides four buckle overshoes, get boots."

"You're right. They're very Goth. I kind of like them."

"And now—" he put an arm around her shoulder and put his lips next to her ear "—unless you have some in that leather bag of yours, get underwear and a toothbrush and whatever you need to spend the night here."

"Cora and Ethel are expecting me back today. What

will I tell them? Given what happened last week, if I don't show up, they'll send a posse after me."

"Make a couple of appointments for tomorrow and tell them you have to stay."

"You have things all planned out."

He nodded.

"I like the way you think."

He nodded again. This time he added several eyebrow flicks.

They didn't shop or explore lumber and supplies for long. The motel they checked into was much newer than the Easy Breezy Inn, but KayLee honestly wouldn't have cared.

When she came out of the bathroom, Baylor was sitting on the edge of the bed looking darkly pensive.

She stopped beside him and put a hand on his shoulder. "What?"

"I guess I should have told you this earlier, before I talked you into staying the night with me." She sat on the bed next to him and he continued. "I don't plan on staying in the valley. I have a job lined up in Denver."

Okay, so it was true. "It's hard to imagine you off the ranch."

"I'll be managing several ranches outside of Denver, but I'll most likely live in the city."

"Oh. Won't your horse miss you?" She couldn't even think of anything sane to say.

"I'll take Blue Moon with me."

"The cowboy takes his horse—of course." It occurred to her in that instant if he asked her to come with him, she'd have a terrible choice to make. She had found a safe place to bear her child and a village of people to fall in love with. Not to mention, she had a job and she had promised to be there until the construction was completed.

"I wanted you to know. I wanted to be fair. I won't leave until I'm sure everything is going well with the construction project."

She scooted closer to him, until the length of her thigh was pressed to his, and reached up to kiss his mouth.

There had been no mention of "come away with me" or "happily ever after," but she was a grown-up. She knew he didn't want her any less than she did him. That was all that mattered for right now.

She kissed his neck, behind his ears and down his throat until he groaned and pulled her onto his lap.

Soon they were naked and she was showing him she wanted to make love with him until he disappeared from her life and she'd find a way to live without him.

She hoped he got the message.

A few hours later they were making their way up and down the aisles of the indoor lumberyard checking types and quality of wood. He stayed at her side, not touching her, but driving her mad anyway.

"I never thought of the lumberyard as sexy before," she said as she climbed down off a low pile of lumber she had stepped up on to closely inspect the wood behind it.

Baylor pulled her behind a stack of two-by-fours and pressed her against him as he kissed her over and over.

She pushed back in his arms. "I've got work to do. My customers are counting on me."

When a store employee came around the corner, ostensibly to examine the ends of the lumber stack, but more likely to see what they were up to, she smiled at the man. Baylor quickly let her go, then she took his arm and they strolled away, trying to look casual as they struggled to keep their hands off each other.

They checked out stain colors, examined and compared roofing materials that would work best in Montana's weather, found an expert woodworker in need of a job and found several types of nonpolluting fireplaces and stoves for keeping the cabins warm for the cross-country skiers and winter snugglers.

Outside the fireplace and stove store, Baylor put his lips next to KayLee's ear. "It must be time to get back to the hotel."

"Got a TV show you want to watch?"

"I'll give you a show."

"I've got an appointment in just over an hour with the manager of Bullet Lumber, but I need food first."

"I could eat."

"How about eating at the Umbrella Room?"

"Sounds fancy. Do you have enough time?"

She grinned and pointed.

On the corner of the street, flaunting the melting snow all around him, stood a street vendor—the hot dog guy. With a large red umbrella opened over the cart.

"Ah, the Umbrella Room."

"I'll see if we can get reservations."

THE NEXT MORNING Baylor held a sleeping KayLee in his arms. She was the most amazing woman he had ever met. She didn't look to anyone to solve her problems. She didn't expect to be handed things because she was pregnant, and she had more daring than might be sensible. And the way her golden hair fell over her shoulders and her full pink lips parted in sleep were almost more that he could resist.

Almost.

Whatever this was between them wasn't going to work out for either of them. He knew he had to be the one to step up—or rather, step away. He could break his own heart, he'd done it often when he was younger, but he would not break hers.

She had found a safe place in the world. She'd have her baby in a few weeks and she'd have the people of St. Adelbert as solid backup—they would be there when she needed them.

He gently eased up from the bed.

He could not give up on finding his sister, or give up the job that could shore up the ranch's finances. He'd leave for Denver as soon as he could get away from the ranch and the less time KayLee and he spent together, especially with no one else around, the better off she would be.

The day was sunny again and more of the snow had melted. When enough of it was gone, they would be able to get the construction started. It might still take a few weeks, but they didn't need his constant presence for the digging to actually start.

He sat in the chair by the window and watched her sleep and when she awoke bleary-eyed and tousled, he wished somebody had tied him to the chair with a rope. When she smiled at him, it was hard to remember what was good for either of them outside of the motel room.

THEY HEADED TOWARD a picnic table in the small park on the way out of Kalispell. Things had changed; Kay-Lee had known as much since she awoke that morning, when Baylor had smiled at her, but he had not come to her.

"Why did we stop here?" she asked. It wasn't much

of a park: one table under a tall pine tree and a flat-
tened space to park.

"Let's sit for a while." He pointed to the table, and
they perched on top with the town at their backs, their
view filled with distant mountains. Sporadic clouds
floated in the sky, a pair of pines and an oak tree stood
in the foreground for contrast.

"This is beautiful." A beautiful place to say goodbye?

"Wait for it." He sat close, but not too close to her.

"We got a lot done today, electrical, water, lumber. I
can see why you trust Bullet Lumber to harvest on the
Shadow Range. Walter knows a lot about forestry, and
thank you for pointing me toward the environmental
engineer." She smiled when she thought of the bearded
man with the red suspenders and his jeans tucked into
his dark wool socks.

Now that Baylor was comfortable with the vendors
and materials, he would be free to leave.

"He's a character."

When she glanced at Baylor, the deepening glow of
the sunlight had turned his hair to a rich shade of gold.
She had a feeling if she asked him to stay, he would.

"I thought I knew a lot about green building," she
said in a tone to match the quiet of the park, "but the
man's information still has my head spinning. I wanted
to run outside and stay there when he told us most products used in our homes and businesses outgas volatile
organic chemicals."

"Made me kinda glad to live in a hundred-year-old
house."

A house he wouldn't be living in much longer, she
thought. They watched the sunset with the sounds of
nature around them.

"In fact, thanks for the past two days." She shifted to get more comfortable. "We got a lot more done together than I could have gotten accomplished by myself. The Doyle name carries a lot of weight."

The sun dropped to sit on the mountaintops. The sky to the right and left of it began to thread pink into the purplish-gray clouds.

"How did you get into the business of design and building?"

She watched the bottom of the sun disappear behind the mountains. "I was brash and gutsy when I was young. I borrowed money to get my company off the ground."

The faint smile he gave her could have been for anyone, not a lover.

Though her heart wanted it, it wouldn't be a favor to either of them for her to ask him to stay. No permanent relationship could be built in a week.

"The second job I landed was with a forward thinker who wanted to build a concept community from scratch, a place where he and like-minded people could live and thrive, he said, no matter what was going on in the rest of the world. And he wanted fresh, rockin' ideas. I'm sure I looked rockin'. Skinny. Crazy blond hair. Lots of fun jewelry. Juls was my favorite jewelry maker. My tan was sprayed on and I applied my makeup with a trowel."

He stared at her as if he were seeing her for the first time.

"I know. I'm a different person. You would have been scared by the old me. Anyway, the concept community guy decided to go with K. L. Morgan and Associates because he said I wasn't tainted by real life yet. I was so happy at the time, I didn't care if he was leveling some sort of insult at me."

She was yammering on, probably saying way more than he cared to hear, so she shut up, and the sun dropped a little more until it was half-gone.

"Go on."

His quietly spoken words gave her the feeling of intimacy like nothing else they had done, as if he wanted to know her, to be able to carry some part of her away with him.

"You sure?"

"Yep." He gave her a small smile.

"The job went well. One of the community's biggest features was the shared facilities where the people could congregate, share meals, share a garden, have classes if they wanted. Every home, every building was built for green living, right down to the solar panels and adequate green spaces."

"Your enthusiasm bodes well for the Doyle family."

"I'm excited for the digging and hammering, but I—"

The sun seemed to just disappear and suddenly the western sky burst with a pink like she had never seen. It shot through the clouds, and when she looked around her, she could see it banded the horizon for three hundred and sixty degrees.

"It's beautiful." And the sun set on their relationship that was never there.

"I thought you'd like it."

When the pink began to fade, he pushed off the table and held her arm while she climbed down.

"Thank you." For the sunsets.

When he stopped in the driveway at Cora and Ethel's house, the lower apartment was ablaze with lights and populated by at least a dozen people.

When KayLee got out of the SUV, three teenaged girls flew out of the house and ran toward her.

"Ms. Morgan! Ms. Morgan!"

Even the teenagers knew who she was.

Baylor came around to where she was standing. "Hang on, ladies," he said to the teens. They all grinned at him. Baylor Doyle commanded attention even from the young. "Give me your keys, Ms. Morgan, and I'll put your things in your apartment."

She handed Baylor the keys to what she was sure was the only locked household in town.

"We need you, Ms. Morgan," said another of the girls. She was about fourteen with red curling hair. "We need you to help us."

The girls took hold of her arms and "helped" her into the lower apartment. Cora and Ethel welcomed her with big smiles.

"They've been waiting for a couple of hours for you," Cora said.

"We're all out of cookies." Ethel bobbed her head.

"Girls, let her catch her breath." Cora directed them all to the dining room and sat them around the table. "Now introduce yourselves and tell Ms. Morgan who you are."

Lexie, the red-haired girl, Becca and Samantha each introduced herself. They were students at the local high school.

As they spoke, KayLee tried not to listen to Baylor's footsteps as he climbed the stairs to her apartment or when his boots tread on the hardwood floors above, heading to her cheery little kitchen. She was sure her milk and the rest of her dairy products would be in her refrigerator when she went upstairs.

"It's our very first play and we've been trying to get

it together for weeks," Lexie began with more enthusi-asm than KayLee could remember having at that age. "We heard you're from Hollywood and your husband was a movie producer."

Cora cleared her throat.

"We're so sorry he's dead," said the pretty, brown-haired girl who called herself Becca Taylor—Rachel's daughter, she assumed.

"Thank you." At the sight of the solemn expressions the three faces suddenly held, KayLee held her grin. "So tell me what this is all about. What do you need me for?"

"We ne-e-e-d to do a play." Lexie's *need* had become a three-syllable word.

"Okay." KayLee had no idea how that involved her, but she was sure the girls would explain it.

"We need you to be our director."

"Ah."

"There are so many roles and it's really funny and we can't get enough boys to do the male parts." Samantha, who spoke for the first time, was no less enthusiastic than the others.

Headlights popped on in the driveway and the Shadow Range's big SUV backed up and drove away with Baylor in it. KayLee couldn't help thinking a part of her life had driven away with him—a wonderful, glorious part of her life.

"Ms. Morgan?"

"Yes, Lexie." She gave her full attention to the girl almost dancing in her chair.

"Would you direct our play?"

"But I've never directed a play before."

"Yeah, but you're the closest thing we got to a director."

The girls must have realized how that sounded as soon as Becca said it because they all giggled.

"So sorry," Lexie said. "So will you?"

"Tell me about the play."

With antics and role-playing they described a play about the cheapest airline in the world. KayLee had to admit it sounded funny and intriguing.

"When is your next practice?"

"Thursday after school. Come and check it out. You'll see we need you," Lexie said as she twirled her red curls around her finger.

Very intriguing. Outside her work, she hadn't been needed for a very long time.

"You're the only person in town that can help us," Becca insisted, looking more and more like her mother.

After KayLee promised to come after school on Thursday, the girls clamored out the door and dashed down the street.

"Well, wasn't that exciting," Ethel said as she sat back in her chair. She didn't even have the energy to bob her head as she spoke.

"They wanted to wait in your apartment, but we talked them into staying here."

"Thank you."

"How was your trip to Kalispell?"

"I couldn't believe how big the town is and how fun the Old West buildings are downtown."

"We enjoy spending the night there from time to time."

Not doing what I did.

"Excuse me, ladies, but I need to go up to my apartment and decompress and go over the information Mr. Doyle and I collected yesterday and today."

"Yes, you go upstairs, now. You must be tired." Cora

studied her as if she were trying to learn something. KayLee hoped no telltale signs showed of the time she and Baylor had spent together.

Ethel went into the kitchen and came back out with a plate covered with a blue-and-white-checked kitchen towel. "We thought you might need something already prepared to eat when you got home."

KayLee took the warm plate gratefully. She might want it later. She wasn't the only one eating in this body these days. "Thank you. That was very thoughtful."

"Well, we sort of encouraged the girls to ask you to help, so we sort of owe you."

"You did, did you?"

The ladies grinned from ear to ear—Cora's wider than Ethel's—as they saw her to her door. A plot was afoot and she was the mark.

She climbed the stairs to her apartment, inhaling what was left of Baylor's scent. What a great two days they'd had. She'd be a mark, she'd be a friend with benefits, she didn't care. All she found in her heart tonight was happiness with a touch of melancholy.

Mr. Doyle. Baylor. She missed him already.

A bad habit to get into.

As she suspected, the chilled and frozen food she had bought at their last stop on their way out of Kalispell had been put away, too. She tucked the covered dinner plate in the refrigerator and made her way to the bathroom.

Tears streamed down her face.

CHAPTER TWELVE

Baylor.

Do not go there.

KayLee leaned on her elbows in her sunlit kitchen overlooking Cora and Ethel's side yard, which was almost empty of snow. The April day was mild and the kitchen curtains—with their red tulips, green stems and leaves on white panels—fluttered in the breeze of the open window. Working at the old maple table was far cheerier than the office she'd set up, so she did most of her planning and designing there.

She was going to have to go call or visit the ranch to see what was available there for onsite storage. Although she had been putting that off, hoping she could get her rampaging hormones in check, or at least stuffed down where they could not cloud her brain.

She spread the papers she had collected the past few days with price estimates and availability of supplies in front of her. If she got a stretch of this warm weather, she'd need to hit the ground running. Who knows, they might even get the concrete poured for the cabins before June.

Once the concrete set, things would fly along. When the building materials were ordered, the second payment from the Doyle family would be due. Baylor or Curtis Doyle was most likely in the process of negotiating that now.

Baylor.

No. She couldn't think about him.

She had other important things to concentrate on right now anyway. It was Thursday already and she had a play practice to check out in twenty minutes.

She organized her things and shut down her laptop.

KayLee Morgan, director. It had a decent ring to it. An interesting addition for her résumé.

She shook her head. If she said yes—uh, *when* she said yes—she would be digging herself deeper into the structure of this small town. That would be good, wouldn't it? The more she incorporated the town into her life, the more she would feel secure and that would trickle down to her child.

What if she decided to live in St. Adelbert for the rest of her life? She could commute to jobs, couldn't she?

Baylor wouldn't be here.

He would be off in the world making a life for himself. *I'll most likely live in the city,* he had said. He'd be living the less-than-stable life of a single with no kids. She had enjoyed that part of her life and now she intended to enjoy motherhood and stability.

The bluest of eyes, riots of blond curls.

Yes, she missed him, and he wasn't even gone yet.

She yawned again and put her head down to rest on the table for a moment. The school was only two minutes away and she didn't need much time to get ready.

When she was no longer pregnant, she'd come to her senses and remember Baylor as the man she most liked to lust after.

She smiled at the memories they had made together. Those she'd get to keep forever.

Oh, yeah.

Her phone rang and the sound startled her. Oh, no, it

woke her up. She thought she had learned that lesson. Guess not.

"Hi, Ms. Morgan. It's Lexie Daley."

"Hi, Lexie."

"You can come to the school anytime and see what we've got so far for our play."

KayLee's watch told her she was fifteen minutes late. What a tactful child. "I'll be there shortly. I need to do a couple more things."

Like use the bathroom.

"See you soon," Lexie said and then the line went silent.

KayLee gripped furniture and doorways to get her groggy self to the bathroom. In the mirror, to her horror, she saw a round sleep mark on her forehead from the tabletop.

"Good job, Morgan," she scolded her image.

She rubbed and powdered her forehead, fluffed her hair and put her California coat on again. It hadn't taken long for her old life to creep back in.

Not totally, she hoped. She had been an idiot not to know how much debt Chad had dragged them into and he had been a shocking fool for buying into so many failing projects.

She tugged the collar of her coat up fashionably and hurried down the stairs.

As she approached the high school, Lexie Daley charged out of a side door and ran up to her. "There you are."

KayLee could hear an unspoken *finally* in the girl's tone. She had been an impatient teenager once and thought her problems had been the most important in the world.

"Yep, here I am." *Yep?* She was beginning to talk as though she belonged here.

Lexie took hold of KayLee's arm. "Let's go in, Ms. Morgan. We're all waiting."

They entered a gymnasium with a stage at the far end. She liked gyms with stages better than cafeterias with stages. The high ceiling gave the illusion of grandeur.

"I can't wait. Tell me more about your schedule."

Becca, Samantha and two other girls ran up to join them.

"Well, we wanted to put the play on in May," Becca said.

"Do you have a date in mind?" May was nearly upon them.

KayLee realized she must have looked shocked because the girls laughed. "Mrs. Pierre said we could do it the last weekend—the Friday and Saturday." Lexie shrugged one shoulder. "It's Memorial Day weekend and we'll have Monday off, but nobody goes anywhere and it's the only time we could get the gym."

She had the kids sit in a circle on the stage facing the rear, while she paced in front of them facing the gymnasium. She listened to their visions of what the play should be. Then she had them tell her how far they were into production. Finally, she asked about a faculty advisor and was told by one boy about Selma Pierre, who mostly made sure they didn't break things or plan anything too sexual. The way the boy made the word *sexual* sound prissy must have been an imitation of the way Mrs. Pierre had said it to them. And they all giggled.

"So will you do it?" Becca asked as she leaned forward over her crossed legs, and put her palms on the floor, fingers in pointed supplication aimed at KayLee. "Will you help us?"

"Will you?" Samantha and Lexie echoed in chorus.

"Well, I—"

KayLee knew she was being watched by more than the eager, pleading teenagers and shifted her gaze to take in the expanse of the room.

Baylor lounged against the wall in the back of the gymnasium. The sight of him sucked the air out of the room as surely as if the gym had been launched into space. He was dressed in a shirt the color of his hair, jeans and—if she could see correctly from that distance—his good black boots. He held his good Stetson in his hands.

"Well?" Lexie demanded.

KayLee breathed and wondered if her whole body was blushing. If she was, the kids were thankfully self-absorbed enough not to notice.

"I'd like to give it a try. Sorry, that was a half answer. I'll do it."

Cheers went up from the group and a couple patted each other on the back. She was officially a stage director.

"I'll need a copy of the script."

A sheaf of dog-eared pages magically appeared under her nose.

She took the well-loved copy of the play's script and looked up at Baylor. He gave her a friendly grin that made her heartbeat jump.

She huffed and gave her attention to the children.

Baylor waited while she revved the kids up for starting a real practice tomorrow. By the time they were finished she was sure she'd have more boys, enough if she doubled up a couple of the roles.

How could she have said no to such enthusiastic people?

The kids ran out of the gym. "Hi, Mr. Doyle," some called. Some giggled and one boy, who was obviously sweet on one of the girls giving Baylor attention, made a rude face.

When they were alone she crossed the gym and when she closed in, he held his ground, but she got the feeling he wanted to step back so she wouldn't get too close.

"This is a surprise," she said.

"A good one?"

"Congratulate me. I've been chosen by default to be the new director of the school play that will be put on in an impossibly short time frame."

The room had become deafeningly silent since the children left.

"Going home?"

"I am."

"I'll give you a ride."

"I was going to walk home, but I'll take that ride."

He held his hat out for her to precede him.

He had driven a silver truck today and he held her hand as she stepped up onto the running board and slid onto the seat. She almost scooted all the way across the bench seat so he would have to press his body to hers when he got in. Almost.

He held himself distant and she should be doing the same thing.

Sitting across the cab of the truck, so close to him and so far away, was painful. It was a good thing they weren't going far. She didn't know how long she could keep her sanity when it came to Baylor.

"Now what made you stop in at the school?" she asked as they began the short trip to her apartment.

"Evvy wanted me to invite you to a celebration on Sunday afternoon."

"What are we celebrating?"

"Trey came home today and she thought we should try to make up for the day you came to sign the papers and there was no fanfare."

"I understood." Sheer joy at the thought of Seth and Amy bringing Trey home colored her world and she smiled.

"Then you'll understand why Evvy wants to make things right."

She did know. Evvy would always want to make things right. "How are Amy and Seth?"

"Seth says he feels like he could sleep for a week."

"Yeah, I can see that happening. I am so happy for them."

"I could tell." He shot a smile at her that she felt to her toes, although she was certain he meant it only as friendly. Though when he put his hand on the seat and reached out to her, she met him halfway with her own and squeezed when he closed his fingers around hers.

She glanced at him from across the cab. "Me, too," she said, of them not quite being able to completely let go of each other.

The grin he gave her this time radiated heat with a touch of regret.

In the driveway at Cora and Ethel's house, he jumped out and came around the truck to help her step over what was left of the snow.

He walked her to her door and then backed away.

"You're not coming in?" she asked.

His expression resolute, he shook his head.

"Thanks for the ride. Please, tell Amy and Seth I'm happy for them and tell Evvy I'd love to come to a cel-

ebration on Sunday. What time and can I bring anything?"

He didn't answer for a moment. "If you need anything, let somebody know. There are a lot of people here
who care about you, KayLee."

"It is nice to know many of the townspeople have
my back."

"Someone will pick you up at about two o'clock and
if you bring anything more than a smile or an appetite,
you'll insult my mother."

"I can drive myself."

He ignored the comment and she forced herself not to
stare longingly after him as he walked away. He didn't
have to extend the invitation in person.

When the truck backed out, she waved and went upstairs.

Maybe she could rest if she tried now.

Maybe not.

Abby Fairbanks, the helpful nurse from the clinic,
lived right across the street, with her new husband and
her sister's son, Cora had said. Apparently the child's
mother was in the army overseas and the boy's father
was getting his life together.

Abby had said they could discuss KayLee's problems
anytime, one of them being Baylor.

Was Baylor a problem?

There was a car in Abby's driveway, so KayLee
headed across the street and rang the doorbell of the
small white house with the brand-new wooden porch.
It was a nice porch, the kind where one might put up a
swing in the summer.

"Aunt Abby!" Inside the house she heard a child's
voice calling. "There's the baby lady on the porch."

A moment later, Abby opened the door. She had a

kitchen towel in her hand and a smudge of flour on her black turtleneck sweater.

"KayLee, are you all right?"

"I'm fine. I'm fine." KayLee tugged at the tails of her sweater.

"I can't turn the nurse off. It's good to see you. Come in." Abby stepped back and let her into a small foyer.

"I don't want to be a bother."

Abby motioned her in. "No bother. My husband should be in any minute. He flies out most weeks, and the day he comes home, nothing bothers me."

"Hi." Behind Abby, a small boy, six years old or so, with curling blond hair clutched a big yellow dump truck to his chest and looked up at her with curiosity.

"There you are," Abby said and smiled broadly at him. "KayLee, this is my nephew Kyle."

The boy grinned at her. She suspected he'd be a shy child for, oh, about the first ten seconds.

"I was going to bring a meal over to you this weekend. Sort of a welcome to the neighborhood," Abby said.

"Can she stay for dinner tonight?" the child asked eagerly.

Okay, shy for five seconds. It made her wonder what her child would be like.

Abby looked between KayLee and the boy. "She could if she likes hot dogs in blankets. Kyle got to choose what we're having for dinner tonight."

"Thank you for thinking of me, Kyle, and I love hot dogs in blankets—the big ones, right, not the little ones."

He nodded enthusiastically. "Yep, I like big ones better."

"Me, too, but I already have a dinner Cora and Ethel

made for me." And she'd better eat it before her land-ladies found out she hadn't already done so.

"Okay." He spun around and ran away carrying his truck. Life should be that easy for all wee ones, but she bet even that little boy had a story.

Abby smiled appreciatively at her. "So what's up?"

"It's complicated."

"Come in. I'll make tea."

"Are you sure?"

"Things were complicated between Reed and I when we first met, so we have experience with such things in this house."

"Good. I was hoping you wouldn't think I was too crazy."

Abby chuckled and led her into a small tidy kitchen. "Sit. Be comfortable."

Steam was already wafting up from the mustard-colored teakettle on the stove, so all that was left to do was for KayLee to choose a tea from the basket in the middle of the table. She picked a soothing ginger spice and dunked the bag into the steaming cup of water Abby poured for her.

Abby sat down across from her with her own cup of tea. "Okay, spill."

"No bush-beating here. I love the frankness in this town."

Abby laughed. "That's good because there's a lot of it."

"You already know my husband died several months ago."

Abby nodded and sipped her tea.

"Well, there wasn't much left of our marriage when he crashed his boat."

Abby sipped more tea without passing judgment and KayLee continued.

"He left a lot of debt behind, and my attorney and I got the creditors to divide almost all of what Chad and I had left and agree not to pursue me anymore. I thought things would start to get better. When I came here…"

"Things started to get complicated again?"

"And then some. Being pregnant doesn't help. My attorney called and told me Chad's attorney has a letter from Chad."

"Oh, dear."

"Yeah. I don't even want to imagine what's in it."

"Bring it to me when it gets here. I'll open it first to see if there is anything you need to know and bury it until you're ready to know the rest."

"That's sweet."

Abby covered KayLee's hand with hers. "I'm a nurse, KayLee. I can take a lot."

KayLee knew it must be true. The clinic was the only medical facility in over a hundred miles and so they must see a broad range of illness and injury.

"I'm—um—I've not had much in the way of backup the past few months." KayLee shrugged. "If it was just me, I'd just—I don't know, survive. But I feel like I need to do so much more."

"I'm glad to hear you say that."

KayLee looked up from her tea.

"There are birthing classes going on at the clinic and I wondered if you could use a birthing partner. If you don't already have a coach, that is."

KayLee straightened in her chair. "Abby, that's a wonderful offer. Are you sure?"

Abby nodded. "The classes are on Tuesday and Thursday mornings at ten o'clock at the clinic."

"I'd love to have you as my coach."

"Dr. DeVane says you plan to use the clinic birthing room. It's great. You'll love it. I'll arrange my work so someone will take my shifts for as long as necessary when you're in labor and for the first twenty-four hours afterward."

"But what about Kyle if your husband isn't here?"

"My mother will gladly babysit. You saw her at the diner. DeLanna Fairbanks, the auburn-haired vixen." Abby shrugged and grinned. "She would have been with Kenny Fuller."

"The man in the three-piece suit."

"That would be him."

"They looked like a hot couple."

"My mom has chosen a winner this time. Kenny and his son, Travis, are great guys and together they own the funeral home here in town." Abby held up crossed fingers.

The side door opened and a dark-haired, very handsome man in a well-filled business suit stepped into the house carrying a laptop bag.

Abby's face burst into a huge smile and she sauntered to the man.

"Uncle Reed!" Kyle flew into the room sans truck.

Uncle Reed set aside his laptop case and picked up his nephew, then he scooped his wife into his other arm, planting a kiss with promise in it on her lips.

"Honey, our new neighbor is here," Abby said and half turned. "KayLee Morgan, this is Reed Maxwell, my husband."

KayLee chuckled when she realized Reed was seeing her for the first time since he entered the house. That's the way a man should love his family. The world had been totally excluded until Reed Maxwell had greeted Kyle and Abby.

"Nice to meet you, KayLee. Welcome to the neighborhood."

"Uncle Reed, come, come." Kyle squirmed down and pulled on his uncle's hand until the man followed.

"Nice to meet you, too," she called after them.

When they were alone in the kitchen, Abby sat back down at the table and KayLee leaned forward lest she be overheard. "Let me apologize before I say this, but my hormones prompt me to say the strangest things."

Abby leaned her elbows on the table. "Okay, you've got my attention."

"That is one good-looking man."

Abby grinned and waggled her eyebrows. "And good-looking does as good-looking is. Speaking of good-looking. It might not be just your hormones. I have heard your name in tandem with Baylor Doyle's."

"Yes, he's in charge of the ranch revival project I'm working on."

"That project will bring long-term growth into the valley. We're all looking forward to it."

"It's kind of saving my butt, too."

"About Baylor."

"About Baylor," KayLee repeated. Be nice to him? Don't break his heart? He's a nice guy leave him alone?

"He's had it rough."

Of all the things about Baylor she could imagine, that wasn't one of them. "He doesn't let on."

"He wouldn't."

"Has he told you he plans on leaving the valley as soon as he can?"

"He did. He said he has a job outside of Denver."

KayLee wasn't sure she liked the look on Abby's face. She seemed worried.

"Baylor and I have been friends since the day he stood up to the bullies for me in junior high." She glanced up at KayLee. "He shouldn't be leaving the valley. There will be a big hole for many of us if he does."

"He's going out into the world so he can have new experiences. You know, live a fuller life."

"That's what he tells himself."

"And what can I do?"

"You can spend time with Baylor."

"But I—"

"I've seen how he looks at you."

She nodded.

"Help him see that whatever it is he thinks he'll find out there in the world, it's not there. You know, you've been there. Leaving behind everyone who loves him will not fix things."

"Have you tried to tell him?"

"He thinks I'm too in love with this place to be objective. I left and came running back."

"Someday, I hope I get to hear that story."

"There are lots of great stories in this valley and I hope you stay long enough to make one of your own."

"That's kind of you to say. And me, too. I'll do what I can about Baylor."

"I'll meet you at class on Tuesday at ten o'clock at the clinic."

Reed chose that moment to return to the kitchen.

"I'll see you Tuesday, Abby, and I gotta go. Reed, nice to meet you. I insist on seeing myself out."

"It was nice to meet you, KayLee," Reed said.

"Goodbye, Kyle," KayLee called over her shoulder and detected a distant reply.

"Your mother will be here in five minutes to pick up Kyle," KayLee heard Reed say. "Says she needs him urgently for something."

Whatever Abby said must have been disrupted by lips meeting lips.

KayLee headed down the steps and across the street.

Spend time with Baylor, Abby had asked. She'd like that, if he didn't run away at the sight of her.

CHAPTER THIRTEEN

KAYLEE DIDN'T KNOW where all the energy came from early on Saturday morning, especially after the week she'd had—Kalispell, Baylor, signing a contract with Martin Homes, Baylor, becoming the director of a play, Baylor, gaining a birthing partner...

It was a good thing she had so many distractions, like the rehearsal this morning. The kids had come so far on their own and with leadership, they would shine.

She didn't want to let herself need anything from Baylor Doyle except to work alongside him to get this project underway. No matter what Abby thought was best for him, he was leaving the valley. Her duty and her love had to go to her baby who would be born to a single parent. She needed roots, and she knew she could put them down here in St. Adelbert.

She scooped oatmeal into a bowl from the pan on the stove, sliced banana onto it and covered it with milk. At the small kitchen table she filled her stomach with food that would nourish her and make her baby grow stronger. It felt good not to eat the junk she and Chad used to eat. In fact, it was amazing in the best sort of way to leave all that behind, the rubbing elbows with celebrities, the champagne on a whim, the all-night parties, the keeping up with every new trend.

With all she had to do, she wouldn't have time to think of Baylor and how he could... Never mind.

She ate faster, concentrating on the food. When the clean dishes were back in the cupboard, she pulled on her lightweight coat, grabbed grocery bags full of apples, bananas and paper cups and started off down the street toward the school.

With the first performance of the play only twenty-seven days away, they had a lot to accomplish. The kids had volunteered to meet at nine that morning and work all day if they had to. All day might be a little long, but the deli at the gas station had volunteered to donate sandwiches and pop. KayLee had turned down the pop, hence the fruit and cups for water.

The day was warm. As she made her way down the street, she zigged and zagged to stay out of the puddles of meltwater. If the weather kept up, even the piles plowed up in parking lots would be nothing but low gray berms of ice in a couple of days.

Blocks from the school, Clem from the post office was out delivering mail and looking as if he enjoyed it. He waved to her and gave her a shrug, which she took to mean not to bother looking in her mailbox today.

No surprise. She hadn't gotten anything yet, not even junk.

As she arrived at the school, Vala, the dark-haired waitress from the diner, waved to her from the other side of the street. Vala must be going home from an early shift. She often left and came back at lunchtime.

As she neared the school, pounding footsteps came charging up behind her.

"Ms. Morgan," a breathless voice called.

Lexie, Becca and Samantha each carried a bundle of what she supposed were the costumes they had been collecting. The play didn't require anything special, but KayLee had no intention of squashing the enthusiasm of the teenage thespians. They had decided the plane from Cut-Rate Airlines was going to the island of Cozumel and they all needed appropriate clothing.

"You ladies look as if you've been busy."

Lexie pulled a bright aqua-and-pink-flowered shirt from her bundle. "I thought we should wear bikinis, but Uncle Guy said this would be more appropriate." She made a face, and the other two giggled.

KayLee laughed. The shirt was much better than the scandalous reaction teens in bikinis would cause, though she was sure the shirts would end up with their tails tied in knots just above the girls' navels. "I think your uncle is right. Remember, we want the audience concentrating on how cleverly you deliver your lines."

Samantha gave Becca a poke. "Yeah, not on how good *our* lines are."

Becca outlined with her hands the form she probably hoped to have someday and wiggled her hips. "Too bad."

KayLee was sure their overseer from the school, Mrs. Pierre, would have seen to it that there was no play this year or any other if she had said yes to the scantily clad version of the show.

Although more boys might join the cast and crew.

They hustled her into the building where several more teens had gathered.

Some of the actors had arranged themselves onstage in folding chairs as a mockup of an old, beaten-up airplane cabin and cockpit they would use for the play. Others were arranging the characters so everyone could be seen and some with artistic and carpentry talent worked offstage on the actual scenery for the play.

As the work progressed, they read lines or recited them from memory. She was proud of them all.

More than once during the morning KayLee looked up to the back of the gymnasium and then made herself look away. He wouldn't be there. She shouldn't want him to be. Baylor Doyle had been as honest as he was sexy. The only harm he could cause her is if she let him, if she had expectations that he could not fulfill.

Ha. That was a lesson she had already learned well. Her expectations were her own and others got to choose to comply or not. Even her own heart didn't do a very good job of falling into line.

"Ms. Morgan?"

Becca motioned her up on stage to the cockpit.

"Don't you think Peter should be the pilot instead of me?"

"Because?" KayLee didn't want the girls here in St. Adelbert to think of themselves as less than the boys and thought quickly to find a way to say that without seeming preachy.

"Because he's taller than me and if he sits in the co-pilot's seat, I'll have to lean forward, and I look better like this." She drew herself up and thrust her chest out just enough, but not too much.

"Becca, you are so right. Peter, what do you think? Can you do the pilot's lines?"

Peter shrugged. As he glanced at Becca his face turned pink. "Guess so."

Becca elbowed him and he got red, but popped out of his seat closer to the audience and let Becca have it.

"All right, then the two of you work the lines while I get Grandma to stop fixing her mascara and the movie star to stop trying to make his hair stick up."

The buzz of laughter and talking filled the gymnasium. Three more boys had joined them and they now had twenty-three actors, as well as a stage crew.

They were so much fun. A few spats, but only a single tantrum.

She turned away from the activity on stage. At the back of the gymnasium, he was leaning against the wall the way he had been the first time.

"Baylor," escaped softly from her lips almost as an explanation of surprise.

She had taken one step in his direction when Samantha whipped past her.

"Daddy," the girl cried excitedly. "You came."

She ran to the man leaning against the wall who bent forward and scooped his daughter into his arms.

Not Baylor.

She wasn't doing very well at all in complying with her expectations that Baylor Doyle would not play a big part in her life. Yet, he didn't have to invite her to the celebration of Trey's homecoming and the signing of the contracts. That the Doyles expanded it to include her at all was so nice, but a phone call would have been sufficient. Holly could have stopped in after she got off work at the law office.

KayLee shook her head. Since she'd be seeing Baylor tomorrow, she had better study her part of designer, general contractor, vendor and possibly friend, but nothing more.

ON SUNDAY AFTERNOON, Baylor let himself into the barn and Blue Moon nickered a greeting. The day had rolled in warm and sunny at the ranch. May Day, appropriate for a celebration for the homecoming of a boy who was lucky to be alive.

The dregs of snow from the storm a week and a half ago were in the process of melting away quickly. The snow here didn't get gray and dirty the way it did in

Denver. Most of it was still icy, glistening and clean, or else it was trampled mud.

Baylor snipped the wire on a bale and shook the hay out so Blue could get at the fodder more easily. When he patted the horse's neck, Blue twitched his ears in anticipation and dipped his head to grab a mouthful.

"Glad your life is so easy, boy."

It was good see Seth and Amy's two-year-old begin to perk up. The boy got tired easily, but Baylor was willing to bet if any of the adults around him had a surgery as invasive as Trey had, the adults would be dragging their butts around looking for someone to help them blow their nose. This boy plopped down with the other kids to build a castle of large, pegged blocks or giggle at some funny kid movie.

Baylor gave the horse another pat and left the barn to check the fence section that would isolate the new livestock when it arrived.

Then he went to see the hangers-on in the birthing shed. There was another pair having trouble bonding and one of the last dams still heavy with calf.

He checked the cow and calf and it seemed as if their issues were over. They'd be put with the rest of the pairs tomorrow. The cow in waiting was still not in labor. He made sure the water was working and grabbed the bucket of towels soaking in disinfectant and in need of laundering.

He was heading past the barn toward the house to get cleaned up for the party when the ranch's SUV pulled into the yard. Lance had been elected to go fetch KayLee. His folks had delegated that kind of running around to their sons a long time ago. The women had been too busy with the preparations, Seth was with his son and wife every minute he could be and Baylor had made the animals a top priority when the choosing was done after lunch.

The passenger door opened and when KayLee stepped out, he was not prepared for the sock-in-the-jaw feeling at seeing her. Hair blowing in the wind, smile making her glow from the inside. She laughed at something Lance said, or knowing Lance, had not said. In one arm she clutched brightly wrapped presents.

Neither saw him as Lance held her elbow as they climbed up the steps and entered the house. It was the first time in a very long time he'd been jealous of his brother.

Maybe he could go back out to the birthing shed and induce that cow into labor. He'd happily spend two minutes in the house making nice and the rest of the party tugging on the hind feet of a calf.

It wasn't fair to KayLee. Hell, it wasn't fair to him. The more time they spent together, the more chance he had of breaking her heart and his, too. This coming week of a million decisions was going to be hell. If he felt he could, he'd delegate choosing the details to KayLee, but his family's livelihood depended on this project, and he had pledged to make sure it would be the best it could be.

He cleaned his boots and let himself into the mudroom where his mother waited with her arms crossed and a frown on her face. She wore her bronze-colored dress, belted at her ample waist and the turquoise necklace and earrings he knew had been handed down from her mother's mother.

"I was about to send the cavalry out after you, Bay, dear."

"Don't you look pretty. Something special going on today?"

His mother's expression didn't change. "KayLee's here."

"I'll be in as soon as I'm cleaned up."

"Did that man from Denver call you again?"

Baylor stopped for a moment. His mother couldn't possibly know about the investigator looking for Crystal; she must mean from J&J Holdings about starting the job.

"Not yet. I expect he'll call soon."

"I worry about you, Bay."

She gave him a long look that he knew meant she wanted to ask him to stay in St. Adelbert. If the only thing at stake was his desire to get out of the valley, he could reconsider leaving, but he couldn't tell her that. The family would feel even more broken without him there, but somebody had to find Crystal and somebody needed to bring money in from outside the ranch. He was the only logical candidate.

He leaned in and gave her a kiss on the cheek. "See you in there."

Baylor headed toward the rooms beyond the kitchen that he assumed had at one time been set up as the housekeeper's quarters, but the rooms had been given to him when his brothers married and built their own houses on the property.

It had all seemed so simple. Go to college and move on, leave St. Adelbert and the Shadow Range behind. It hadn't taken him long to grow up and realize there was no leaving family behind no matter where you went or how educated you got.

He stood under the shower until he was sure all cow and horse was washed away and then some. By the time he was finished dressing he had on clean jeans and a plain white shirt. He snugged the dark blue stone of his bolo tie up under his collar and pulled on his black boots. Because his mother had been wearing a dress, he put on the leather sport coat that always made him feel like a bit of a dandy.

What else could he do to stall?

THE FIRST THING KayLee noticed about the comfortable den the Doyles had collected in to celebrate Trey's homecoming—and Evvy still insisted in spite of KayLee's protests, the signing of the contract—was Baylor's absence.

"Are those for us?" five-year-old Matt asked as he ran a finger over one of the wrapped gifts KayLee had placed on the small table beside the chair where she sat. Katie, his younger sister, stood at his elbow looking eager for KayLee's answer.

She wasn't sure what protocol should be and looked up at Holly for help.

"Matt, Katie, come over here. If KayLee has gifts she gets to give them to whoever she wants."

"Me?" Matt asked as he pointed to himself.

"Come here, you guys." Lance swept up a child in each arm and giggles prevailed. "You don't want to send KayLee running to the hills, do you?"

"Want presents." Katie kicked her feet and Holly grabbed for the little girl's hat as it flipped off her head.

Everyone was dressed up today. The children each wore a pint-size version of a cowboy hat. The stone in Curtis's tie matched the color of Evvy's dress. Lance and Seth wore Western-style string ties and sports coats, and Holly and Amy wore dresses that made them look more like California women than ranchers. It was easy to see they did get farther away than Kalispell once in a while, whether in person or via catalogues, she wasn't sure. She realized she didn't even know if Holly and Amy were from the St. Adelbert area or outside.

Trey seemed so small, so young to have been through surgery. On the nearby couch, he sat on his dad's lap and eyed the bright packages beside KayLee. She caught his gaze and smiled at him and he dimpled back.

"Uncle Baylor," Matt cried, pushed down from his father's arm and raced toward the doorway.

Baylor looked so good KayLee wondered if anybody heard her draw in a quick breath of amazement.

How was it possible he was better-looking? Blond hair darkened with moisture and slicked back made the planes of his face more distinct. The dark leather jacket hugged his broad shoulders, and the blue stone at his color almost matched the blue of his eyes. When he smiled, she admitted if he had been in a tuxedo it might actually have knocked her unconscious.

She felt a hand pat her arm. Amy was smiling at her.

Amy knew. They probably all did, but at least they were polite enough not to show it as the rest watched Matt try to bowl Baylor over.

Baylor snatched the boy up just before the crash and lifted him to eye level. "Grandma tell you there'd be no cake until I got here?"

Matt put a finger in his mouth and nodded.

"Or presents," the boy said around the finger.

"Presents. Somebody got presents for me," Baylor teased.

Matt turned and looked at KayLee pleadingly.

She shook her head and he turned back to Baylor. "No, for us kids."

Baylor quickly lowered Matt to the floor. "I guess we'd better start this party."

"Yippee!" Matt cried.

"Yippee!" Katie echoed.

Yippee, KayLee thought. She wondered how much yearning after one rancher one heart could take until it just refused to beat anymore.

"Now?" Matt had climbed up on the arm of the chair and almost pressed his nose to KayLee's when she turned to face him.

"I think we should let your grandmother call the shots."

Evvy nodded approvingly, and Matt settled back against the chair and folded his arms. Evidently, he wasn't going anywhere as long as there were presents to be had.

KayLee liked the warmth of the little shoulder pressed against hers. She was going to love holding a bundle of baby in her arms. She was sure holding her own child would make up for whatever else she didn't have in her life.

Baylor took a seat on the couch directly across from her, and watched her as if he knew what she was thinking.

For distraction, KayLee picked up a present and whispered in Matt's ear.

He jumped off the arm of the chair and grabbed the package and lunged at Trey with it. Amy caught him and placed him on Seth's other knee.

"Gently, now," Seth said to his nephew.

"This is for you, Trey," Matt whispered loudly and gave the package to his cousin.

Trey held it but didn't open it.

Matt eyed Trey's present and then the others on the table. He wanted a present so badly he nearly wiggled himself to death.

KayLee was sure she knew how he felt.

"Would you like Matt to open your present, Trey?" Amy asked her son.

Trey handed the present to Matt, who tore off the paper. KayLee had no idea what to get a child who had just come home from the hospital. A soft brown bear was apparently a good choice as Trey hugged it when Matt handed it to him, and he didn't look as if he intended to let it go for a long time.

As soon as he handed the toy off, Matt came charging back. She handed him another package, and he gave it to Katie, who ripped the paper off the dolly and grinned a two-year-old toothy grin.

"Katie?" Holly said.

"Thank you," came Katie's auto-response.

Matt returned and sighed comically when KayLee handed him his package.

"You are such a gentleman, Matt," KayLee said to him as he ripped and tore. While the dump truck inside wasn't as big as Abby's nephew Kyle had, Matt seemed to like it.

Baylor smiled at her and mouthed his own thank-you. He had told her not to bring anything, but KayLee's reasoning had been that even the fiercest hostess wouldn't begrudge a few toys for the children.

After the cake was served, the congratulations, the thanks and well wishes were passed around again and again, it was time for KayLee to leave. She was prepared for an excruciating trip back to town with Baylor, but Lance smiled at her as he brought her jacket.

"Go with your husband, Holly," Evvy said. "Even a man can clean up after a party."

Curtis smiled as if he'd been there, done that before.

KayLee, Lance and Holly were headed to the door

when Baylor stopped them. "I need to borrow KayLee for a second."

"Anytime, Bay," Holly said.

Baylor led her into the office, stepped a safe distance behind the desk and moved the mouse for the computer screen to pop to life.

"I looked over the list of things you need opinions on, but most of them are areas where it would be best if we did them together. I'm available every day this week—"

Oh, no! He wanted her to sit by his side and stare a computer screen and not have her hand wander to his thigh or into his hair even once. He gave her so much more credit than was humanly possible.

"—and there is the one supplier in Missoula we might need to meet with about the flooring."

Missoula: that was hours away from St. Adelbert. He was going to have to handcuff her to her side of the truck.

If he heard her thoughts it might not be too late to toss her off the ranch once and for all.

"KayLee, do you want to do this out here, or do you want me to come into town? We can do whatever's best for you."

"Best for me would be for me to—" run away "—come out here. It's easier if we need to go visualize one of the locations. And for heaven's sake, I can drive myself. Today was special. It was Evvy's party and I let her be the boss."

Trey came running into the office with his bear. "Thank you, KayWee. I wuv him."

Yeah, me too. Oh no, that could not possibly be true.

Baylor thanked her again for coming and for the toys for the children. With every word he spoke, she had wanted to pull his mouth down to hers and kiss him, to hold him close. To boot herself out of the county.

"I'll be here by eight o'clock." She managed not to say any of the insane things floating around in her head.

Baylor snickered. "The crack of dawn every day?"

"The sun's up long before... Hey, you'd be surprised. I've been practicing."

"Eight o'clock it is. Have a good evening and sleep well."

"I will." She left him in the office scrolling screens. *If I learn how to stop dreaming,* she thought.

As they sped down the highway, she grinned, not because she was a senseless pregnant woman who could not control her libido, but because she had actually had a conversation with Baylor and had made no overt comments or even innuendo. She had wondered if she was still capable of such a thing.

The crack of dawn every day?

Wait, did he mean they would spend five days straight together?

Fine. Whatever got the job done.

THE WEATHER REMAINED her friend. Almost two weeks passed. She and Baylor lived through a week of settling details and even survived a trip to Missoula together.

Nothing had changed except she was sure she had not one nerve left unfrazzled.

A couple days of rain had washed away the dirt from the roads and melted the snow away. She had signed contracts with electrical and plumbing contractors. And praise be, Al Martin had laid the road and had prepared the cabin sites for the concrete pads.

Two weeks before the Cut-Rate Airlines would be

performed and twenty days before she was due to deliver her child the concrete was about to be poured.

KayLee paced in front of the beds of gravel with the footings already solidly in place. Wooden frames would be filled and would be removed after the concrete hardened.

Workers stood ready with tools as the gray concoction slushed in two portable mixers. Al Martin and the concrete contractor had been like mad scientists when they were adding cement, sand and water to the revolving tubs. And now they waited for just the right amount of time.

A shadow fell over her right shoulder and she turned to see Baylor standing behind her. Her heart did its usual flop. She gave him a small smile and made herself watch as they began to pour the concrete into the waiting bed.

Arms folded over the top of her stomach. "I feel like getting in there and helping myself."

Baylor didn't say anything but she knew he heard her. The workers were all in a flurry, pushing, tamping and flattening the gray mass.

"That would be quite a sight." His words floated softly over her shoulder and she strained to collect every nuance.

"Al would have a heart attack if I even looked cross-eyed at one of those tools."

"Al's a good man."

And a good man will always do right by a woman. A Montana rule it seemed.

"Hurry up," Al called to one of the men who seemed to be playing with concrete like a kid with his mashed potatoes. "We don't get a do-over here."

"I'll be in the office when you're ready to go over that list of materials."

Even over the hubbub created by the men and concrete, she heard his footsteps retreat.

KayLee waited an honest ten minutes before she followed. The surface of the first concrete pad was smooth and shiny when she left and the men were adding the finishing touches.

In less than a week's time the wooden frames would start going up for the first two cabins. The project was ahead of schedule and she was feeling great about that part of her life.

She let herself into the mudroom and cleaned off her shoes. Suddenly, she was nervous. Not about the doorknobs or how many data outlets were enough. Baylor was in the office and as often as she worked at his side, and as often as they pretended it was best that they be just friends, she could not find the strength to move on, to let him go.

She stepped into the office and he glanced up at her.

Yep, even though another week had passed this day would be no different.

She knew she still couldn't approach Abby's request without losing her heart in the process.

"How did the concrete pouring go?"

"As well as you'd expect it to go. Al's a good man, just like you said."

He studied her for what seemed like minutes, but was probably less than ten seconds. She studied back. There was nothing she could tell him that wouldn't dig her in deeper, make her fall in love with him, if she already wasn't.

"I think you should take a break," he said as she continued to study him intently. "Let's not do this today."

She sighed and didn't care if he saw. He smiled as if he knew he had made a correct guess.

"Did your special beef arrive?"

"Yesterday. Better late, you know. They're in quarantine right now. Are you going to the ice cream social Sunday?"

"What?" Her brain had trouble making the switch for a moment. Cora had mentioned the town's first social gathering of the year. It was a way for all of them to keep in contact. They were far flung and the winter was long. This event would be held in the school. A later one as well as the town picnic would be in the town square. "No. I have too much to do."

"You should, KayLee."

"That's what Ethel said."

"You'll disappoint a lot of people. Would it help if I told you I wasn't going?"

She nodded as tears rose, and she took the red-and-white hankie she had so wisely kept in her pocket and dried her eyes.

CHAPTER FOURTEEN

KAYLEE PUT ON THE LAST touches of her makeup for the ice-cream social. It had been three weeks since the celebration at the Doyles' house for Trey's homecoming. The contract signing seemed like such a trivial thing to celebrate when compared to the health and welfare of a child.

Child. KayLee examined her body's profile in the mirror and rested a hand on her growing belly. She wondered, as she often did, how much bigger the child inside her was going to make her. "Not complaining, little one," she said to her belly.

Yesterday she had watched as the large trucks poured concrete from their revolving tanks. At last real progress had been made at the ranch. The weather had outdone itself for the last week, and had grown increasingly warm for the area. Construction of the wooden skeleton frames would begin as early as next week.

But today she would attend her first ice-cream social.

She packed up her leather bag with essentials and was ready to head out when her phone buzzed. The caller ID said Martin Homes. On Sunday?

"This is KayLee Morgan," she said.

"Mrs. Morgan, this is Curly Martin."

"Good morning, Mr. Martin." The old guy with the purple cast on his arm. Al Martin had said "the old coot" was his granddad. He was apparently trying all of Dr. DeVane's cast colors. Third broken arm in two years.

"Yep, call me Curly. Too many Mr. Martins in this valley."

"Yes, Curly. What can I do for you?"

"My son asked me to call you. He needs you to come out to the Doyle ranch."

"Is tomorrow soon enough?"

"He needs to…uh…see you now. I mean, he said you didn't have to hurry or anythin', he'd wait."

"Can it wait until after the ice-cream social?"

"Awww, those things last for hours an' he wants you to come soon. Somethin' about the concrete crackin' up or somethin'."

The concrete? Literally the foundation for the whole project? It couldn't be.

"Is Mr. Martin there now?"

"He's on his way and that's why I'm callin' you, 'cause his mobile won't work well out on the highway. I don't have much in the way of detail 'cept he wants you there soon. But safe."

"Thanks, I hear you, Curly. I'll be there soon."

She thumbed off her phone. She could call the ranch, but she was the buck-stops-here person. If there was a problem she wanted to be on top of it now.

She tried not to think too much and concentrated on getting there. Had they failed to prepare the beds for the concrete pads properly? Did they pour the concrete too soon, was it too cold, was the mix wrong?

She tried not to think too much and concentrated on driving. She also tried not to envision the disappointment on the Doyles' faces that something had gone so awry.

Who would be at the ranch? They should already be

in town for the ice-cream social. Most of them should be. Curtis and Baylor might be there to meet her and Allen Martin would have called the concrete contractor.

In short there might be a crowd to stand around and stare at her first big failure. She wouldn't blame anyone else. It was she who had promised due diligence for the Doyles' money.

KayLee drove past the ranch house and out to the cabin area. The main house looked deserted. Hopefully, that meant most of them were in town. The new gravel road to the construction site was a solid bed and easy to drive on. As she approached the area where the concrete pads had been laid, there was no one there. Not Curtis, not Allen, no one, not even Baylor and she found herself disappointed he wasn't there.

She leaped out of her car—okay, fine, she didn't leap…. She *heaved* herself out of her car, but in her mind she leaped. Then she hurried as fast as she could to the first slab of poured concrete. The pad was the correct shape and it was smooth. There were no cracks, bumps, heaves or other disruptions that weren't supposed to be there. She raced to the second. She could see nothing wrong with this one, either.

What was going on?

She heard a vehicle's engine and expected to see the Martin Homes dark blue pick-up truck. What she saw was the silver truck she had come to learn was Baylor's personal vehicle, approaching rapidly.

The truck skidded to a stop on the gravel surface of the road, Baylor jumped out and ran toward her.

"Where is Allen Martin?" she called as he closed the gap between them.

"What's wrong?" Baylor's demand was tinged

with anger. He studied her from head to foot and then frowned.

She had put her blue dress on for the social. Did it look that bad?

"What's going on, Baylor?"

"Why did you tell Cora you were hurt and needed help?"

"Okay, I'm going to gape at you here because I have no idea what you're talking about. I haven't spoken to Cora since last night."

He looked full-on suspicious as she talked and aimed silent accusations directly at her as he stared unblinkingly.

"Your eyes are so blue in this light." She couldn't help herself, didn't care to.

He closed the gap and took hold of her upper arms as if he intended to shake the truth out of her if he had to, but he still didn't speak.

"I haven't spoken to Cora since she grilled me in detail…" she said as answers dawned "…about what we had gotten done out here yesterday. Concrete!"

"What does Cora have to do with the concrete out here and why would she say you were hurt?"

His eyes reflected all the blue in the Montana sky. "Curly Martin called me and said Al needed to meet me here because there was some sort of disaster with the—the—" All she wanted to do was climb up this man and start kissing from the top down.

"Concrete?"

She swallowed and kept her feet on the ground. In her condition, she didn't think that climbing up anything would work very well anyway.

"You're sure you're okay."

She swallowed again.

"No." She shook her head and then nodded. "I mean, yeah, I'm fine."

He let go of her and whipped around so fast, she lost her equilibrium for a moment, then righted herself quickly.

"Is there anyone here at the ranch besides you and I?" she asked.

He stopped. "Not that I could find."

"We've been had and very cleverly, I might add."

"Who? What are you talking about?"

"Well, at least by Cora and Ethel and they somehow got Curly Martin in on their plan."

"Their plan to get us out here without chaperones?"

"Precisely."

"It worked."

"I hope so, Baylor." She took two quick steps closer to him. "Make love to me again. It won't break my heart and I won't try to keep you here."

"KayLee, I can't protect you from this if you won't let me."

"Baylor, I have to protect myself. If I don't, I'll always need someone there to bail me out."

She reached out to him.

"We're going to disappoint a lot of people if we don't show up at the ice-cream social," he said stiffly, but he didn't back away.

"We're going to disappoint some if we do show up."

"So somebody's going to end up disappointed either way."

"Yep, they are." She reached a hand up to his cheek. "It might as well not be us."

"We are crazy if we do this."

The rough tone his voice had taken told KayLee she

had won this round. He leaned in to kiss her sweetly on the mouth.

"Yes, we are, and I'm afraid I'm not as easy to get close to as I was the last time."

When he smiled, there was smoke in his eyes. Before she knew what he was doing, he was tugging her hand. "Let's go up to the house."

He led her into the main house and down the hall past the kitchen to the opposite end of the first floor. When they entered the room, she was surprised to see a small apartment with a sitting room and a kitchenette.

"Impressive. Take me to your bedroom."

"Pushy."

"Horny."

When he kissed her she wanted to be immediately naked, to have him touch her all over, and then she was and he did.

And she did him.

Several times.

"I might have to come to Denver once in a while to get me some of this," she said as they lay in each other's arms.

"You'll forget me when I'm gone."

"Yep, I'll be too busy to think of you."

What sounded like footsteps on the stairs told them they might not be alone anymore. A tap on the door confirmed it.

"It's me and Amy. Trey got tired so we brought him home."

"How much time do we have?" Baylor called out.

"Not enough. An hour. Forty-five minutes to be safe."

"Thanks, Seth."

"You betcha, bro."

"Cora, Ethel and Curly had a lot of accomplices," KayLee said as Seth's bootsteps faded.

"We need to get you out of here," Baylor told her.

"I'll go, but please, don't shut me out from now on. I'll be able to take it when you're out of the valley, but knowing you're so close and I can't touch you, can't even be friends with you, makes me crazy." She kissed the spot behind his ear. "And it's not nice to torture a pregnant woman."

"I try not to torture any women."

"I'm afraid you come by it naturally, sweetheart."

He dipped in and kissed her until she got up and crawled on top of him. "Don't torture me one more time."

He groaned and pulled her down onto him. "Yep."

On her way back to town, she waved to the oncoming traffic. They probably all knew who she was, where she was coming from and what she'd been doing there, she might as well be friendly about it.

And it was too late for ice cream.

KayLee stood in her small pink-tiled bathroom and brushed her hair back into a ponytail. Several days had passed since she and Baylor had made love as if they intended to do it forever, as if they belonged together. Each day since, she had seen him or heard from him. Tomorrow when the framing for the cabins began, she would probably see him again, and break her heart again, too.

She had gently admonished Cora and Ethel and let Curly buy her a cup of apology coffee, but she loved every one of them for what they had tried to do for her and Baylor.

She tried not to think of Baylor and heartbreak as

she finished her make-up quickly and hurried to the gymnasium for play practice.

"Ms. Morgan, we're all set," Lexie said as KayLee entered the gymnasium.

"Look." Becca pointed at the stage where a group of students struggled to hold the airplane together. The section of a plane's fuselage with one side of the aircraft's skin and interior wall missing sat nearby. With the exception of one unpainted section in the rear, it looked spectacular.

"Wow. It's come a long—"

Just then the middle section of the bank of faux windows wobbled and flopped down over the seats. Laughter and squeals ensued, followed by scrambling and one "Sorry" from somewhere behind the fallen scenery.

"Well," Lexie said from beside her, "it isn't fastened together yet, but you get the idea."

"It looks great!" KayLee shouted and clapped for the group up on stage who worked so hard conceptualizing, drawing, sawing, painting, hammering and all that went into making the mock airplane cabin. Then she turned to the actors who were awaiting direction. "Set up the chairs and let's see how things are progressing."

Lexie took off like a shot and started gathering people. They lined up the chairs as if they were plane seats. Four were line up separate from the others. These were for the cockpit crew.

Becca and Peter took their seats in pilot and copilot chairs. The other two chairs in the cockpit always remained conspicuously empty. It was Cut-Rate Airlines after all.

A tall woman with short graying hair approached from the doorway. "Hi, Mrs. Pierre," KayLee called to the woman.

"How are things going, Ms. Morgan? They look like such a ragtag bunch."

KayLee wanted to jump to the kids' defense, but she knew their appointed overseer didn't mean any harm.

"They have their costumes." KayLee pointed to the every-color-in-the-world pile of shirts. She tried not to wonder what Mrs. Pierre's face would look like if that pile was a heap of tiny bikinis.

The costumes, such as they were, got a nod of approval from Mrs. Pierre.

"Good. Let me know if you need anything." The tall woman walked quickly away and disappeared into the hallway.

They wouldn't see any more of Mrs. P for a couple days.

KayLee listened while the kids practiced their lines.

"Peter, see if you can project your voice more, and, Mandy, if you emphasize *reptile* in that line, the joke will come across better."

They were amazing teenagers. They could almost direct themselves by now.

KayLee noticed a couple of teen boys milled nearby waiting for definitive direction.

"I like what you're doing with the scenery for the third act, Benjamin and Marshall. Get started on that last piece," she called to the pair of set painters.

"Samantha and Becca, I want to see what you've done with the changes we made for the beginning of act two."

The two girls jumped up, scripts in hand.

"Can you do it without your scripts today?"

Alarmed, Samantha tugged her long blond hair back, but Becca took her by the arm. "Sure we can."

When they performed flawlessly KayLee applauded them and had all the actors run the entire scene.

After they had worked for over two hours, KayLee gave them their assignments, extracted promises that all homework would get done and sent them on their way.

KayLee slowly walked home. The weather was still getting nicer by the day. Several people waved at her and when a silver pick-up truck passed, she thought of one blond rancher. There were many silver trucks, and she didn't need them as a reminder to think of him.

They would work side by side in the paneled office at the ranch, blinking at the computer screen or pouring over drawings. Now that they were friends, the details were easy, but spending time with Baylor was starting to make her fearful at the day he'd leave St. Adelbert.

For the good of all involved, KayLee and Baylor decided to avoid letting people think they were a couple. None of them believed in temporary. Cora and Ethel would be planning a wedding and the whole town would have unfair expectations. Here in St. Adelbert it seemed that most of the village would suffer from a broken heart if KayLee and Baylor let them believe what could never be true.

Never be true. All she had to do was remember how she and Chad thought they were in love, enough to get married after a week. Okay, so she was jaded, but she'd never wish that on anyone, on Baylor, on herself again.

When KayLee arrived at home, Abby was across the street sitting on her porch with a knitted throw over her lap and reading by the warmth of the late afternoon sun. KayLee waved.

Abby put her book down and started to get up. "I have something for you."

KayLee waved her off. "Stay there. I'll come over."

KayLee clutched the orange canvas bag she was carrying over one shoulder and crossed the street.

When she approached the foot of Abby's porch, her friend held up a FedEx envelope.

KayLee stopped dead still.

The letter from Chad. She wondered if she should run away or get it over with.

"Come up here." Abby smiled kindly at her. "If you make a break for it, I'll chase you and I'll win."

KayLee slowly climbed the stairs. She dropped the canvas bag on the porch and huffed out a breath as she sat in one of the forest-green plastic chairs.

"Make yourself comfortable. I'll get some tea and leftovers. You have got to be hungry after play practice."

KayLee started to protest, but Abby insisted. "It's the least I can do for someone who volunteers to work with a bunch of the town's teenagers."

When Abby returned a few minutes later, she placed a tray on the table between them with a steaming cup of tea, a plate of food that really smelled good and the envelope. She had also brought a lap blanket and handed it to KayLee.

KayLee put the colorful throw on her lap and reached for the envelope.

Abby stopped her. "Eat first. Your baby will appreciate it."

KayLee nodded and smiled. "You know how to apply torque to the right screws."

Abby grinned.

KayLee chewed and swallowed a bite of food. "Where are your guys?"

"Playing soccer. It's kind of nice to get to read in

peace once in a while. Reed's here in town this week. I'm in heaven."

"Cora says your sister is coming home soon."

"Kyle is so excited he can hardly wait. He keeps asking if it's really true."

"How long has she been gone?"

"Over a year."

"That's harsh."

"It has been good for her. She's a different person. I'm so proud of her."

They chatted and KayLee ate. When she had eaten all she comfortably could, KayLee sipped tea, while Abby packed up the leftovers.

"Now that you're fortified, you can tackle the letter," Abby said as she sat back down in her chair, wrapped in the blanket.

KayLee paused, the envelope in her hands. "I guess so."

She removed the contents and scanned the documents briefly. The top one was a copy of Chad's death certificate with a note attached by Randolph Sharring. *You will need this.* For what, KayLee had no idea. The rest seemed to be legal-sounding stuff, but then the letterhead caught her attention.

"Life insurance. Chad had a life insurance policy?" KayLee was stunned.

"I take it you never knew."

"No."

When tears flooded KayLee's eyes, Abby reached out a hand. "Do you want me to read it for you?"

KayLee shook her head.

"The beneficiary. He made his child the beneficiary."

KayLee took the red-and-white hankie and wiped her face. "He did love our baby."

Abby got up and hunkered down beside her and Kay-Lee appreciated the support.

She turned the page and wondered if she was seeing correctly until she read the words that spelled out the policy amount.

She looked at Abby, who grinned at her.

"Oh, my God. Oh, my God. Five hundred…"

"Thousand dollars," Abby continued when she could not.

"Abby. Oh, my God."

"You could live anywhere for a long time."

"But it's the baby's money."

"Check with your attorney. It most likely belongs to you, since your child hasn't been born yet and your husband's estate went to you. It did, didn't it?"

"It did. Five hundred thousand dollars. He's been gone for almost seven months and he can still surprise me."

"You and you're child are set for a long time, but right now, however, you need to go home and put your feet up. Speaking of things on your plate—Baylor."

Abby nodded toward an approaching vehicle. This time the silver pick-up truck was Baylor's. He stopped across the street and got out.

Every time KayLee saw him she was amazed all over again. He pushed his hair back with his hand and put his hat on.

"I love it when he does that," Abby said. "He's the most manly man I've ever known."

"Mmm," KayLee said. "The two of you never…?"

Abby laughed. "I'm older than he is and in grade school and high school, that meant something."

"Me, too." KayLee grinned. "But it doesn't mean as much now."

"As adults, it can be an advantage for you two."

By then Baylor was standing at the bottom of the steps with a questioning look on his face. "What's an advantage for the two of us?"

"Age is, if you must eavesdrop," Abby said. "Now whatever outrageous compliment you are about to pay us, Baylor, I graciously accept and I gotta go."

She grabbed the blankets, leaving KayLee with cold tea, the dish of leftovers, the contents of the envelope and Baylor.

"Hi. You scared her away." She drank down the tea and collected the food and papers.

"I don't think much scares Abby Fairbanks anymore."

"I'm not going to like what brings you to my neighborhood, am I?"

"We need to talk."

"Okay. Let's walk down toward the river. I could use a little exercise."

They moved amicably in the direction of the river.

"It looks as if you have everything under control with the construction," he said quietly, almost too calmly. "Lance and Seth have a handle on the new livestock."

She nodded and for sure didn't like where this was headed. He had said when everything was under control he was leaving. She had hoped that meant after her baby was born.

"The first batch of framing studs had more bad than good pieces in it. I sent the whole lot back. I can't have the laborers sorting wood when they should be building and ending up short in the middle of the day." She didn't know why she was telling him this.

"You will be the hardest thing for me to leave in this valley."

"I had trouble getting them to match the stain on the spindles and the banister, but I think that's all straightened out."

"KayLee." He reached over and touched her cheek. "I got a call from Denver today."

KayLee wanted to shove her fingers in her ears. Instead she smiled not quite directly at him, more like over his left shoulder. "I suppose they want you there yesterday." It felt like what it was—a preemptive strike—but it didn't feel like much of a victory.

"They want me there tomorrow. They're having a problem with scours, a disease in the calves."

"Babies. Using the big guns, huh. How can you turn babies down?" How could she even think of asking him not to go yet, to stay until after her baby was born? Hers was safe inside and would be for another three weeks.

"That's kind of what I thought. I'm not sure when, but I'll be back for my things."

Suddenly she wanted to kick and scream. How could she possibly tell him? Her feelings for him might be changing from lust to something more. She had practically promised not to hold him back. Their friendship was built on "you go your way and I'll go mine."

Was it fair not to tell him? Could she let him walk away believing they were friends with benefits and nothing else? She had hated that term, never understood it, until she met Baylor.

Did he deserve to know her feelings for him could change or would she be selfish to tell him?

CHAPTER FIFTEEN

KAYLEE HAD A DECISION to make.

Was it more important to keep her bargain with him or tell him things might be changing for her? If it would make a difference for him, she should tell him. But it couldn't make a difference for him. He needed to get away from the valley and entanglements. And she could be a big-time entanglement.

That wasn't all.

Something deep and painful pierced the heart and soul of Baylor Doyle. She'd like to think she could help him with it, but he kept everything too close, too buried, for her to even guess what it was.

Even if she found a way to keep him at her side, that wasn't where he wanted to be—whether she was in St. Adelbert or Denver.

Baylor stopped her with a hand on her arm.

"What are you thinking so hard about?" He ran a fingertip along her jawline that started the usual fires and sent flashes of need sparking through her. She would deeply miss that when he left her.

She captured his finger and kissed its fiery tip, then continued walking toward the stream of gray tumbling water. "When do you leave?"

"Before sunrise tomorrow, that's why I came this evening."

They stopped under the budding trees, where the

stream ran inches from their toes. He put a hand on her shoulder and she smiled. He couldn't help himself. He'd safeguard her as long as he could, until the deep and dark thing that drew him from the valley took him away from her forever.

She started downstream, stumbling over a root her belly did not let her see and Baylor gripped her arm harder. "I take it scours is a serious problem."

A much as she tried to douse it, a fire burned where his hand touched her arm and the blaze spread.

"Once scours gets started, it can sweep through the calves, killing many of them if they aren't treated and many times even if they are treated."

"So it's a disease then."

"It's a symptom, and the Shadow Range seems to have a formula for treating it that's superior to what's out there."

"Saving the lives of babes, even if it's baby cattle, seems like something you're perfectly suited for."

He stopped again and brought her around to face him. "I didn't come to see you so I could talk about calf diseases or banisters."

She looked up into his eyes and saw the pain there that Abby had talked about. He needed a friend and she'd be that for as long as he needed her to be. With benefits for as long as they both shall need. Well, that was out of line, but at least she didn't say it out loud.

He studied her face as if he might find some answers there, as if he were cataloguing her features for future reference.

About the control? Maybe not.

She rose up on her toes and he lowered his lips to hers. His kiss was long and soft and it was saying goodbye. No matter how often he returned to the St. Adelbert valley, his heart was leaving tomorrow and for good.

And taking a big chunk of hers with it. Guard it well, my friend, she thought.

He lifted his mouth from hers and she dropped back down into her flat shoes. "Abby asked me to see if I could use my influence to convince you to stay in the valley. I assured her my sway over you wasn't as great as your need to leave."

"It's the kind of thing she'd do. She left and when she'd been kicked around enough times, came back and found the love of her life. She feels safe and secure here. This valley is a good place for that."

"And you don't like safety and security?"

"Are you asking me why I'm leaving?"

"It was just an observation, but if you wanted to tell me why you're leaving, I'd listen."

He started them moving back upstream. "The bank needs the stability I can provide by taking this job."

"That was something I never thought of."

"The stability that will provide the next loan for the materials, and to keep the job going."

As he placed his hands on her imaginary waistline, she brought her hands to his powerful forearms.

The fire never got old. Like chocolate and presents never got old. Like sunrises and new snow. Like looking up into the fathomless blue of Baylor's eyes as she was doing now.

"So you're leaving to save them," she said into the blue.

KayLee thought of the five hundred thousand in life insurance, but knew that was the last money on earth Baylor would take to further his own agenda.

His solemn nod felt like another door closing between them. He wasn't telling her everything. Frustration crowded in, a hum inside her head until if felt like a high-pitched whine. She could help, she knew she could. If he'd just let her.

"I'm the only one who can do this."

"Bullshit." She stepped back and her hand flew to her mouth.

He gave her one of his classic smirks. "I'm glad I'm finished kissing that mouth."

"Yeah, over the top. Sorry. You try being pregnant and starting a new life." And loving a man who couldn't love her enough. No, that wasn't true. She had no idea what love was, but she knew what it wasn't. "But those reasons you gave are so, so...so monetary."

"And your point being?"

"You don't play for money points in life."

"I don't? Money makes a lot of people comfortable in this world. What kind of points *do* I play for?"

She started for home again.

"It's the kind of thing a person needs to figure out for himself or herself."

He was right to leave.

A tear trickled down her cheek.

He reached over and touched the wet trail. "Yeah, me too."

Just as they stopped in front of KayLee's apartment, Cora and Ethel bustled out their front door, grinning.

"Bridge night." Ehtel's voice sounded like an excited chirp.

"We'll be gone for hours," Cora clarified. She took her friend's arm and the two of them hurried away without looking back.

KayLee took her bag from Baylor and started up the sidewalk to her apartment.

"Wait a sec," Baylor called after her as he retrieved a foil-wrapped package from his truck.

He held it up. "For you."

She reached for it and he held it away from her. "I get the feeling most of the people in this valley are trying to get us together."

"What does—" She nodded toward the package.

"Cake."

"Oh, cake. Yummm. What does cake have to do with getting us together?"

"Evvy Doyle raised responsible sons."

"She did, and…"

He tipped his head back and peered down his nose at her. "My mother knows there is no way I'd let you carry a package up the stairs, that I'd have to bring it up myself."

"And are you going to?"

He nodded solemnly. "A man doesn't want to disappoint his mother."

She handed over Abby's leftovers and led the way.

Once inside her apartment, he placed the cake and leftovers on the old oak table.

He stopped, his expression part sheepish, part hopeful.

The deep purple light of the evening cast shadows that made the blond rancher seem troubled.

"Are we freaks?"

"You mean because we have sex whenever the opportunity presents itself and then we do it again."

"And again. What would happen to us if we were in a position to get married and live together forever?"

"You mean we'd end up dry husks because we were too crazed to eat or drink?"

"Maybe."

"Or that we'd get tired of each other?"

She couldn't reply. What could she possibly say to that besides the tired old things she had been telling herself for so long?

"Afraid of repeating your marriage?"

She nodded.

"This valley is the best place for you and your baby. You'll be safe here."

KayLee tried to smile. There was something in his voice that was more desperate than two lovers who couldn't get what they wanted.

She did the only thing she knew he would let her do to soothe him—she brought his mouth to hers and she made long sweet love to him.

BAYLOR SAT BEHIND THE DESK in the ranch office, in the dark, and he felt like a damned heel. He had not lied to KayLee—exactly—but she hadn't heard the whole truth, either. They *had* called from J&J Holdings. They had said they had a problem with scours, and they had asked him to come early—and he had turned them down flat, but gave them help over the phone.

The second call he had gotten had been from the investigator he had looking for his sister. He'd found a woman he was sure, this time, was Crystal and the woman was in trouble.

Trouble he could deal with, if Crystal was all right, he could deal with anything.

The office light flipped on, and Baylor looked up to see Lance in the doorway.

"That about her?" his brother asked.

"KayLee?"

"We're not all hicks." His brother leveled a gaze that demanded truth. "Crystal."

"She's in trouble in Denver and I'm going to go bring her back."

"Did you plan on telling anyone—ever?"

"I didn't know anything for sure until this afternoon and it's not much."

"You know enough if you're going to run after her. Does KayLee know you're leaving?"

"Yes."

"Does she know why?"

"Not all of it."

"She doesn't deserve to know?"

"What do you know about such things?"

"I know what I'd tell Holly, and I know what I'd catch hell for not telling her because it was for her own good."

"KayLee's got enough on her mind."

"Haven't you figured out that woman doesn't need you to save her?"

Baylor looked at his brother.

"What she needs if for you to love her," Lance said in his quiet way.

This time Baylor dropped his chin to his chest. The more he had found out about KayLee Morgan, the more he found out she was doing one heck of a job taking care of herself and her baby. "I know."

"You leaving now?"

"Yep."

Lance walked him to his truck.

"Driving won't get you there any faster than a flight in the morning."

"I know, but I can't sit here and wait."

"Bring her home, bro." Lance gave him a handshake and then a brotherly hug.

KAYLEE SPENT MOST of Friday trying to convince herself it didn't matter that Baylor was in another state. She had filled the day with the ranch project, contacting the insurance company about Chad's policy and running through the play again with the teens. When she woke up on Saturday morning, she wasn't any more inclined to believe it was okay that Baylor was gone.

She sat on the deck outside her bedroom, soaking in the sun, sipping the coffee she had ground and made in her press pot. Her back hurt most of the time these days and the Braxton Hicks contractions were more noticeable.

Her phone on the deck table buzzed. The caller ID didn't have a clue and said "unknown."

"Hello?"

"Hey, what can I say. I'm gorgeous and the man can't get enough of me. So he's bribing me with free use of his satellite phone. No way am I telling him I've fallen in love with his smile and his hot bod. So, what's the haps."

"Is this Cindy or some crazy person? What time is it there?"

"Both. You're minus ten hours in the boonies, eleven if you were still home."

"So late evening then and I am home."

"You're in California? No, I get it, St. Albert—"

"Adelbert."

"St. Adelbert is home. Well, it's almost party time here. Say, are you still preggers?"

"Yes. Cindy, are you sure you haven't started partying already?" KayLee shifted to get more comfortable in her chair, closed her eyes and let the breeze blow over her face.

"I've partied a little already. So did you reel in that rancher man yet?"

"He's not available."

Cindy snorted. "He have a wife somewhere?"

"He has commitments."

"Whoa, honey, I can tell by the longing in your voice are you in l-o-o-ove."

"No, but…"

"Marry him, give your baby a daddy."

"That's ridiculous, especially since he's gone."

"So finish your cabin-building job and follow him."

"And start my old life all over again? No, thanks."

"Chad was a bully."

KayLee opened her eyes and sat up. "What? No, he wasn't."

"Tell me—how many friends do you have left from California?"

"Um, you." KayLee rubbed the sore spot in her back muscles and then rested her hand on top of her belly.

"You did Chad's stuff, lived Chad's life."

"I did not."

"What happened to your business?"

"I wanted to be on the set more with Chad."

"How many of our trips did you cancel?"

"All of them." KayLee brushed away the strands of hair the wind had stuck to her lip balm.

"Why?"

"Well, the first time Chad had already planned a surprise second honeymoon for us. And the second time because he decided to bump his knee surgery up a month."

"That wasn't knee surgery, was it?"

"Well, no." KayLee paused. "I'm an idiot."

"You're not an idiot, KayLee, but you were an inno-cent when you married him."

"I was twenty-six and running my own company."

"Almost twenty-six and you had yet to run with the celebrity crowd. You've heard of stars in your eyes? You had stars in your brain."

"But—"

"It was subtle, honey. You found ways of convincing yourself and everyone around you that it was all your idea."

"Farly Longwood thinks Chad's death was my fault."

"Farly Longwood's a jerk. And when your husband died, so did Farly's meal ticket."

"Really?"

"Really." Cindy chuckled, but she sounded defini-tive.

Farly Longwood was totally blowing smoke. A weight lifted.

"Let's go back to what's-his-name—Baylor, you said?"

"Baylor." Oh, yes. A weight not lifted.

"Dark hair and eyes. You looking for another Chad?"

"I'm looking for no one, but he has blond curls and the bluest eyes."

"So you've been gazing into them, have you? And he's gone?"

"Yes."

"Are you in love?"

"I thought I wasn't."

"Oh, goodie. A wedding. Wait until I get back in the States, please."

"Cindy, I told you—he's gone."

"If he hasn't gone to Mars, then follow him, or use

your considerable feminine wiles on him to keep him there."

"He doesn't want me to follow him and my feminine wiles are temporarily distorted." KayLee took a sip of the dregs in the bottom of her cup.

"Sorry, sweetie, I'm being paged. Change his mind and have a happy birth if I don't talk to you again before hand. Ta and ta!"

"Goodbye," KayLee said to the dead phone line.

This valley is the best place for you and your baby, he had said when she practically proposed to him last evening, not *come away with me, my love* or *together we can do anything.*

CHAPTER SIXTEEN

BAYLOR GLANCED UP AND DOWN the trash-covered street outside the dive he'd been given as the address where his sister lived.

The crooked and cracked concrete steps led him up to an unlocked front entrance, where inside, the individual apartments mailboxes were ripped open and useless. The stairs creaked wildly as he made his way up past trash and filth.

On the third floor he found the door with an imprint of the letter *C* and knocked.

Silence answered his first and second knockings. The third brought a croaking "Go away."

"Crystal, are you in there?"

More silence.

He tried the handle. No luck.

"Crystal, let me in."

Nothing.

"Crystal, I've got the stuff you asked for."

He heard shuffling inside this time and the door snapped open.

He stared into the dull-eyed look of his sister and the sharp eye of a gun barrel.

"What the hell do you want?" She wore dirty sagging gray sweatpants, a torn undershirt and no shoes. Her matted blond hair was clumped on one side of her head.

"It's me, Crystal, your brother."

She looked more closely at him, lowered the gun and slammed the door in his face.

Or she tried to slam the door, but it stopped on the toe of his boot and rebounded open, exposing the stooped posture of a broken woman.

She crouched and aimed the big gun at him again. "Go away. I don't have any brothers."

"Shoot me if I don't mean anything to you."

She snapped the gun down with a heavy sigh and turned away from him. She did recognize him, and to some degree, she still trusted him or she wouldn't have turned her back.

In the dim light of the sparsely furnished apartment, she went over to the couch with a faded throw, swept aside food wrappers and sat down on the edge. She placed the gun—a Glock, he decided, one that had seen lots of service, and a big weapon for a woman of his sister's small stature—on the couch.

He had taught her to shoot a handgun. He had taught her to stand up to people.

"What do you want, Baylor?"

"I want you to come with me."

"Still the blunt and honest guy?"

"You're my sister and I can help you."

"And still trying to save the damsels in distress. Get over yourself. We damsels don't need you."

She didn't sound strung out when she spoke, yet she thoroughly looked the part.

"I'm taking you to drug rehab today."

"The hell you are." She got up, leaving her gun on the edge of the couch as if she'd forgotten she had it. "Get out. Go back to the ranch where you belong."

"I'm not going back to the ranch. I've got a job here in Denver."

"I don't care if you move into the apartment upstairs. I don't want your help. I don't need your help."

"You need someone's help."

"Don't move here, Baylor. Things happen here. It won't be good for you. You belong in Montana." There was a pleading in her voice that ripped at his heart.

"I belong here for as long as you need me."

She sat down on the couch again and put her hand on the gun. "If I go to the rehab center, will you go back home?"

"I have a job here."

"Damn it, Baylor. Go home." She glared at him, but had a clarity in her eyes that gave him hope. Maybe Crystal wasn't as far gone as she looked. She had been brilliant, one of the smartest kids in St. Adelbert.

"I'm not leaving you."

"I need you to leave me."

"What does that mean?"

"If you stay here, you'll get sucked in with me. I've seen it happen to too many people. I can't let it happen to you."

"You're worried about me?"

His gut clenched. There was something he didn't know.

He sat down in the chair opposite from her. "What happened to you?"

A dark, wiry man appeared from what must have been the bedroom. "Crystal!"

Crystal scooped up the Glock without taking her eyes off Baylor and then whirled in a wobbly pivot and fled down the dark hallway. A door slammed.

He followed her and knocked. "I'll be back, Crystal."

She didn't answer, so he left her in the filthy apartment, crawled back into his truck and drove away—for now.

That his sister didn't want him there didn't mean he was leaving town.

He did return the next day and if she was there, she didn't answer.

Alone in his motel room, he wanted desperately to call KayLee, to see her, to hold her in his arms. He had fallen in love with her the first time he saw her freezing on the porch at the ranch, before he realized she was pregnant. Every time he saw her, every time he had sex with her, he fell in love some more. He knew it was unfair to her, but he couldn't help himself.

On the third day, he went back to his sister's apartment, and he planned on coming back a fourth and for as many as were needed to talk her into getting help.

THURSDAY MORNING, the day before the play performance and a week and a half before her due date, KayLee took a long shower to help ease the aching muscles in her back. When the water cooled, she got out of the shower and dressed. Today, she needed to assure herself the construction materials had arrived on schedule.

Tuesday she had seen Dr. DeVane, who had pronounced her as healthy as she could possibly be for a woman who might be overworking herself and who could deliver any day now.

After the appointment, she and Abby had attended the last of the birthing classes. Abby had been a superb partner.

Dr. DeVane would attend the birth and examine the child afterward, and if for some reason Dr. DeVane could not be there, her husband would fill in for her.

Abby would be at the clinic and at home with KayLee for the first twenty-four hours and then Cora and Ethel would keep an eye on mother and baby.

KayLee had no doubt the women who lived downstairs would be attentive and helpful.

Her mother had said she might be able to come out in a couple of weeks and her father was on yet another honeymoon. Her family might not be much help, but she really did have a village to care for and to help her welcome her baby.

Just yesterday, the sheriff's wife and the mailman's wife stopped by. They had a little green sweater, hat and booties set from their knitting group. "We always have a set on hand because you never know," Flora Potts had said.

Baylor's face played through her mind often. She hoped he was happy. Though her bigger concerns at the moment were the construction project and staying healthy for her baby's sake.

When she arrived at the storage facility she had rented in town for the building materials, it was empty and dark. The shipment had been due before eight—it was now after ten o'clock. No materials meant idle workers—unpaid workers who would scatter and might be hard to get back and impossible to replace.

She headed for the ranch to see how close they were to running out of materials. And she couldn't help herself if Baylor were there—she wanted to see him for herself. She wanted to look into his eyes and see if going to Denver had lessened his pain or made it worse.

At the ranch house, Evvy greeted her at the door with a worried expression on her face and let her into the foyer.

"Is Trey all right?"

"Oh, my goodness." She put a hand on KayLee's shoulder. "The baby's fine. Seth and Amy took him to the city for a doctor's appointment. They were making a day of it."

"What's wrong?" Had something happened to Baylor in Denver?

"You should go talk to Lance. He's out in the shed, the one where the calves are born. You know which one I'm talking about. He'll be needing to talk to you, so you should go out there right away." Words tumbled uncharacteristically out of Evvy's mouth.

"Evvy, as long as every one is okay, we can fix whatever's wrong. I'm sure we can. Is Baylor back?" KayLee was sure she knew the answer to that question. Evvy wouldn't be sending her to talk to Lance if Baylor were there.

"He hasn't come home yet."

The hand on KayLee's shoulder trembled.

"I'll fix it, Evvy. Whatever it is, I'll fix it."

KayLee hurried at her best rate from the house toward the shed. She could see in the distance the skeletons of the two cabins. What she could not see were any workers. She knew why.

Please, don't let them all disappear, she thought.

Lance was in the only occupied pen with a cow and calf. He seemed intent on trying to get the cow to let her calf nurse, and the cow seemed equally intent on not letting man or little beast near her.

"Hi, Lance."

She hadn't realized how much dark-haired Lance looked like his youngest brother, the set of his chin, the shape of his nose and ears.

"KayLee." He acknowledged her but went back to what he was doing. First things first. Even a nonrancher like herself knew a calf would be better off if the mother let it suckle the first milk.

KayLee reached over the wooden pen and touched the tethered cow on the neck. "What's her name?"

Lance gave a rough sound that might have been a laugh.

"You don't give them names?"

"We give them numbers."

"She looks like a Candy to me. I think I'll call her Candy. Hi, Candy."

He pretended to study the animal. "She looks like a cow to me. I'm going to call her Cow."

"Come on, Candy. Let the kid eat. You are the mother after all."

Instantly, the calf lunged in and the cow let it take the teat without protest.

"Thank you, Candy." She grinned at the taciturn rancher. "It's a mother-to-mother thing."

Lance gave her a long look, shook his head and then came out of the stall and around to where she stood.

"Evvy's upset. What's happening?" she asked as she moved away from the calf-cow pair. She didn't want to mess anything up that Lance had accomplished.

"Our cash on hand for the project has run out."

"That would be why the building supplies didn't show up." KayLee didn't have to search very hard for what would be the long-term ramifications of the Doyle's failure to procure funds. All she could come up with was project failure. Well, that sure wasn't going to happen.

"Harder to get the supplies back if they've already been hammered in place," Lance said in his economical way. "So they held up the shipment."

"What does Baylor say?" Surely they would have called him in Denver.

"Haven't been able to get a hold of him. Before he left he told me to handle things until he got back. Guess he meant it."

They had called Baylor and he hadn't answered, hadn't even called them back. A flash of cold fear swept through KayLee, held her in a tight taloned grip and kept her scrambling for a reason—any reason. "Why wouldn't Baylor call back?"

"J&J Holdings hasn't heard from him, either. They phoned last Thursday for him to come over for a few days. He turned them down. Said he had something else to deal with."

No. No, he didn't, she thought, still grasping for the logic and not finding it. "How could that be? J&J had some calf disease he was going to go help them with."

"Scours. He handled that on the phone." Lance stared at her hard. "Have you got any idea where my little brother might be?"

"Me?"

"Holly says somebody's been using our...um...the supplies we keep in the trucks."

She wasn't sure who was more embarrassed. "So everyone knows?"

He nodded.

"He—no, I don't know. He said he was going to Denver." *He lied to me.*

They started for the shed door in silence.

She sifted through Lance's information and decided she had to think about getting the flow of materials restarted. She could think of Baylor when she had the time and the courage. She had made it very clear he didn't owe her anything, apparently not even the truth.

"I thought Baylor's job would swing the bank loan in your favor."

"He hasn't taken the job yet and the bank said they couldn't release more money on a promise like that. Holly took Dad into Kalispell to see what he can do."

"What are the chances?"

Lance glanced at her and then stared forward as they headed for the house. "Slim to none. We're pretty extended."

"Are there other arrangements that might be made?"

"Sell some land, but that's not a real solution. Eventually you have to sell the house out from under yourself."

And then it would all be gone. The lifestyle. The family would, out of necessity, shatter.

She couldn't let that happen. This family gave her a chance when no one else would. They saved her from isolation and abandonment. She needed to keep her promise and bring this project in on schedule.

"We'll work it out," she finally said. "We'll work something out."

No way would the Doyles consider borrowing her child's life insurance money. What if *she* bought the land for her child with the money, stipulating she would not sell, except to the family, unless the Doyles wanted to sell the rest. Land was a good investment, wasn't it? She had to invest part of the proceeds from the life insurance policy and her baby wouldn't need it for at least eighteen years, when he or she started college. She could put, say, a fifteen-year limit on her not selling outside the Doyle family.

As they reached the ranch house, Holly and Curtis arrived. At Lance's questioning look, Holly shook her head and pressed into his arms for a comforting hug.

Curtis, in the meantime, put his arms around them both; an obvious slump to his tall physique.

The more she looked at the Doyles, the more she knew she had to make it right. No one would release supplies on her word, but they would release them for a solid promise of cash.

"I need to go," she called to them. "Don't give up hope."

She climbed in her car and headed toward town. She wiggled in her seat as she gripped the wheel. She hadn't realized how much worse her back pain had gotten.

When KayLee got home Abby was in the yard hanging sheets and towels on the clothesline in the warm afternoon sun.

KayLee greeted Abby, grabbed the other end of a sheet and together they shook out the wrinkles. They folded it in half as if they had done this before, and they had. KayLee had learned to love the smell of line-dried sheets and towels. Abby tossed her a clothespin from the pouch at her waist and they each pinned their end to the line. Abby put the third clothespin in the center.

"S'up?" Abby asked as she grabbed the empty basket to take it back into the house.

"Can I run something by you to see if I'm totally crazy?"

"Come inside."

KayLee followed Abby into her kitchen and sat at Abby's table.

"Shoot," Abby said as she put on the kettle.

KayLee told her about her idea to invest in the Doyle ranch. She also told her about the back pain.

Abby smiled as if she knew something KayLee didn't. "The back pain is pretty normal during this stage of pregnancy. Let me know if it gets worse."

"Do you think the Doyle family would go along with my providing the cash by way of a sale?"

"They might. I don't know if you've noticed or not, but they are a pretty stubborn bunch." Abby sat down across from her.

KayLee laughed. "As a group, that family is quite formidable. As a part of this community, I used to think they were invincible, but I guess everyone has places where they need help."

"They might consider it if it was presented in a way that made it seem fair and even beneficial to you and your little one. Wouldn't that mean you sticking around in St. Adelbert? Wouldn't that be too—"

"Painful? Yeah. I've been a fool, Abby. I told myself in the beginning not to get too close to him, but I convinced myself it was lust and lust is a great deal of fun and then it fades. Thought I'd be fine."

Abby grinned. "Well, one of you two seeing the light is good news."

KayLee frowned. "It won't change anything. He's driven to leave the valley for something and he needs to do it without me. We thought we were being so honest with each other. At least, that's how it started. We'd just be friends."

"Just friends?"

"I love him, Abby. For whatever that's worth, and he's gone."

KayLee hugged her arms around her chest. *And he lied to me.*

Abby put her hand on KayLee's. "Don't lose faith in him. Whatever is bothering him, he'll tell you, it just may take some time."

"He hasn't involved me so far." The cup of tea Abby had made her was hard to swallow.

"That's Baylor. He'd take a hit for you, but he won't show you what's in his heart."

Talking about Baylor only made the ache worse. Kay-Lee expelled an exasperated breath. "So about offering to temporarily own some of the Doyles' ranch. Is that ridiculous?"

"They decided to trust you, KayLee. They might be willing to extend that trust, especially since you are living here and not commuting back and forth to California. The people here feel more comfortable if they can look a person in the eye and make a judgment. The world might be a small place these days, but it's always been small in St. Adelbert."

"I'm going to see what I can do."

"Finish drinking first."

KayLee did and then got up to leave, anxious to find out what she could do next.

"Keep me posted on that back pain."

"Yep."

Abby grinned again and KayLee marched across the street with hope for the construction to restart. She'd check to see how much time it would take to release money based on the life insurance policy and then— She paused in the middle of the street when a sharp pain seized her lower back.

When the pain subsided, she continued across the street and up the stairs to her apartment. When she arrived at her door, a flood of liquid soaked her clothing and splashed all over the landing.

CHAPTER SEVENTEEN

KAYLEE STOOD AT THE TOP of the stairs and cried with overwhelming happiness. She was going to meet her child at last. Nothing in her life had ever been better than that.

Boy or girl, dark blond hair like hers, dark hair and eyes like Chad. Cute. The baby would be the cutest thing she'd ever seen. She'd hold and protect her child for as long as needed. She'd love that child for no other reason than she or he was her child.

She took the first of many deep cleansing breaths.

Here goes, Chad, she thought as she let herself into her apartment to get dry clothing and to make all sorts of phone calls. She'd take good care of their child.

Whatever she and Chad had done to each other and to themselves was all in the past. Her child would know the fun, wild and exciting side of his or her father and would know that Chad had loved his child.

"Ow!" Now that was a contraction.

When the back pain she had been experiencing found its way around to her abdomen, KayLee admitted that she must have been in labor for a while. Now that her water had broken, the pains came harder and there was no doubt.

She called Abby and Dr. DeVane, cleaned up the landing and then she made sure the coffeepot was unplugged and the garbage disposal had baking soda in it. Silly things, as if she'd be gone a month.

She went into the nursery and ran her hand over the rocking crib that Baylor had brought up the day he carried the rest of the things Amy and Holly loaned to her. The newborn Doyles must have slept here.

The crib didn't belong where it was. She grabbed an end and tugged until it rested beside her bed. No way was her baby sleeping in the next room. There would be plenty of time for that when the child was older. Ten, she thought and smiled. Twenty.

While she waited for Abby to get her nephew squared away, KayLee mused about her own calmness at this critical moment in her life. Then she realized it was numbness to disguise the gaping, echoing hole in the middle of her.

Somewhere deep inside, she had come to believe with all her heart Baylor would want to be a part of this birth. That, at least for that, she would have her friend nearby.

Now that wasn't going to happen, and she wanted to feel like kicking something. Instead she felt an emptiness on what should be one of her happiest days.

She brushed at the new tears as she opened the bag she had packed and repacked to take with her to the clinic. She held up a tiny onesie with a baby dinosaur on the front and green trim. She had been an outside-the-box girl and had preferred dinosaurs to little purple ponies, rag dolls to the ones that talked and played alphabet games.

She snapped the lid to the suitcase closed and found her mobile phone.

"Sharring and Sharring, how may I help you?"

"Put Mr. Sharring on the phone."

"I'll—"

"No, Ms. McCall. This is K. L. Morgan and I don't have time for the games today."

"Yes, Ms. Morgan. I'll put him on right away."

KayLee could hear the amusement in Randolph's assistant's voice and wondered how long she had been waiting for someone to insist she bypass Randolph's screening process.

"KayLee?"

"Randolph, tell me again about the insurance policy proceeds, please."

"As part of Chad's estate, the funds belong to you. You may do with them whatever you choose."

"Randolph, I need your help."

She asked Mr. Sharring to make inquiries at the bank in Kalispell about using the insurance proceed to restart the materials flow.

She put the papers she'd need to fax to the bank into her leather bag and went downstairs to tell Cora and Ethel she was on her way to the clinic and the next time she'd see them, she'd have her baby in her arms. The two women danced and hugged and promised to have things perfect for her arrival home. KayLee smiled at their antics and wondered what *perfect* meant to them. She didn't care, they would do well.

On the way to the clinic in Abby's car, she couldn't help but notice her friend's grin. Sure, Abby would be happy for her, but...

"Abby, you seem overly happy with my condition. Is your husband looking more sexy to you these days?"

"Outrageously," Abby replied.

"When?"

"December. A Christmas baby."

"Congratulations. I'm so happy for you and, Abby, you will make the most perfect mother."

"I'll look to you for helpful hints."

They passed John Miller and his partner in front of their hardware store. The men grinned and gave a thumbs-up.

"They know?"

"You live upstairs from Cora and Ethel."

"I do."

KayLee sat forward suddenly. "Oh, my God, the play." The words came out as a strangled squeak as another forceful contraction squeezed.

"Don't yelp," Abby said with a hand to her chest. "You scared me to death."

KayLee leaned back into the headrest as the contraction subsided. "Sorry. I'll have to call Becca Taylor. She's only sixteen but she's really stepped up. She was *my* understudy. And Mrs. Pierre. She'll help Becca if she needs it, but she probably won't need it. They are going to do a full dress rehearsal tonight, and I'll miss the first performance tomorrow. Unless—"

"No unlesses. You'll miss the play. They'll do fine and it'll give Becca something great to put on her résumé. So, how are you feeling?"

"Excited. Scared, but not so scared as I'd be if you weren't with me." KayLee rubbed an ache in her side. "And I know it's silly, but I miss him."

"It's not silly. If you feel half as much for Baylor as I do for Reed, then it should be driving you nuts."

"It is, but he was so very honest about it. I knew he was leaving."

"Do you think he was honest?"

"What do you mean?"

Abby continued up Main Street, and they were

almost at the clinic. "Well, he knew he was leaving and when he told you that, it gave him free reign to feel whatever he wanted about you. If he broke a heart it would only be his."

"Does it matter?"

"It might. How would you feel if you thought he felt about you the way you feel about him?"

"I don't know. Mad at both of us for doing that to ourselves. Depressed because when we're together it's so right, but it's not our time."

Abby drove up the ramp to the emergency entrance of the clinic and KayLee got out of the car and into the wheelchair that Phyllis—another nurse—had waiting for her.

Abby waved and left to park the car.

Another contraction distracted her from anything except herself and her baby.

"Thank you, Phyllis," KayLee said when the nurse stopped the chair in the birthing room. "I love this room. The green and yellow colors are so soothing, kind of nonjudgmental under the circumstance."

She and Phyllis chatted about when her water broke, how long she had been having contractions, how Kay-Lee felt in general. Phyllis measured her vital signs and said, "Dr. DeVane will be in to examine you in a short while, so put on the gown and robe, but you can pace or sit or whatever feels best until she's ready."

KayLee sat. She had things to do before she got down to baby-birthing business. She called about the play and then she called the bank. Randolph Sharring hadn't failed her. The branch manager took her call right away. A couple of faxes back and forth on the clinic's fax machine, and everything would be set to start the supplies moving again.

Abby stopped in but left again when she saw Kay-Lee didn't need her at that moment.

KayLee supposed she should talk to the Doyles about the bank transactions, but the most harm she could do was a few loads of building materials. Unlike the bank, KayLee trusted the Doyle family to make good on the money.

Besides they'd already be "hammered in place" as Lance had said before anybody knew she put up the money. The details of what could be done in the future could be figured out after her child was born.

When she finished her business calls, she dialed Baylor's phone and it went directly to voice mail.

As the afternoon finished up, the contractions came harder and longer and Abby stayed with her while Kay-Lee walked, sat, curled up on her side in bed—whatever felt best at the time.

As the pains occurred closer together, KayLee found herself longing to see the face of her friend, of the man who could love her if he tried.

"I hope he's okay, Abby. Lance said he didn't call them back. They don't know where he is. Maybe he didn't even go to Denver. Maybe he's never coming back."

Abby smoothed her damp hair away from her face. "I know you miss him and I also know you will do a great job giving birth to your child."

Out the window of the birthing room, the sky changed to a purple-red before falling into darkness.

Abby rubbed KayLee's back and gave her sips of water and apple juice. "You are doing so well, KayLee."

"Thanks, Abby. I don't know what I'd do without you. I guess I'm going to try to rest now. You can go out for a while if you want."

KayLee faced the far wall and tugged the sheet over her to keep the chill of the ventilation away. She was tired, but sleep didn't come. She forced her eyes to stay closed, but a couple minutes later they popped open again.

She heard voices in the hallway and Abby came back into the room. "Are you up for a visitor?"

KayLee sat up, her heart beating fast with anticipation. "Who is it? I mean, sure."

"Come in, Sheriff."

A second later Sheriff Potts entered hat in hand.

KayLee smiled at the man who had been so nice to her the first day she was in town.

"How are you, Ms. Morgan? My wife, Flora, sends her best wishes and says if it's all right with you, she has families ready to drop food off at your house for the next couple of weeks."

KayLee felt a new rush of warmth for this small town. "I'd love that. Tell her thank-you."

Abby handed her a tissue and she wiped away a tear.

"And I have someone else who wants to see you if you're up to another visitor."

She nodded, wondering who the sheriff could possibly have brought to see her.

Sheriff Potts stepped back and Baylor filled her field of vision. The world could have fallen away then and she wouldn't have noticed. Her friend had come back. He wore a stoic rancher expression and the "uniform" she had come to love, the open-necked, button shirt of soft sandy-colored cloth with faded jeans and boots.

"Yep. Love," Abby whispered in her ear and walked out of the room.

The sheriff spoke to KayLee. "You tell him, if I catch

him driving that truck of his over a hundred again, I will put him in jail. Nothing that fast is reasonable and prudent."

"I will definitely speak to him about it, Sheriff."

KayLee drew in a sharp breath and the pain in her lower abdomen swelled.

"I'll leave you to it now, Ms. Morgan." He nodded once and disappeared.

In an instant Baylor was at her side. She wanted to be angry with him, but he hadn't made any commitments to her that he had broken.

"How did you know?" she asked.

"Abby left me a message I couldn't ignore."

"I love her. Why didn't you return Lance's calls? We didn't know where you were—if you were safe or dead by the side of the road."

It sounded like the accusation it was. She didn't care, she was owly now and anyone who wanted to tell her to be nice could take a flying leap.

"I'm safe. I'm here now." He tucked her hair behind her ear and searched her face.

Her mobile phone on her bedside rang. It was Lance Doyle's number. She glared at Baylor and opened her phone. "Lance, he's here."

"Kick his butt for me."

"Count on it."

"I don't know how you did it, KayLee, but we've already finished unloading a truckload of materials. The contractor says construction will begin again tomorrow morning early. KayLee, you rock."

She smiled. That was an awful lot of words all at once from Lance Doyle and she knew it was a *thank-*

you and a *well done.* "Thanks. We'll talk about it in a few days."

"Holly says she'll see you tomorrow if you're up to it."

She closed her phone. "He said to kick your butt for him. I won't be doing that today, but I want you to you know it will happen."

He dared a small grin and she smiled back. "I hope you know how much it means to me that you're here."

He sat on the edge of the bed and let her squeeze his hand as hard as she wanted to during the next contraction. When the pain eased, she kissed him long and hard and he kissed back the same. "I'm so glad you're safe. Knowing my friend is out there gives me strength. Don't do that to me again."

"I'll try to keep in touch next time."

Somehow that wasn't as comforting as she thought it should have been. How about "come live with me forever" or "I'll never leave you."

Abby swept back into the room. "Enough alone time for you two. This woman needs her coach."

Abby sat on the opposite side from Baylor and when the next contraction came quickly she helped KayLee through it. "Baylor, I need you to leave now for a couple minutes."

He left the room. "Are you sure you want him here?"

"I do, Abby."

Abby nodded. "Phyllis is going to do an exam. I think it's time we get Dr. DeVane back in here."

KayLee smiled.

With Abby on one side and Baylor on the other adjusting to her every mood, KayLee brought her child into the world.

DR. DEVANE HELD UP the squalling infant for KayLee to see. She then put the child on KayLee's chest for her to touch. "Welcome, MaryRose."

With her dark-haired beautiful girl and Baylor, she knew that was enough for right now.

KayLee was reluctant to give her child up when Phyllis came to take her away. "We'll only be gone a short while. I've got a nice warm place to give her a bath and for Dr. DeVane to examine her."

Abby and a new tech KayLee had never met cleaned up the room while KayLee rested. Baylor sat quietly holding her hand. His small act of assurance let Kay-Lee drift off.

When she awoke, she was alone and the lights were dimmed. She barely had a chance to collect any concern when the door opened.

Phyllis and Abby breezed into the room.

"I'm going to check you and make sure things are returning to normal," Phyllis said.

"And I have someone who wants her mommy."

When Phyllis declared KayLee progressing wonderfully, Abby placed her daughter in her arms.

KayLee tugged the blanket down so she could look into her daughter's face...her tiny nose, two chins, so much brown hair and the blue eyes of a newborn.

When Phyllis left, KayLee looked pleadingly up at Abby.

"He's on his phone. I'll send him in when he's finished. In the meantime, let's see how hungry MaryRose is." Abby grinned.

After a sharp rap, Baylor opened the door and motioned Abby out into the hallway. KayLee couldn't hear what they were saying, but she could see that Abby was upset.

When Abby turned toward KayLee, there was no difficulty hearing her words. "Go in and tell her. She at least deserves to hear it from you."

CHAPTER EIGHTEEN

WHAT BAYLOR HAD TO TELL her was that he had to leave. There was an emergency in Denver and he didn't say what kind, but she was sure it had nothing to do with the job at J&J Holdings and they both knew he wouldn't be explaining to anyone in St. Adelbert anytime soon.

Whatever his secret was, KayLee knew it was not about her, though she knew Baylor well enough to know at least some of the pain she saw in his face was for what he was doing to her.

She let him leave without protest.

She allowed nothing and no one to eclipse the joy that met her daughter on the day of her birth.

A week later, she sat on the edge of her bed, staring into the tiny crib where MaryRose slept peacefully. No one had ever adequately described to KayLee the feeling of being a parent. She could not get enough of gazing at her daughter, awake, asleep, crying, feeding and especially when her daughter stared back at her.

When she looked at MaryRose, she had no regrets about her past. She missed Baylor and the hole he left in her heart had not lessened, but even he, especially he, would tell her the baby had to come first.

The doorbell rang. "It's me, KayLee," Abby called up the stairs. They had an agreement, Abby would let herself in. It was easier.

Abby had been a great helper the first twenty-four

hours. And good as their word, Cora and Ethel had added a few features to her apartment. There was a rocker in her room in front of the windows overlooking the street and the mountains beyond. There had been a new fluffy robe with matching slippers and nursing nightgown laid out on her bed when she arrived home. There were pink decorations added to the nursery. And every few days, they placed fresh cut flowers on the dining room table.

So much food poured into the house that when she was full and her freezer was full, she had to start insisting people come over to visit and help her eat.

But the dark loneliness always woke her from a deep sleep or snuck in when her daughter was napping—there was a space in her life that refused to be filled.

No one had heard from Baylor.

"Hi," Abby whispered, although it seemed MaryRose could sleep through anything. Must be from bouncing around for months totally at the mercy of another human being.

KayLee hugged Abby and they went into the kitchen.

"My mother finally called," KayLee said over a cup of tea. "Says she is excited to be a grandmother and she'll come and visit soon."

"And your dad?"

"Still honeymooning, but Chad's parents sent a baby gift and a request that I bring MaryRose for a visit sometime in the undefined future."

Abby frowned. "I'm sorry."

They sipped their tea and enjoyed the warm breeze coming in the window near the table.

Well wishes had showered KayLee from all directions, even from Mrs. McCormack, the wife of the dreadful man in the diner.

When she was up to it, she had as many places to go and people to see as she could possibly want if she were looking for distraction. There was even an elderly couple who would celebrate their seventy-fifth wedding anniversary this summer and had invited KayLee and MaryRose to the party.

There were tired times when she wondered if she was cut out to be a mother, but the encouragement of the other women helped soothe those particular jangling nerves.

Abby finished her tea, washed, dried and put her cup away. "Well, this villager has come to scrub your kitchen floor and to clean your bathroom."

"But I—"

Abby held up a hand. "Before you protest, hear me out." When KayLee nodded she continued. "I expect quid pro quo. Next to cleaning my refrigerator, and I noticed you have already done yours, I hate scrubbing my kitchen floor and cleaning the bathroom."

KayLee nodded again. "I'll be there after Christmas to clean yours."

"It would be a little bit of heaven."

While Abby worked, KayLee stared into her cup and wondered if the tea leaves in the bottom would tell her if a certain rancher would come back into her life. When the tea leaves told her nothing, she realized the pain at his absence did not lessen as time passed.

A tear slipped down her cheek and she angrily wiped it away. She wasn't pregnant anymore and she shouldn't be crying over things she could not change.

As the days passed, KayLee and Abby shared many cups of tea and each of MaryRose's accomplishments. The ranch project went well and by the end of the second week of her daughter's life, she had made the arrangements with Curtis and Lance Doyle to sell her enough land, in her daughter's name, to finish the initial cabins and start the next pair. And she had celebrated her daughter's first smile.

By the time MaryRose was three weeks old, KayLee had agreed to redesign the town hall to help ease some of the burden on the gymnasium. Since Cut-Rate Airlines, by all accounts, had been a smashing success, she had tentatively agreed to direct a new play in the fall.

Her daughter met the three Doyle children for the first time and the mothers agreed MaryRose had been fascinated and very pleased to make their acquaintance.

On a bright, warm Sunday afternoon, Abby and Kyle came up to KayLee as she was about to take MaryRose for a stroller ride.

"You could use a break," Abby said. "Program my number with a special ring and don't answer anyone else's calls. MaryRose, Kyle and I will be busy for three hours, so go in the house and pump and then go away and leave us alone."

KayLee didn't want to take her friend up on the offer, but after she saw how tickled Kyle was to be able to help with the baby and how proud Abby was of him, she knew she had to go. And MaryRose did love to stroller ride and to look at people's faces, especially children.

With the vision of the three of them happily heading down the sidewalk, KayLee headed out, by herself for the first time since giving birth, to the ranch to inspect the progress of the cabins.

She ignored the normal ring of two phone calls, bypassed the ranch house and drove out to where the outside of the first cabin was almost completely finished. The inside, with its naked beams and exposed wiring, was a different story, but that would change in the near future.

Her phone rang and she read the screen by reflex. *Lance.*

The man had grown downright loquacious toward her since they sort of bonded over the delayed supplies and his missing brother.

"Hi, Lance."

"Thought I should warn you, Baylor is here. He's come to collect his things."

She hadn't expected that, now Abby's urgent need to take MaryRose made more sense. "How's he look?" Not the question she really wanted to ask.

"Loaded for bear."

"Does that mean mad?"

"And then some."

"So he knows what I did?"

"On his way out there now."

"Good." She closed her phone. Lance had told her at one of their visits to the bank, he didn't think Baylor would take to her bailing the ranch out.

He'd have to live with it. She'd had to live with a lot since he was gone. She wondered if she could speak to him without wanting to touch him and decided she could. In fact, it would be best if she kept her distance.

She stepped out of the cabin to see he was almost there. Big man, blond hair blowing in the wind, Stetson probably on the seat of his truck. Jeans telling of solid muscles and the open *V* of his shirt giving a glimpse of the blond curls that she knew created their own *V* over his tight belly.

Showdown time.

"Hi, stranger." She smiled in a friendly manner. Let him fire the first shot.

He took her arm and led her back inside the cabin.

He slammed the door with a backward kick and lowered his mouth to hers. All the feelings she thought she could keep bound up slipped past her control and she snaked her arms around his neck and pressed her body against his.

She hadn't felt these things in the weeks, not since they last made love in her apartment before he disappeared the first time. She welcomed the rushes and the swell of need.

He let her go and stepped away.

"We can't take your money."

"I'm not giving it to you." She clenched her hands into fists to try to dissipate some of the fire that burned inside her. "My daughter and I own a quarter of your family ranch."

He closed in and took hold of her upper arms. "Lance told me about your deal. You can't do that."

She smiled up at him. When he didn't let go and flee, she kissed inside the open *V* of his shirt. "How does it feel to be saved for a change?"

Now he left her standing by herself and ran both hands through his hair. She almost smiled at the familiar gesture, but she seemed to have lost her mirth.

"KayLee, there is no guarantee you will ever get your money back."

"Baylor! There are so many things in my life that did not come with a guarantee attached. My parents for starters, my marriage…you. You know before you disappeared again, I actually found myself wishing MaryRose was your daughter."

He captured her with his blue eyes and didn't blink. "I started wishing you'd let me be her father."

KayLee couldn't get air into her lungs. He stood there

under the raw beams of the soon-to-be loft and looked like a man who knew the ache of a heavy burden.

"But…" he continued.

KayLee kicked aside a chip of stray wood with the toe of her shoe, and her breath came rushing in on a wave of disappointment. "There is always a *but* between us, isn't there."

"It's up to me to make sure my family stays together even if it means…"

"To hell with your own life?"

He didn't say a word. She knew he didn't really want to fight with her, and she didn't want to fight with him. There were only a few people who Baylor fought with and that was more out of…brotherly love.

She suddenly realized the source of his pain.

"It's your sister, isn't it? She is the only person who can rip your heart out and stomp on it."

"That's not exactly true." He pivoted until his back was to her.

"Me?"

"You." He'd said it so quietly she almost didn't hear the word. That one word gave her hope.

"I've kept my part of the bargain."

"You did and that makes you the best friend anyone could have. I abused that friendship and you let me."

She dropped her head. There was no denying it. "That's apparently what I do. I play for security points and to be secure, I need people's approval."

"And that's when you stomp all over my heart. Don't let me do that. Don't let anyone. Punch. Kick. Spit. Do what you have to do, but don't let a single one of us take advantage you."

She marched over and punched him hard on the arm.

With a gentle laugh, he rubbed the spot and then reached out for her.

She backed away to keep her brain functioning. "I don't know what's happening with Crystal, but I would never, ever tell you to desert your sister or to give up on her or whatever it is you think I might do to stand in your way."

"It's not that." He stared up at the naked rafters.

She circled around him and stared at him until he relented and looked at her. "I want to know what it is because I've learned something, Baylor Doyle. I loved you. I was willing to give up all I've been given here in St. Adelbert, all the security and approval in the world, if it meant MaryRose and I could spend our lives with you because without you the rest had so much less meaning. So tell me. What is it? You owe me that much."

The sound of the wind and the creaking of new lumber filled the space. "She's an addict," he eventually said with the sharp edge of pain in his voice. "I arranged for her to enter a rehab program."

"I'm so sorry. Is she doing all right?"

He barked a rough sound. "She had thanked me and praised me even. Told me how much she loved and appreciated my making the arrangements. And she didn't even bother to show up at rehab."

She wanted to touch him, to hold and comfort him.

"That was the call I got at the clinic the night Mary-Rose was born. If I could have talked to her alone, if I could have gotten her to go to the rehab facility with me, but there always seemed to be someone around and she was always trying to get rid of me."

She wanted to tell him it wasn't his fault, but she let him talk.

"She's on the edge, KayLee, and someone has to be there to bring her back before it's too late."

He spun away and walked out of the cabin.

BAYLOR LEFT KAYLEE with a shocked look on her face. She could be crumpled to the floor by now and there was nothing he could do to fix that. She was healthy and well off here in the valley and that's where she needed to stay.

That she had loved him in spite of all their pledges of friendship only…

Clouds had crowded out the sun while he was in the cabin with KayLee, and rain threatened to fall. As he covered the ground between the cabin and the house, he hoped, chicken that he was, that KayLee would stay out of sight until he was gone.

She was what they would call some kinda woman. Her defiance about helping out had poked a hole in the head of steam he had built up and he hoped for her sake and her daughter's she had made a wise choice about buying into the ranch.

He hadn't come here to inflict more pain on her. He'd come to get a few of his things and maybe a few things that would make Crystal think of home, of her roots.

Footsteps closed in behind him. KayLee coming in for more pain? She said she played for approval points. He approved, more than he could ever remember approving of anyone. He was glad she had her daughter.

She had loved him. He had that. He slowed and let her catch up to him. He studied her profile, buried a picture of her face in his heart where he could find it when he needed it.

As they approached the house, he recognized Colorado license plates and his heart nearly stopped beating. J&J had no reason to be here. This could only be word about his sister and that could not be good.

A dark, wiry man got out and leaned against the rear quarter panel of the old Oldsmobile. His hands rested on the car on either side of him, knees slightly bent, he was ready to spring at any moment, in any direction. He reminded Baylor of a hungry wolf.

Baylor signaled KayLee to stay back.

There were some things he wasn't willing to risk. KayLee Morgan was one of those things. MaryRose's mother. His friend. If he couldn't keep her safe on the ranch, he might as well give it all up.

Suddenly, Baylor knew he'd seen the man before. A flash of his face was all he had caught before his sister had dragged the man away on that first day at her apartment. The man was clean-shaven, wearing khaki pants and a golf shirt. He didn't look much like the druggy from Denver, but he was.

Baylor stepped aggressively close, allowing the guy no access to KayLee except through him.

The man didn't flinch or cower as Baylor expected and that might be the reason Baylor didn't punch his lights out.

He looked up at Baylor and spoke calmly. "I'm Carlos Ramirez, Crystal Doyle's partner."

"KayLee, get out of here." Baylor kept his voice dangerously low as he spoke. "I don't care what you call yourself. Whatever it is you came to say, say it and get out. And if you're looking for Crystal, no one here will help you."

"I see you've met Officer Ramirez."

It wasn't KayLee speaking, but the familiar voice couldn't be real. It was too clear, like the old Crystal. He stayed where he was, afraid to break the spell.

"Bay, if you've already punched him, don't worry. Ramirez usually has one or two coming anyway."

This was his sister. Funny, irreverent and took no prisoners.

He turned slowly. She wore jeans and a T-shirt, had cut her blond hair short, and there was only a clean, clear look in her eyes and a smile on her face.

"Give me a hug," she said. "Or punch me."

The words lifted the sluggishness that had descended over him. He grabbed her and hugged her tight.

Crystal pushed away and went to her partner. "Thanks for the ride, Ramirez."

The man nodded and was soon leaving a trail of dust on his way off the ranch.

"Well, I'll be damned," Lance said from the porch behind them.

"Lance Doyle, I heard that," Evvy called as she stepped out beside her oldest son, ready to continue her chastisement. The words never came out of her mouth and her eyes filled with tears.

"What's going on out here?" Holly stopped beside her husband and grinned. She figured out right away what was going on.

Soon all the rest of the Doyles were out of the house except Curtis.

Amy shrieked, which made Trey cry until Seth picked him up and popped him on his shoulders and did the "daddy's a horsey" thing.

Crystal took the steps slowly as if testing to see if anyone would fend her off with a punch or a kick. Then she caught each of her brothers and her sisters-in-law with a big hug, but when she got to Evvy she stopped and curled her lips in as if she was thinking whether or not to hug her mother.

The children dutifully hugged their aunt but soon lost interest in the surprise and ran inside to play. Trey did a good job of keeping up with Katie, who was only a month older than him, and both of them did their best to stick with Matt.

Baylor took the steps two at a time and motioned KayLee up on the large porch. He walked over to stand beside his mother, facing Crystal, arms crossed, feet spread. Lance and Seth flanked him and stood in identical poses. Their wives stood at their elbows.

None of them spoke as Crystal shifted her gaze between them one at a time. "I didn't know how bad it was for you at school until another girl stepped forward." Evvy spoke first. She looked as if she were glad to be facing her demons. "By the time I found out, you were gone."

She turned to her youngest son. "I know, Baylor, that you blame yourself for not being here for her."

"She told me those two guys dragged her into the locker room, so I had a talk with them." He remembered Crystal's face when she told him and afterward when he assured her nothing would happen to her now, but it had. "Somebody had to do it."

"It was my duty. She told me, twice."

Baylor faced his mother. "You knew about the second time and let her go back for a third?"

He felt his older brother's hand on his shoulder.

"Of course I knew, but not until it was too late. You are her brother, Bay. This was not your burden—"

"Hey, I'm right here," Crystal interrupted her mother, commanding attention. "I like to think I can take care of myself. Baylor didn't give those boys black eyes that weekend he came home from college."

A smirk played around Cyrstal's eyes, but she wasn't being given any quarter by her family.

"Why didn't you let us know where you were?" Lance asked.

"I was mad, at first, and then I was stubborn. So to get even, I became a cop. Turns out I have good instincts for undercover work." She turned her lips in again and shrugged one shoulder. "And as far as they knew, I didn't have any family that I was close to. Names in a file. You know."

"A letter? A phone call was too much?" Seth prodded.

"The longer I was away, the harder it got."

"Why didn't you tell me? You could have gotten away, found me," Baylor said. "I made no secret of where I was."

"Think about it, Baylor. It wouldn't have mattered if I was a drug addict or a cop trying to bust the biggest drug trafficking ring in the whole region. You would have tried to save me and no matter how that went down, there would have been consequences."

"So what?" Lance asked. "You'd still be lost to us if Baylor hadn't sent somebody snooping around."

"You both knew?" Evvy asked, looking between Lance and Baylor.

"We didn't know much," Baylor admitted.

"Enough to almost blow my cover."

"I wasn't—" Baylor started.

Crystal made a chopping motion with her hand to silence him. There must be things he didn't know. Things she didn't want to discuss in front of everyone.

"You're staying?" Evvy asked.

A light rain had begun to fall, splattering on the wooden porch and most of the Doyle family.

Baylor reached for the bags sitting on the porch that he assumed were Crystal's, but she got there first.

"Put this somewhere safe." She handed him a locked box he assumed must be the Glock he had seen her handle so well in Denver.

Lance shepherded them into the house, into the large living room where someone had built a fire to ward off the chill of the coming rain.

Baylor placed the box in the locked gun cabinet along the wall near the entrance to the room.

Then they all stood around the square wooden coffee table as if no one was willing to commit to a seat.

"Are you staying, Crystal?" Evvy repeated the question she had asked outside.

"We got the job done in spite of Baylor's—" Crystal gave him a look of stubborn thanks "—intervention. I need a place to be out of sight for a while. I'll stay if I'm welcome. Seems I can't hide from you people very well anyway."

"This is your home," Evvy said. "Of course you're welcome."

Crystal looked directly at KayLee, then she stepped around Seth to where KayLee stood apart from the group. She put out a hand. "Hi, I'm Crystal Doyle and you look like somebody I should get to know better."

Put on the spot, KayLee glanced at Baylor and then took Crystal's hand and introduced herself. The smile she gave his sister was a sad one and it pained him.

Evvy stepped forward. "KayLee is the designer and general contractor for the cabins you can see we're building."

Crystal looked from Baylor to KayLee and back again.

"What's all the racket out here? Man can't even get

a good nap these days." Curtis Doyle filled the doorway. His hair was smashed on one side and his shoulders slumped.

Then he spotted his prodigal daughter.

Curtis almost flew to Evvy's side, drawing up tall, looking bigger and dangerous like a stallion whose territory was being challenged.

"What's happening?" he demanded.

Evvy backed into the curve of Curtis's arm and spoke to her husband. "It's all right, Curt. We're about to work out a few things."

Curtis relaxed visibly.

Baylor hadn't seen his dad look so vigorous in a long time.

Crystal's homecoming was already having resounding ripples in the family, good ones. He hoped she'd stay.

"I'd like to speak with Mom and Dad alone," Crystal said. "And I'm glad to see all of you."

Lance gathered up the rest of them and herded them down the hallway to the den.

When KayLee tried to back out of the family crowd, Lance practically dragged her along. Baylor wasn't sure if that was a good thing. She might just want to go home to her daughter and leave all this drama behind.

Amy and Seth took one couch. Lance and Holly took the other, leaving the two chairs. KayLee sat in one of the chairs and as Baylor started for the other, Seth called out, "Wait. Chair's broke."

Baylor didn't believe him. "Doesn't look broke."

"We can't help how it looks." Amy backed up her husband "It's broke."

Baylor took a seat on the arm of the chair where KayLee sat and they all grinned at him.

He shook his head, but what he wanted to do was to pull KayLee into his lap and demand she learn to love him all over again.

Because damn if he didn't love her, probably always had, no matter what his head tried to tell him was right and fair.

"Do you suppose," Holly asked from across the room, "Crystal found anyone to love in Denver?"

Baylor glanced at KayLee and then began to explain what the apartment building was like where Crystal lived.

"But was there a special guy for her?" Amy asked. "Because every woman deserves a special guy."

"What's wrong with you people? Our sister lived a horrible life. Lonely, most likely. She probably didn't have time to get close enough to anybody to fall in love." Funny, they didn't look chastised.

Holly was rubbing Lance's thigh and he was twirling her long red hair between his fingers. Seth was...

"What?" Baylor demanded. They were going to kill him with innuendo if he didn't stop them.

"We got fence posts smarter than you, Baylor," Lance offered.

"If it was up to you, our family tree would be a shrub." Seth raised his eyebrows and ran a finger down Amy's forearm to her wrist.

"All right. All right. I get it, but there's nothing here for you all to be poking in."

That brought snickers all around.

"Kinda like the chair's broke," Lance mumbled loud enough for all of them hear.

Holly patted Lance's stomach and the snickers evolved to chuckles.

From KayLee's expression, she was looking for a way

out. The best thing he could do was to help her escape. He stood and pulled KayLee from the chair. "Come on. I'll get you out of here."

"Now hold on just a minute," Lance said as he glared at Baylor and then at KayLee. "We've all had about enough of the foolishness the two of you have been perpetrating over the past few months," Lance finished.

"Perpetrating." KayLee nearly choked on the word.

Baylor didn't know what to say. If it were up to him, he'd take it all back, and would never have left KayLee's side.

She had loved him, but now she wanted to make a life with her daughter and she hadn't even hinted there was room for him anymore. What did his hick brothers know about love he hadn't figured out yet?

He looked to his brothers.

"Don't look at me," Lance said. "I told her to kick your butt."

"Sounds about right to me," Seth added.

Baylor grabbed KayLee's hand and dragged her down the hallway toward the office. In the dim light, he stopped and put his arms around her.

"Wow, I love how close you can get to me."

"Is that what you dragged me down here to say?"

He drew her close and put his chin on the top of her head, afraid of getting the wrong answers to the questions he had.

"I love you. I want another chance. I know I've hurt you too many times, but if there is some part of you that still loves me, please give this sorry ol' cowpoke a break."

She didn't say anything, but she didn't stiffen or try to flee.

"We can live anywhere you want to, though I

wouldn't mind living here. I won't ask you to give up anything you don't want to give up."

She stayed quiet and he got more scared.

"I want to be a part of your life. I want to love you forever, and if the offer is still open, I'd like to be Mary-Rose's father."

From the den Holly laughed and Amy whooped.

"I guess we aren't as alone as I thought we were." He put his cheek to her soft hair.

"Marry you? I didn't hear 'marry you' anywhere in that nonsensical rambling."

"Ask her, you idiot!" Seth yelled.

Baylor realized they weren't alone at all. His brothers and their wives now lurked arm-in-arm in the hallway outside the den.

"Do it right, boy," Curtis Doyle advised as he flipped on the hallway light. "I taught you better than that."

They were all there, including his sister and the kids. Baylor looked down as KayLee lifted her face to smile at him. All he found there was love and acceptance, and possibly even a yes to his unasked question.

He might not be able to live with the answer, but he sure as hell couldn't live without asking the question.

She put a hand on his shoulder and her cheek against his chest. She was either settling in or getting ready to push off.

He took a deep breath. "I love you with all my heart and soul, will you marry me?"

"Yes!"

He's never known such joy—or relief.

In a blink, they were surrounded.

"Well, I'll be damned," Lance said as he saw his brother's face.

"What?" Holly asked as she craned to see. "Oh, man. Oh, wow! About time. Amy, you gotta see this."

KayLee looked up and laughed. "I'm sorry. I am so sorry."

"You don't sound very sorry," Baylor said as he swiped at the tears in his eyes.

That started them all laughing.

KayLee's eyes were so full of tears they had begun to run down both cheeks.

She reached into her jeans pocket and pulled out the big red hankie he had given her that first day. She wiped her eyes and then his. "Okay, so I still can't stop crying."

Amy laughed. "Give yourself about, um, about twenty years, or longer."

"There is one problem," Baylor said as he held Kay-Lee close to his heart. "I'm not sure I can make my family accept you, you being such a pushy outsider and all."

"Forget it, Baylor," Holly said. "We love you, Kay-Lee."

Crystal approached, smiling, and put a hand on each of their shoulders. "Thank you, KayLee, for saving my brother from himself."

"Welcome, sister," Lance said and kissed her on the cheek and then led the rest of them down the hallway and out of sight.

"I guess we'll have to build another house on the Shadow Range," Baylor said as he looked into the face of his world.

"I might know somebody who can get that done," KayLee said as she reached up and kissed him. "We still need to get a few more issues taken care of."

"Okay."

"Don't ever lie to me again. I've learned a lot about

taking care of myself in the last few months and I can't do that if you lie to me."

He kissed her soft lips and hugged her close to him. It was great, arousing, to be able to hug her face-to-face.

"Baylor, do you have to think about it so long?"

"I was thinking about you and I got lost. I won't lie to you. I'm not sure I even could anymore. What else do we need to deal with?"

"You gave me a two-week trial when I got here. Did I pass?"

"You've earned a lifetime warranty. Anything else?"

"There is." She smirked. "I still need to kick your butt."

"I think we can work something out."

She put her palms flat on his chest and pushed up on her toes. "I love you, Baylor Doyle."

"I love you, K. L. Morgan."

When she kissed him this time, she almost crawled up him.

And he liked it.

* * * * *

Harlequin Super Romance®

COMING NEXT MONTH

Available October 11, 2011

#1734 IN THE RANCHER'S FOOTSTEPS
North Star, Montana
Kay Stockham

#1735 THE TEXAN'S BRIDE
The Hardin Boys
Linda Warren

#1736 ALL THAT REMAINS
Count on a Cop
Janice Kay Johnson

#1737 FOR THEIR BABY
9 Months Later
Kathleen O'Brien

#1738 A TOUCH OF SCARLET
Hometown U.S.A.
Liz Talley

#1739 NO GROOM LIKE HIM
More than Friends
Jeanie London

You can find more information on upcoming
Harlequin® titles, free excerpts and more at
www.HarlequinInsideRomance.com.

REQUEST YOUR FREE BOOKS!
2 FREE NOVELS PLUS 2 FREE GIFTS!

❖ Harlequin®
Super Romance®

Exciting, emotional, unexpected!

YES! Please send me 2 FREE Harlequin® Superromance® novels and my 2 FREE gifts (gifts are worth about $10). After receiving them, if I don't wish to receive any more books, I can return the shipping statement marked "cancel." If I don't cancel, I will receive 6 brand-new novels every month and be billed just $4.69 per book in the U.S. or $5.24 per book in Canada. That's a saving of at least 15% off the cover price! It's quite a bargain! Shipping and handling is just 50¢ per book in the U.S. and 75¢ per book in Canada.* I understand that accepting the 2 free books and gifts places me under no obligation to buy anything. I can always return a shipment and cancel at any time. Even if I never buy another book, the two free books and gifts are mine to keep forever.

135/336 HDN FC6T

Name	(PLEASE PRINT)	

Address		Apt. #

City	State/Prov.	Zip/Postal Code

Signature (if under 18, a parent or guardian must sign)

Mail to the **Reader Service:**
IN U.S.A.: P.O. Box 1867, Buffalo, NY 14240-1867
IN CANADA: P.O. Box 609, Fort Erie, Ontario L2A 5X3

Not valid for current subscribers to Harlequin Superromance books.
**Are you a current subscriber to Harlequin Superromance books
and want to receive the larger-print edition?
Call 1-800-873-8635 or visit www.ReaderService.com.**

* Terms and prices subject to change without notice. Prices do not include applicable taxes. Sales tax applicable in N.Y. Canadian residents will be charged applicable taxes. Offer not valid in Quebec. This offer is limited to one order per household. All orders subject to credit approval. Credit or debit balances in a customer's account(s) may be offset by any other outstanding balance owed by or to the customer. Please allow 4 to 6 weeks for delivery. Offer available while quantities last.

Your Privacy—The Reader Service is committed to protecting your privacy. Our Privacy Policy is available online at www.ReaderService.com or upon request from the Reader Service.

We make a portion of our mailing list available to reputable third parties that offer products we believe may interest you. If you prefer that we not exchange your name with third parties, or if you wish to clarify or modify your communication preferences, please visit us at www.ReaderService.com/consumerchoice or write to us at Reader Service Preference Service, P.O. Box 9062, Buffalo, NY 14269. Include your complete name and address.

HSR11

*Harlequin Romantic Suspense presents the latest book
in the scorching new* KELLEY LEGACY *miniseries
from best-loved veteran series author Carla Cassidy*

*Scandal is the name of the game as the Kelley family fights
to preserve their legacy, their hearts...and their lives.*

Read on for an excerpt from the fourth title
RANCHER UNDER COVER

*Available October 2011
from Harlequin Romantic Suspense*

"**W**ould you like a drink?" Caitlin asked as she walked to the minibar in the corner of the room. She felt as if she needed to chug a beer or two for courage.

"No, thanks. I'm not much of a drinking man," he replied.

She raised an eyebrow and looked at him curiously as she poured herself a glass of wine. "A ranch hand who doesn't enjoy a drink? I think maybe that's a first."

He smiled easily. "There was a six-month period in my life when I drank too much. I pulled myself out of the bottom of a bottle a little over seven years ago and I've never looked back."

"That's admirable, to know you have a problem and then fix it."

Those broad shoulders of his moved up and down in an easy shrug. "I don't know how admirable it was, all I knew at the time was that I had a choice to make between living and dying and I decided living was definitely more appealing."

She wanted to ask him what had happened preceding that six-month period that had plunged him into the bottom of the bottle, but she didn't want to know too much about him. Personal information might produce a false sense of intimacy that she didn't need, didn't want in her life.

"Please, sit down," she said, and gestured him to the table. She had never felt so on edge, so awkward in her life.

"After you," he replied.

She was aware of his gaze intensely focused on her as she rounded the table and sat in the chair, and she wanted to tell him to stop looking at her as if she were a delectable dessert he intended to savor later.

Watch Caitlin and Rhett's sensual saga unfold amidst the shocking, ripped-from-the-headlines drama of the Kelley Legacy miniseries in

RANCHER UNDER COVER

Available October 2011 only from Harlequin Romantic Suspense, wherever books are sold.

HRSEXP1011